TOOLS OF THE TRADE

AN ANGUS MURDERS MYSTERY

ALLAN L MANN

NOIR CAFÉ PRESS

First paperback edition published: July 2019

This edition: October 2019

Cover design by Nick Castle

Author photograph by Allan L Mann

Library of Congress Control Number: 2019908991

ISBN 978-1-7329227-0-9 (paperback)

ISBN 978-1-7329227-1-6 (ebook)

Published by: Noir Café Press, LLC

www.NoirCafePress.com

To my family and friends, who politely listen.
You are all too kind.

ONE

Wednesday, 26th March, 2014

That was the clever part: Bobby had been shackled to the cliffs and left to watch the tide rise, death creeping slowly up the rocks.

A thousand years had passed since the red sandstone was quarried to build the abbey at Arbroath. Cart tracks, rutted deep into the sandstone rocks leading back to the car park at the start of the cliffs, were said to have been made by the monks as they hauled the stone away from the shoreline quarry for the sixty-year building project. The iron rings were probably a much later addition to the scene. Now they held ropes tied around the wrists of Bobby Gant.

He had been beaten to the point of unconsciousness, gagged, and arms and legs bound with ropes. The assault had taken place in a dimly lit building. His mind had raced as the two men beat him with a long strip of leather. Or had it been a belt? He knew it was leather because he could smell it when they whipped it into his face. Funny, he thought. Why was he trying to work out what they'd beaten him with? His mind went back to the one time he had been punished at school, when the ultimate discipline was six of the best with a leather strap. The "belt".

Another blow seared his cheek. This one opened up a deep cut and the blood flowed into his mouth. The pain was immense, but the involuntary cry wouldn't come. It was as if someone had tackled him to the ground and winded him, his breath forced from his body without the accompanying groan. Tears did come, mixing with blood and filling his eyes so that the one naked light bulb sparkled and morphed like an exploding firework when his head fell back, and he looked up with eyes still barely open.

Bobby had lost all sense of time. The beatings had gone on for some time, and he had lapsed in and out of consciousness. He had been bundled into the back of a van and driven out to the cliffs, bag over his head and trussed up with those ropes which were now cutting into his wrists and ankles. They had pushed him out of the back of the vehicle with a few kicks and he hit the ground on his side, popping his shoulder out of its socket. This time the cry came, and he let out a scream that was muffled by a gag in his mouth. He was lifted to his feet and shoved forward. He could hear the waves to his right and felt the unevenness of the ground as he walked for about five minutes.

Grass gave way to rock. He stumbled and, unable to steady himself or break his fall with his hands tied behind him, he crashed down landing on his right knee and upper thigh on the rough terrain.

A hand under his disjointed arm brought him to his feet again as more tears fell with the pain. After just a few minutes he was pushed down and told to sit. The rope around his wrists was untied and his arms were pulled to the side. He almost fainted as bone was ground against bone in the shoulder. Tied to the rings he sat on the rocks. The bag was removed from his head, but the gag remained, and his two companions said nothing as they turned and walked away.

He blinked as he tried to work out exactly where he was. It was cloudy and dark - evening or morning, he couldn't tell as he didn't know where the sun was - but he could see jagged red sandstone rising above him ten stories and the North Sea was in front of him like a dirty blanket laid over the rocks in the grey gloom fifty yards away. He tried to think. Where was he? He had to be at the cliffs on the edge of town. He looked around again and in an instant he knew the sea was not going to keep its distance and would slowly come towards him, creeping up as if it were a wild animal curious about the stranger in its environment. The realisation made Bobby start to kick and pull at the ropes tied to the rings, every movement causing searing pain to shoot through his body.

Slowly, inexorably, the cold sea made its way up to Bobby. He continued to struggle, lashing out with his feet as if he could kick it away, but the ropes held fast until, eventually, he could no longer keep his head above the waves. *At least the pain will go away*, he thought. It wasn't long before he stopped kicking and slipped into unconsciousness.

Death had washed over him.

TWO

"You have *got* to be kidding?"

"No, Tom, there's no-one available. My hands are tied. We need someone there A.S.A.P. You accepted the assignment, you'll just have to suck it up and do your best to get this one figured out quickly if you want your holiday any time soon."

"Sir, with all due respect..."

"No use arguing, Tom," interrupted Chief Inspector Brian Campbell. "Get yourself up there as soon as you can. The Duty Sergeant has all the information you need."

Recently retired Detective Sergeant Tom Guthrie stood up, wanting to protest some more, but knew it would be fruitless. He turned to leave his former boss's office, resigned that his long-awaited holiday would have to wait some more. Wait until... until who knows when.

"It's murder trying to plan anything round here you know."

"Very funny, Tom."

***

The police service in Scotland had undergone its biggest change in years, with regional forces being brought under a single command structure. Police Scotland, they called it. Gone was the Tayside Police that Guthrie had been a part of for just over twenty years, slowly progressing from fresh-faced recruit graduating from Tulliallan, to Detective Sergeant based in Tayside Police Headquarters in Dundee. His career had stalled, and he became more and more frustrated with how things were done. Perhaps he was just a little old-fashioned and unable to move and adjust to the environment, but with the changeover to Police Scotland on the horizon came the excuse to pack up his desk in Dundee and take his leave.

It took less than a year for Guthrie to realise just what a large part of his make-up was the old copper. One he could not easily set aside. The whole retirement lark was not something he was ready for. He was barely forty, after all. He had spent most of his time working on his 1973 MGB GT, a project he had promised himself since he was young. As soon as the car was at a stage he could rely on it for daily transportation, Guthrie had sold his "every day" car and enjoyed the slower pace of classic motoring. He enjoyed it until he needed to actually go somewhere or do something, then he regretted his decision.

Once the MG project was completed, Guthrie found the hole in his routine, once filled by suspect interviews and door-to-door inquiries, could only be filled by getting back in the game.

Doing so was surprisingly easier than he figured it would be. There were no licensing requirements for private investigators in Scotland. Guthrie formed a company, joined a couple of professional associations, arranged insurance and had some kid—at least that was Guthrie's assessment of the impossibly young-looking website designer—to produce an online presence.

It was shortly after this that his old boss in Dundee had called him to tell him that, due to the upheaval of Police Scotland, his services would be required. The summons turned out to be a short-lived investigation of a murder that took place in one of the poorer areas of the city. This, however, led to a more permanent arrangement whenever Dundee needed someone with Guthrie's experience, and now he was considered a civilian contracted consultant. The only promise being that it wouldn't last forever. "Just until the senior officers get their arses in gear and SCD can supply us with the manpower we need," said the Chief Inspector.

The newly-formed Serious Crime Division was responsible for the investigation of all major crimes, such as murder. Cases were handled on a relatively local basis but sometimes this stretched the organisation beyond the point they had enough manpower to cover the work. A special commission approved the formation of a small cadre of former officers who were drafted in to help with incidents. The use of civilians was not publicised for fear of questions being asked, but crimes had to be investigated and this was the stopgap solution they had settled on as the internal battles over budget were hammered out between the police bosses and the politicians. Tom Guthrie was one of the few they called.

He pressed the accelerator pedal of the MG hard to the floor as he passed the speed limit signs on the A92 heading northeast out of Dundee. The car made some more noise but didn't seem to go any faster. He cursed under his breath.

It wasn't too long, however, before Guthrie stopped worrying about the lack of horsepower as he went over in his mind the quick and dirty synopsis the Duty Sergeant had given, before he headed north from Dundee.

"You're a lucky sod!"

"And how, exactly, do you come to that conclusion, Sergeant Davey?"

"Well, it's a beautiful day, and it seems like you're off to get your fill o' sea air."

Guthrie smiled inwardly at Davey's slight Glaswegian accent, tempered as it was by the last fifteen years on the east coast. "Aye, well, that's as may be, but apart from seagulls and fishing boats, what exactly am I to expect at the end of this particular rainbow?" Guthrie asked. "No pot of gold, I should think."

"No' even a poke o' chips. The lads up in Arbroath called about a couple o' hours ago with the news they'd found a body up by the cliffs. The boss called you when he found out SCD didn't have the resources locally."

"A floater? Great. Who knows where the thing could have come from." Guthrie could feel his face turning red as he realised all hopes of his holiday were quickly disappearing. "And why do they need me, for crying out loud? Can't they handle this themselves? How do they even know it's a murder, anyway? Could be some poor bloke's gone and fallen off the cliff while taking his dog for a walk. I can see this being a complete waste of time."

"Perhaps if you'd allow me to give you one or two wee snippets o' information, you'd be more willing to see this one may need your talents," Davey responded, throwing on a little forced country bumpkin accent to emphasise to Guthrie that he let him ramble on a little. Tom looked at the floor and kicked an imaginary pebble down the hallway.

"Sorry, Davey. Not exactly what you'd call thrilled about being launched off to look at some auld codger that fell off a cliff." Guthrie leaned against the counter and, at last, looked at the desk sergeant. "Please. Fill me in."

Davey picked up a dark brown file folder, opened it and, with a flourish of someone who was about to announce the winner of the biggest jackpot in lottery history, pulled out the single sheet the folder contained. Pausing for further effect, Davey straightened his tie and cleared his throat with a sham cough.

"Oh, come on you old bugger!" was all Guthrie could manage, trying not to laugh.

"Okay, okay." Davey began to read the details from the sheet. "At 0913 hours this morning we received a call from the station at Arbroath requesting support from Divisional HQ for a CIO, with respect to the discovery of a body. Said body was found at the cliffs on the north side of the town at approximately 0730 hours. The deceased was pronounced as such by a local doctor at 0823 hours." Davey looked up from the paper and saw that Guthrie was looking down at the floor again. Guthrie looked up when he realised the sergeant had stopped and was now looking at him.

"Sorry, Davey. I'm riveted. Please do carry on."

Davey raised an eyebrow, but continued, "A Chief Investigating Officer was requested from Divisional HQ due to the state of the body when found."

"Oh, come *on* Davey, cut to the chase will you. Stop dragging this out and let me get up and back so I can..."

"The deceased was found tied to the rocks below the high tide line."

Tom Guthrie was now looking straight at Davey. "I thought that might get your attention. Oh, by the way, they haven't moved the body yet. They're waiting for you to show up. SOCO's already there doing their thing, the pathologist's already on his way and the scene needs to be cleared well before 1525 hours."

"Three-thirty? Why three-thirty?"

Davey shuffled some papers around the counter, then looked up at the recently retired detective sergeant and smiled. "High tide."

THREE

The A92 was, in parts, quite picturesque, cutting as it did through farmland that snuggled up to the edge of the North Sea. Relatively recent improvements had been made to the road. No longer was it the old, two-lane main road typical of less populated parts of the country, but a wide, four-lane artery winding its way north and east from Dundee to Aberdeen. Roughly halfway along that route was Arbroath, a town owing its existence to religion and fishing.

The ruins of Arbroath Abbey dominate the town. From its perch above the north end of the old town centre, the iconic circle, where once a huge, stained glass window was part of a tower, looked down like the eye of God watching over the slow demise of this once bustling fishing port.

Fishing still happened here, but it had been in steady decline for decades. No longer a sanctuary for a weathered fishing fleet, the smell of the daily catch was almost a forgotten memory, the local authority having embraced plans to officially turn the high-walled harbour into a full-blown recreational marina. Pleasure craft outnumbered working boats ten to one.

Guthrie paid the harbour a cursory glance on passing. Looking up he saw the red sandstone circle of the Abbey window but ignored the speed limit signs as he made his way into town. He had done well. The MG had surprised him with its willingness to cruise along the main road north from Dundee at almost fifteen miles per hour faster than the law allowed. Precious little acceleration, but if you gave it enough time the poor thing finally reached a decent speed. Guthrie had allowed himself to relax in the half hour since leaving HQ, eating a Mars Bar and drinking a bottled water on the journey — the water was his concession to healthy cuisine.

His thoughts were a jumble of images from the past. As a boy, he had come to Arbroath a couple of times with his family. He remembered the outdoor swimming pool and going for a ride on the miniature railway that ran along the links, right beside the real railway line running from Aberdeen to Dundee, Edinburgh and beyond. More recently he had paid a visit to the police station to pick up some little thug who had made his way to Arbroath after jumping out of a bathroom window at Ninewells Hospital in Dundee. He was in hospital after being arrested for explaining how rival football fans were going to go home in an ambulance. Guthrie had enjoyed his childhood experiences of the town and he had enjoyed dragging the wee nyaff Dundee United fan back home. Today, however, he was here on his second murder case as a civilian.

Just beyond the harbour the road curved to the left and Guthrie slowed the car slightly as he flicked on the turn signal and pulled into the car park of the local nick on the right. Turning off the ignition, he stepped out of the car and quickly checked his shirt for any signs of melted chocolate flakes from his Mars Bar lunch, then made his way inside to meet his hosts.

FOUR

Guthrie was escorted up to a large room that had been set-up as the hub for the murder investigation. There were several uniformed officers coming and going, bringing in all the necessary pads of paper, boxes of pens, and the like. Several computer stations had been installed along one wall but, most importantly for Guthrie, two coffee pots were sitting on a table next to the door, and another fresh pot was already halfway through brewing.

"The boss'll be along in just a minute, sir," said a PC who looked all the world to Guthrie like he just left high school. Guthrie nodded and smiled, then helped himself to a coffee.

The station at Arbroath was relatively new. Not like the old Victorian-era building located north of the town centre, this building had an open, light feel to it. Plenty of large windows allowed the sunshine into the incident room and white paint reflected light off the modern furniture's stainless steel and glass. Guthrie took in the scene. Occasionally one of the PCs would catch his eye and flash a polite smile.

The odd "sir" would accompany the smile, but generally every officer seemed to be concentrating on his or her task at hand.

"Bloody efficient lot," he quietly mumbled to no-one but himself.

"Thank you."

Guthrie spun around so fast coffee spilled out of his mug and hit his shoe with a little splat. "Bugger!"

"Sorry, Tom, shouldn't have crept up on you like that." The uniformed inspector offered his hand towards Guthrie. "Long time, no see. I'm the 'boss' you were looking for. Sorry to keep you waiting."

"Hello, Ian. Didn't realise you were in-charge here." Inspector Buchanan responded with a smile that almost managed to hide his obvious dislike of the former colleague heading an investigation on his patch. It wasn't lost on Guthrie. "I was just admiring the efficiency of the operation here. You must run a tight ship." Guthrie indicated the comings and goings of the room with a sweeping gesture, spilling some more coffee on the floor. "Bugger!"

"That's all right, sir, I'll get it." A PC jumped out from behind Inspector Buchanan and almost ran over to the table with the coffee and grabbed a handful of napkins. He bounded back over to the spill like a black Labrador retriever after a downed grouse. Guthrie stood and watched as the spill was wiped up with more enthusiasm than he could have imagined as the PC stood up, looking all the world like the black lab in Guthrie's mind wanting a scratch behind the ear for doing such a great job. Buchanan introduced him.

"Thanks, Alisdair. Tom, this is Alisdair McEwan. I've assigned him as our liaison If there is anything you need from us, Alisdair will be more than happy to oblige. I figured he can work with you as your junior officer. He's completely up to speed on the details of the case — such as they are at this point — and will be at your disposal twenty-four-seven."

The black Lab shook Guthrie's hand a little too enthusiastically for his liking. "Good to meet you, son. I'm sure we'll get on like a house on fire." *Lots of flames and screaming,* he thought to himself.

"Actually can't wait to see how you work the case. My goal is at some point to be assigned to SCD you see, so I'm ready to jump right in."

Guthrie took a long sip of coffee and looked the twenty-something Alisdair McEwan up and down. His build was tall, athletic. His uniform shirt was pressed to within an inch of its life, razor sharp creases running down the length of both sleeves. His trousers had been given the same treatment. The black, standard-issue police boots were so highly polished that Guthrie could pick out the individual fluorescent strips in the ceiling reflected in the mirror-like surface of the toe caps. "Well, now. With your boss's permission, why don't we start by getting you into some civvies. Can't have you looking all uniformed when you're working as a detective on a murder inquiry, now can we inspector?" Guthrie gave Buchanan a quick, conspiratorial wink and raised an eyebrow questioningly.

"Absolutely correct. Alisdair, get yourself off home and put on something a little more appropriate, and come right back here A.S.A.P. to take Mr Guthrie out to the cliffs."

"Yes, sir!" beamed Alisdair. He spun on his heal and trotted out of the incident room.

"Good kid," Buchanan said as he walked over to the

coffee pot, Guthrie trailing him. "A little too enthusiastic sometimes, but you'll lack for nothing with him working alongside you. He's sharp as a tack and knows this town inside and out — good and bad."

"Well, I appreciate it, Ian. It'll be hard enough not knowing the lay of the land, so I'll be relying on all the help I can get. He's not the son of Jock McEwan is he?"

"Yes, he is. Jock retired a few years ago now." Buchanan looked around the room then lowered his voice, no longer interested in continuing the small talk. "Tom, we all want to see this one sorted quickly. Nothing like this has happened in this town for a long, long time and I want it handled right, and I'll be damned if I let anyone here slip up." Buchanan's smile slipped from his face and was replaced by a sternness that took Guthrie by surprise. "And just for the record, when I asked for additional resources I didn't expect they'd send a civilian to head up the case. I appreciate your experience, but ultimately you're in my town and it falls to me to make sure we don't cock this up. It's no secret that our past collaborations didn't go as smoothly as they could have. I hope you understand my position here." This was the other side of the Arbroath inspector that explained the quiet efficiency Guthrie had seen from the moment he had walked through the station doors. Inspector Ian Buchanan took no prisoners and cut no slack.

Guthrie took another long sip of coffee but kept his eyes firmly on Buchanan. Lowering the mug, he narrowed his eyes and nodded. "Well, let's just see how it all progresses then, shall we?"

Buchanan turned without responding and walked from the room. Guthrie sighed deeply and stared out of the window and down at the traffic outside. The last thing he needed during a murder investigation was the boss of the local nick, and therefore his resources, being hostile. Never mind the fact that they had worked together for years and didn't like each other.

"Bugger."

FIVE

Alisdair had returned within thirty minutes and signed for an unmarked Ford Focus for the short drive to the cliffs. Less than ten minutes after leaving the station, they were at the foot of Seaton Cliffs, looking at the soaked and lifeless body. A lone strand of brown, slimy seaweed wrapped around his left leg, like a vine that had worked its way from the rocks up the trunk of a young tree. The gashes in Bobby's face were wide, clean and white from spending hours soaking in salt water, but Guthrie knew that they were not the result of being beaten against the rocks. It was clear that these were inflicted on the victim before he died.

"Do we have an ID on him?" Guthrie asked one of the Scene of Crime Officers who was walking gingerly around the body taking photographs and trying not to wind up on his rear end in one of the many rock pools.

"Aye. Bobby Gant. Got it from a couple of credit cards in his wallet, along with some other bits an' bobs in his pockets. Doesn't look like there was anything obvious taken. Wallet, watch. Everything's there, so probably no' a robbery." The Scene of Crime Officer wiped his nose with the back of his hand and sniffed. The wind was picking up and coming from the east, from the sea. It was making the wet crime scene colder by the minute.

"Aye, well, I'd have to agree with you there. Anybody seen the doc? Do we have a time of death?"

"He's come an' gone. I asked him the same question, but all he had to say was that it was probably between midnight and six."

Guthrie looked at the SOCO with a furrowed brow. The officer took another picture of the scene, fished a lens cap out of a pocket and snapped it onto the wide angle lens. He gave Guthrie a parting raise of the eyebrows before slowly trudging toward the foot of the sandstone cliffs and back out to the slightly worse for wear Transit van. Guthrie surveyed the landscape, taking his own mental picture. "Low and high tide," he said to himself.

Guthrie knelt down by Gant's side and pulled back the sleeve of his jacket revealing both the watch and the rope that had rubbed Gant's wrist raw. The watch was a Breitling - an expensive, aviation-themed timepiece that cost about as much, Guthrie suspected, as he got paid in three months as a cop. It was still ticking away, keeping perfect time. Standing up, he motioned to a uniformed officer he was finished by making a slashing motion across his neck. Two men stepped forward and unfolded a black body bag and began carefully untying Gant's wrists before lifting him and placing him in the bag. The zipper was closed, and they began their unsteady journey with their cargo across the rocks to the path leading down from the walk at the top of the cliffs.

Alisdair had been careful not to get in the way and had

busied himself taking notes. "Seen enough, son?" Guthrie called over. Alisdair nodded and put his notebook and pen in his inside jacket pocket. "Right. Let's get out of this weather."

They had already made it back to the car, engine running and heater blowing at full tilt, when the van passed on its way to deliver Bobby Gant to the mortuary in Dundee.

Guthrie sat and stared out over the North Sea, the wind now picking up the waves as they broke over the expanse of low, flat rocks. Even though the tide still had fifty yards to go, the wind still managed to carry the spray all the way to the car.

Watching the waves, he was drawn in his mind to whether or not his murder victim was alive when the tide came in. Chances are he was. Both arms tied to rings above the low tide mark, not to keep the body from floating away or tied down to keep it submerged and never found, but to be found. It also looked like someone was giving their victim one last chance to contemplate his pending demise.

Guthrie shivered at the thought and the involuntary action brought him back into focus on the dark water beyond the windshield. He turned the heater down, tapped the top of the dashboard and told Alisdair to head back to the station. Nothing was going to happen, as far as a post-mortem was concerned, until tomorrow. He really just wanted to head south out of town and head home, but he knew he needed to check-in back at the station at Gravesend and figure out a basic plan of action with Alisdair. Gravesend. He mulled on the fact that it was an appropriate location for a police station involved in the investigation of a murder.

Alisdair drove slowly along the road between the sea

front wall on the left and the green expanse of the public park on the right, obeying the fifteen miles per hour speed limit. He let the silence between them linger. He too was thinking about the obvious sadistic mindset that had played with the life of Bobby Gant.

SIX

Once back at Gravesend, Guthrie headed straight for the incident room and the coffee pots. His hands had not warmed up and his fingers were still numb. He just wanted to wrap them round a hot mug.

Alisdair had checked-in with the incident room coordinator, asking for messages and updates. He made some notes then walked over to Guthrie and handed him a piece of notepaper. "Post-mortem scheduled for eight tomorrow morning, sir." Alisdair waited for a response from Guthrie who was too busy trying to get the lid on his travel mug. "I put the time on the note for you, sir, along with my mobile number."

"Huh? Oh, aye. Thanks, Alisdair," Guthrie managed, still fiddling with the cup and lid combination. "Thanks for this." He waived the piece of paper noisily in the air and started towards the door. "Alisdair."

"Yes, sir"

"Look, I'm sorry. I've still to get my head around this...this..." he looked at the room and activity around him. "this *stuff* today. I thought I was going on holiday, a long

overdue holiday, and this came up." Alisdair looked sympa-
thetic and nodded. Guthrie wasn't sure, however, if the
sympathy was genuine or just an attempt on Alisdair's part
to try to understand the concept of a life beyond the
uniform that probably fell completely outside the young
man's thinking, but he kept on anyway. "Never mind. I'll
meet you back here in the morning — let's say nine. In the
meantime, I'll head back south and grab some things that'll
make my stay here a little more productive come tomorrow,
and you can find out as much as you can about our Mr
Gant. Make sure Family Services has made contact with his
next o' kin and get all the relevant details on him. Since the
PM is first thing, we won't have to wait too long before we
get the preliminary results. You and I can work out a plan of
action first thing, brief your boss, and then hit the road. As
soon as the call from the pathologist comes in here, they can
phone us. We'll see what we've got to go on at that point."

"Yes, sir. Of course." Alisdair had been taking notes and
looked up to see the office door closing with a jerk, hitting
Guthrie in the process. The sound of liquid hitting tile floor
was quickly followed by, "Bugger!"

SEVEN

By the time Guthrie made it back home he had finished a Yorkie Bar he had picked up from a vending machine at Gravesend and stopped for a fish supper. He sat in his leather recliner, grabbed the television remote, found a rerun of Top Gear and slowly opened the warm parcel of fish and chips, the smell of malt vinegar filling the flat.

As he picked apart the flakey white fish he tried not to think about the day's events. He really should be driving to the west coast and booking into the bed and breakfast for a week's getaway, but instead was deeper in it than he had been for a while. Fortunately, the B&B had been very understanding and had cancelled his booking with no penalty, wishing him the best of luck for a speedy conclusion to the case, and that they would be more than happy to see him when it had all been settled.

If only it could be as simple as that.

Guthrie knew they had just started, but, from where he was sitting, he couldn't bring himself to think positively about the case. For no particular reason, he had a grim feeling about the death of Mr Bobby Gant. The way he had been left on those rocks suggested a cold, calculating mind had been involved. It appeared to be no rookie bad guy; this was like someone who was playing games to amuse himself. Just killing the guy wasn't good enough.

Guthrie's flat occupied the top floor of a modern, four-story structure on Beach Crescent, overlooking the harbour of Broughty Ferry, on the eastern outskirts of Dundee. From the recliner of his open plan, loft-like accommodations, Guthrie could look out over the River Tay, with Fife beyond, and watch the seagulls wheel around the small castle that had guarded the mouth of this important river for over five hundred years. To the west he could see the city of Dundee and the road bridge connecting Tayside with Fife. His thoughts spun around in his mind like the gulls outside. He realised he was just staring at the scene through the window so he scrunched up the now cold paper on his lap and went over to the kitchen and deposited the ball of greasy newsprint in the chrome flip-top trash can.

Fifteen minutes later he was showered and dressed in tracksuit trousers and a baggy sweatshirt. He poured himself a good measure of Three Wood Auchentoshan single malt whisky in his favourite cut crystal glass and savoured the first taste of the bronze coloured liquid. Guthrie was not one to drink regularly, in fact he had sworn off alcohol completely for years, but every once in a while, he would indulge in his one real guilty pleasure. He walked over to the full-length windows that spanned the entire width of the flat and surveyed the now dark view. The orange glow of the street lights reflected off the water. The blue and white of the saltire cross Scottish flag fluttering over the castle was picked out by a lone spotlight, the wind having succumbed to the overpowering darkness and was now nothing more than a steady breeze. Guthrie had always appreciated the view. It was one of the reasons for buying the flat in the first place, but there were nights like this one that fell into the category of being just a tad more special than the rest. He was never sure why he thought that way, but this was one of those times. Was it the fact he was back on the hunt for a killer? Perhaps it was a little bit of smugness that came with owning his own "penthouse suite," as he liked to call it in a tongue-in-cheek fashion? Or was it just the whisky making him a little more apt to think with a tinge of romance about what was, after all, a very modern flat? These were questions he felt he didn't need to answer.

Another generous mouthful of Auchentoshan finished off the glass. The nectar gone, he washed and dried the tumbler, set it back in its place on the shelf and decided to call it a night. Tomorrow would be the real start to the case.

EIGHT

Thursday, 27th March, 2014

The morning started out before dawn. Guthrie had not slept much during the night, the soporific powers of the Auchentoshan unable to overcome the combination of coffee, chocolate, fish and chips. But that was okay. Once breakfast was polished off Guthrie went about gathering some supplies for the day, checking off the items from a mental list, perfected over a quarter of a century of police work:

Two pens, one cheap and the other an expensive Swiss-made item he had bought during a trip to Zurich several years ago; one small, black Moleskine notebook; his iPhone, which came in handy for taking photographs and even recording short interviews.

That was it. Nothing fancy, no big bag of equipment. Guthrie was certainly a practitioner of the K.I.S.S. Principle — Keep It Simple, Stupid.

He grabbed his travel mug of coffee, car keys and patted his pockets as a final check to make sure he had everything he needed for the day and took the stairs down to ground level. Walking out to the car parked across the street, facing the River Tay, the sun was already well above the horizon. Guthrie squinted and shielded his eyes with his hand. Perhaps this would help get him going, some much needed Vitamin D. He paused, savoured a mouthful of coffee and then inhaled deeply the familiar air of sea water, seaweed, and that fresh, crispness of a morning which is more perceived than physically experienced.

Guthrie unlocked the car and manoeuvred himself into the seat. The bottom cushion flattening to almost paper-thin proportions. That was the next project on the MG - a new interior. Nothing fancy, just fresh foam for the seats and perhaps leather instead of the original mid-seventies vinyl. Turning the key in the ignition and allowing the fuel pump to tick for a few seconds, he pulled out the choke and started the old car. It came to life almost immediately. Guthrie smiled in a self-satisfied way, knowing that weeks of work on the vehicle had paid off handsomely.

He backed out of the parking spot and made his way through town only now beginning to come to life. He had decided not to take the quickest way out of town, so he enjoyed the slow meander through Monifieth, Barry and Carnoustie before cutting north to join the main road into Arbroath. Even though the sun was streaming through the windscreen for most of the journey, the enjoyment of driving his beloved classic car on country roads, window open slightly to let the cold air in, was time in which he forgot about work, forgot about bills, forgot about having to reschedule his vacation. This was why he sold his other car. By the time he had arrived in the car park of the Arbroath police station it was 7:45, his coffee was gone, along with the tiredness.

Guthrie signed in at the front desk and, clipping his visitor badge to one of the belt loops of his trousers, he climbed the stairs to the incident room. It was populated by two uniformed officers who were typing on their keyboards. Much to Guthrie's surprise Alisdair was not at his desk so he made his second big decision of the day — regular or decaf? Looking between the two pots for what was probably longer than the decision required, he decided that half and half was the answer. A generous amount of flavoured artificial creamer and a couple of packets of sweetener were stirred into the mix and he found a desk and took a seat.

It was five minutes and half the mug of coffee later that Alisdair walked into the room. Guthrie raised his travel mug in greeting.

"Good morning, sir," said Alisdair. He walked over and took a seat at the desk next to Guthrie. "How was your evening?"

"Fine thanks, Alisdair." Guthrie nodded in the direction of the coffee pots. "Get yourself a cup and we'll talk about the plan for today." Alisdair got up, strode over and poured himself a small paper cup of black coffee, no sugar.

Once Alisdair had returned to his seat, he pulled a sheet of paper out of the stack he had brought in with him. "Here's the address of Gant's next of kin." He handed Guthrie a piece of notepaper and went on, "He was living in Montrose. Parents are here in Arbroath. Gant worked for a clothing company in town, Ogilvy Outerwear. He was in R and D — research and development. I confirmed Family Services paid the parents a visit yesterday afternoon. No one has been to his work or visited his house in Montrose."

"Ogilvy Outerwear. Where have I heard that before?" Guthrie asked.

"Probably worn one of their foul weather jackets. Standard police issue. They've had the contract for about fifteen years now. They're the one who supply us with the standard black and hi-vis versions for all uniform officers."

"Aye, that's it. Okay. Anything else?"

"Not at this point, sir. SOCO, as you know, was pretty useless, what with the scene being essentially underwater for several hours, but they extended the crime scene cordon back along the path to the car park to see if they can find anything that might be useful in the way of footwear marks, et cetera. Post mortem, of course, should be getting under way in the next few minutes over in Dundee. We'll know more later in the day."

"Fine." Guthrie turned and stared out the window and took another mouthful of coffee. Alisdair had to wait almost a full minute before Guthrie spoke again. "Right. What say we call on Mr Gant's work this morning, take a trip up to Montrose to check out his house, and chat to his parents this afternoon? Have someone organise a time with the parents, while you get us a car. In the meantime, I'll have a chat with Inspector Buchanan and let him know our immediate plan."

"Yes, sir," Alisdair responded. Sliding his chair back from the desk, he gathered up his papers, stuffed them into a black messenger bag, turned and grabbed the first uniformed officer to make the phone call up to Montrose.

Once Alisdair had left the incident room, Guthrie stood up and wandered over to the windows. He fished his mobile phone from his jacket pocket and looked at the time. Last thing he wanted to do was chat to Buchanan, but he might as well get it out of the way.

Buchanan's office was located on the end of the building, along a short corridor from the incident room. He knocked and received a, "Come" from inside.

"Ah, Tom. How are you this morning?" Buchanan stood

up and indicated for Guthrie to take one of the two seats in front of the desk. The office was spartan and utilitarian. A couple of certificates of achievement decorated one wall, a bookshelf, heavy with reference books, covered another. Behind the desk were the same style of windows as the incident room, adorned with the same institutional blinds. There were no signs of any personal life beyond a small trophy indicating some success at a fishing tournament.

"About to get a start on the day, then?"

"Yes," replied Guthrie, easing himself into the chair. "In fact, I just wanted to give you a quick update on the plan, such as it is at this point, before Alisdair and I head out."

"Very good — fill me in."

Guthrie relayed the day's schedule. Buchanan listened intently and his gaze never wavered from Guthrie as he talked.

Once Guthrie had finished Buchanan said, "Okay. I expect to be briefed at least twice a day, regardless of the progress. Should anything significant be discovered, I also wanted to be informed immediately, irrespective of the time or place."

Guthrie tried not to let his dislike for the man show on his face but wasn't sure how well he was doing.

"Remember, Tom," Buchanan went on, "I expect this case to go smoothly, by the book and without hiccup. I may not be hands-on, but I am watching your every move."

Guthrie stood up. "I understand. I'll make it a priority to pass on everything we do."

"I expect nothing less."

"Well, I expect Alisdair is waiting for me, so I'll get on." Guthrie turned and left the office, for some reason, closing the door behind him as quietly as he could. He stopped at the stairwell and frowned to himself. He shook his head as if ridding his brain of some fog. What was it about the man that made Guthrie feel like he was inferior? He reckoned it was just the atmosphere of cold, personality-lacking, efficiency that permeated the entire building getting to him.

An involuntary shiver brought Guthrie back to reality and he headed down the stairs and out to the car park where Alisdair was waiting in the unmarked car.

Settling into the passenger seat he said, "What can you tell me about Ogilvy Outerwear, Alisdair?"

"Well, sir, owned by John Ogilvy. He started the company back in 1977 — working out of his garage and a spare room — but quickly gained several small contracts, basically due to the high quality of the product. The big break came in '81 when they won a contract to supply an oil company with foul weather gear for their offshore workers. That experience eventually led to the police contract in '98, which was just renewed with the amalgamation of all the old forces into Police Scotland." Alisdair spouted off the facts with almost casual ease, continuing to look straight ahead as he drove. Guthrie was impressed. The fact that Alisdair had obviously done his homework on the company either late the previous evening, or early this morning, told Guthrie that he might be doing him an injustice thinking of the fresh-faced PC as enthusiastic, but still clueless when it came to the basics of detective work.

Guthrie folded his arms and slouched down in the seat. "All right, Alisdair," he said, turning to face the side of Alisdair's head, "The obvious question is...?" He let the pause hang in the air like a balloon just out of reach of a small child.

"Any colleague at Gant's work got it in for him?" Alisdair jumped for the balloon.

"Good start, Alisdair." Alisdair smiled, happy that he

was pleasing his passenger. "But we need to make sure we read between the lines when folks answer. I'll ask the questions, but I want you to read the body language, study their tells."

"'Tells,' sir?"

"You know, just like in a game of poker — do they fidget, rub their hands together, scratch their nose — that sort of thing."

"Oh, of course, sir, yes."

"Anything that would give you reason to second guess their answer. Got it?"

"Yes, sir," replied Alisdair with that Black Lab enthusiasm.

"Very good. Anyone we get a funny feeling about, we'll dig around some more, look into their history a little closer, and then we'll come back and have another chat with them."

"Right, sir."

Their destination was on the outskirts of the town, a short drive from the station. The industrial estate consisted of a handful of square, characterless buildings, most of which were relatively small compared to the headquarters and manufacturing facility of Ogilvy Outerwear. Parking was found at one end of the building. The area around the lot was landscaped with small evergreen shrubs, expertly trimmed and tended. There were three flagpoles located to one side of the main entrance, flying the cross of St Andrew, the Union Flag, and one with the Ogilvy Outerwear logo: a stylised depiction of the *Round* O of the town's abbey, incorporated into the Ogilvy name.

Guthrie and Alisdair entered the sparse main lobby and approached the reception desk, occupied by a young woman who appeared to be in her mid-twenties, although Guthrie always had a difficult time guessing the age of a woman. Probably something to do with make-up. The receptionist looked up and smiled a broad, authentic smile.

"Good morning, gentlemen, and welcome to Ogilvy Outerwear. How may I help you?" She swept her auburn hair from her right eye to behind her ear and smiled again at Alisdair, who returned the greeting with a little smirk and a lowering of his head, eyes to the floor.

Guthrie looked at him and rolled his eyes. "Good morning, Miss. My name is Tom Guthrie, and this is my colleague, Alisdair McEwan. We're from Police Scotland. I believe we have an appointment with Mr Ogilvy." Alisdair had recovered enough to produce his Warrant Card ID from his jacket pocket and held it out for the receptionist to inspect.

"Of course. Mr Ogilvy wanted to come down and greet you as soon as you arrived. If you don't mind, would you take a seat and I'll call him."

Guthrie thanked her and Alisdair nodded shyly. Guthrie took a seat in one of the four armchairs arranged around a large coffee table opposite the reception desk. Alisdair walked back over to the floor to ceiling windows that framed the main entrance door and contemplated the car park.

The reception area was a study in white. The floor was white, the walls were white, the furniture was white. The only colour belonging to a display of the company products which consisted of a group of white, featureless mannequins, arranged in what looked like an informal cocktail party gathering for mountaineers, outdoor enthusiasts, police, fire and oil workers. Guthrie wondered if they came to life after hours and sat around reception telling stories about their various adventures.

"Gentlemen." The voice broke Guthrie's daydream. He

turned in his chair and looked towards the source. A man in his late fifties was striding towards him, hand outstretched in greeting. His hair was short, salt and pepper grey and he was dressed in what amounted to golf club casual.

"Sorry to keep you waiting. On a conference call. John Ogilvy."

Guthrie got to his feet as Ogilvy reached him and shook his hand. The handshake was firm and business-like. "Mr Ogilvy. I'm Tom Guthrie and this is Alisdair McEwan from Police Scotland. Thank you for seeing us this morning."

"No problem at all. This whole thing is such a shock. When I heard about Bobby, well, you can imagine." Ogilvy's jaw tightened.

"I understand, Mr Ogilvy," Guthrie motioned for Ogilvy to lead the way. "We would like to talk with you, of course, then with Mr Gant's co-workers, or at least those who worked with him on a regular basis."

"Certainly, Mr Guthrie, I thought you might. Our conference room has been set aside for you. Use it for as long as you want. I told everyone they need to make themselves available to you."

"Thank you."

Ogilvy led them to the back corner of the reception area and through a door leading into a long hallway. On the left side of the hallway were windows that provided a view across the main manufacturing area. Four rows of machines were making pieces of various different garments. One machine looked like a printing press, but instead of paper, fabric was being fed into another part of the process where it was cut by a blade, splitting it in two. Other rows contained individual employees working sewing machines, and what Guthrie assumed to be inspection stations, bright lights and men and women assessing the quality of the finished product.

The noise of the factory floor was muted behind the glass of the hall windows as they walked. Fluorescent lighting arranged in long, continuous rows, hung from a high ceiling. One or two of the tubes were burned out. A break area consisting of two soft drink machines and a snack machine, a small round table with four white, plastic outdoor chairs occupied one corner. A shelving unit was home to a coffee maker and microwave.

No one on the factory floor either noticed or cared to look up at the visitors as they made their way towards Ogilvy's office.

NINE

Ogilvy's office was all the way at the end of the hallway. The three men entered, and the Managing Director of Ogilvy Outerwear took his seat behind a large mahogany desk which sat to the right after entering the room. On the desk was a laptop computer, some files neatly contained by a wire in tray and a large blue coffee mug. Behind him were shelves containing books, an expensive looking crystal decanter set, and what Guthrie assumed were framed photographs of the family. On the long wall opposite the door were large windows which provided a view of the fields beyond the industrial estate. Another set of windows to the left of the door overlooked the factory floor. The two sets of windows provided plenty of natural light and the ability to see his employees and be seen by them. Guthrie noted the neatness of the room. Nothing flashy, no framed diplomas, Rotary Club certificates, or other trappings of a businessman. Clean and efficient.

Ogilvy indicated the two chairs across from the desk, "Please, take a seat. Would either of you like a tea? Coffee, perhaps?"

"Thanks, but no."

"No, thank you, sir," echoed Alisdair who had turned from looking out over the factory and took a seat next to Guthrie.

"Well, how can I help, gentlemen?"

Guthrie took out a pen and his Moleskine notebook, opened it to a blank page and made a note, all the while just letting Ogilvy's question remain unanswered. "First, Mr Ogilvy, thank you for taking time to see us and allowing us to interview your employees." Ogilvy smiled and nodded. "At this point we don't have much information regarding Mr Gant's death, beyond the fact that it's certainly suspicious. Right now, we're bringing together everything we do know, talking to those who knew him, in order to build the big picture."

"I understand."

"Mr Gant worked in your Research and Development department, correct?"

"Yes, that's right."

"What exactly does that entail?"

Ogilvy picked up a pen from his desk and looked beyond Guthrie out towards the factory floor. "Well, quite simply, Bobby helped lead our research and development efforts. He coordinated how we sourced or manufactured new materials for our products."

"Such as?"

"Oh, things like waterproofing agent, for example. Some of our products don't need to be waterproof, but others -- jackets for skiing, say -- certainly do. He also worked with suppliers to ensure consistent quality once those vendors were supplying us. When we developed technologies in-house, he was in charge of that effort."

"Did he travel much or do most of his work here in the factory?"

"A little bit of both. I'd say the split was seventy-thirty with the majority of his time spent here."

Guthrie had been making notes throughout. He glanced over to Alisdair who was just sitting looking around the office, apparently paying only the slightest amount of attention. Guthrie could feel his heart thump in his chest and refrained from slapping Alisdair's arm with his notebook.

Guthrie quickly turned back to Ogilvy. "Who did he work with here on a regular basis? We'll need to interview them this morning."

"Sure. Ogilvy looked up to the ceiling. "Ah, he mostly worked solo, then brought in others from the company when nailing down a particular product..."

"Not much of an R and D department, if I might say," Alisdair interrupted. Guthrie looked at him with a frown and one raised eyebrow, relaying mild frustration at the young officer. Alisdair continued to look at Ogilvy waiting for an answer.

Ogilvy laughed, "Yes, son, you're quite right. Ogilvy Outerwear is a small, family business. You could say we're lean and mean. I hire good people who are excellent at what they do, but we also have to wear many hats."

"And what were they," Guthrie asked.

"Well, because of our size, all departments work together in some way, shape or form."

"Could you give us an example?"

Ogilvy pushed his chair back, stood up and walked over to the office door. On a coat hook was a red jacket. On the neck of the collar Guthrie noticed the Ogilvy Outerwear logo. The company's managing director took it off the hook and returned to sit on the corner of his desk closest to Alisdair. He draped the jacket across his knee, so the inside was visible to his two visitors.

"Well, Bobby essentially ran R and D - no, not much of a department, as I said, technically R and D was just Bobby. He was charged with coming up with ideas that would put our products ahead of our competitors, like the liner in this jacket. It's made of a special material that wicks moisture away from your body, is breathable, yet doesn't allow moisture in from the outside. It's based on something that is fairly common in nature."

"Capillary action? Like plants?"

"Aye. Trees actually. They transport water from their root system slightly differently than smaller plants because of their size. Bobby led a team that designed this liner material for us based on the natural process." Ogilvy flipped the jacket over and grabbed a sleeve. "But the process doesn't stop there. A new waterproof treatment also had to be invented to work with the liner. Same issue there. The moisture could only travel one way and the treatment couldn't degrade the breathability of the garment.

"Not only did Bobby come up with the ideas for these new materials, he had to work closely with contractors, vendors, folks that worked with us to either supply us with the raw material or a finished product, like a liquid waterproofing agent we then apply in-house. So, another hat he wore was procurement."

"Smart fella," opined Guthrie.

"Yes, and a key employee, Mr Guthrie."

"How does this affect your business, then? Seems like his death could pose a problem for you."

"I won't lie, Mr Guthrie. Bobby will be a huge loss. Sad for all of us on a personal, human level. But if you're asking me to answer as a cold-hearted businessman then, yes, it's a blow that will take some time to overcome." Ogilvy stood up and slowly walked back to the office door. He hung the jacket on the coat hook and carefully brushed the back of the garment with his hands, as if wiping away some imaginary lint. He turned to his guests, "Bobby was well-liked here. I can't imagine anyone having a bad word to say about him, never mind wanting to beat him up or kill him."

Guthrie rose from his seat. Alisdair took his cue and followed suit. "Well, we certainly appreciate your time, Mr Ogilvy. We'll just arrange some preliminary interviews with your employees and as soon as we know anything more concrete we'll let you know."

"Of course. I appreciate it." Ogilvy opened the door and shook hands with the two men as they walked into the long hallway.

Guthrie stopped after a few steps and turned. Alisdair, head down, almost walked into the back of him. "If anything comes to mind that might help, no matter how insignificant you think it is, please call the station."

Ogilvy nodded and closed his office door.

TEN

The interviews with Gant's co-workers revealed nothing other than no one had a bad word to say about him; just as Ogilvy had surmised. Gant was a quiet, hard-working man who was on friendly terms with everyone in the company. Even the two employees Guthrie decided to pull from the factory floor, who would not have had a close working relationship with him, knew of his character and friendly nature. No excitement. No dirt. No "ah-ha" revelation.

Back in the car the two men said nothing until they reached the edge of town. It was Alisdair who broke the silence.

"Where to now, sir? Station or the parents' house?"

Guthrie slouched a little in the seat and stuffed his hands into the pockets of his leather jacket. "Let's check with the station first and see if they managed to secure a time for us to meet with the parents. If Gant's workmates are anything to go by, I can't see his mum and dad having anything other than parental pride in who he was." He huffed and closed his eyes as he pinched the bridge of his nose between his thumb and forefinger. "We're not going to get anything helpful, are we?"

"Oh, I don't know, sir. I guess we have to expect the worst but hope for the best."

"Okay, Mr Glass-Half-Full, I'll play along with you." Guthrie looked at the green numbers of the small digital clock in the middle of the dashboard. "Here, it's almost twelve. I'm dyin' for a coffee and a pie. Know of anywhere on the way?"

Alisdair thought for a second. "What do you want, sir? Steak pie? Sausage Roll? Guthrie raised an eyebrow and nodded. "All right. I know just the spot."

ELEVEN

The two men sat in the unmarked police car in a parking spot in front of a hole-in-the-wall bakery. There was nothing remarkable about the shop's exterior. It was sandwiched between a place selling and repairing old electronic equipment, and a charity shop. All three had bars on the windows and the graffiti adorning the grey, harled wall extolled the virtues of various "youth groups," as Alisdair euphemistically called them. Nothing remarkable about the shop at all.

"For crying out loud, Alisdair, whatever possessed you to actually eat something from this place for the first time? It's a dump. It looks as though you could come down with food poisoning just looking at the front door."

"Not bad, though, eh, sir?" Alisdair smiled and took a swig from a bottle of water.

"Not bad? Jeez. I like your style, son. This has to be the best steak pie - well, in the history of steak pies!"

Alisdair laughed in mid-bite of his sausage roll. "I know. Pretty spectacular. One of the lads back at the station was going out to pick up lunch for a few of us who were working some overtime on a Saturday a couple of years back. He said he was going to pick up some hot pies and the like. I just thought it was going to be the usual chain stuff. You know, wrapped up in cellophane and you stick it in the microwave to reheat it, kind o' thing. But then he shows up with these. I asked him where he got them and checked out the place the following week. Thought he was having me on, but I took a deep breath -"

"I can see why."

"- and walked in. I've been coming here at least once a week ever since."

Guthrie lifted his paper cup of coffee in a gesture of salute, "Well, full marks, Alisdair my boy," then took a swig before lifting the pie to his mouth and taking a bite, careful not to burn himself on the steaming chunks of steak.

"Sir?"

"Hmm?" Guthrie responded through a mouthful of pie.

Alisdair put his flakey pastry lunch on the napkin on his lap. He grabbed the steering wheel and shifted slightly in the driver's seat, angling himself towards Guthrie. "I hope you find me more useful to you than grabbing coffee and being your tour guide to the finer parts of Arbroath."

"What?"

"Well, sir, I want to be able to contribute to this investigation in a positive sense. Not just as the token copper, the official representative of Police Scotland. I know I can come across as a bit enthusiastic," Guthrie made another *hmm* sound in agreement, "but I know I can do more than point out hidden lunch spots."

As Alisdair talked, Guthrie had turned and was listening with his head cocked to one side.

"Alisdair, look, to be honest I'm not overly keen to be working here in Arbroath. Your boss and I go back a ways and, well, let's just say you probably wouldn't see us hanging out together down the pub of a Friday night."

"I know, sir."

"You know?"

"Yes, sir." Alisdair looked out across the street. It had started to rain again. A steady rain that seemed innocent enough, but would keep on, not content until, before you even realised, it had penetrated every layer of clothing.

"And exactly *how* do you know, Alisdair?"

Alisdair took another mouthful of water, swallowed, and looked down at his lunch. The sausage roll was still hot and giving off little wisps of steam. "Inspector Buchanan briefed me, sir."

"*Briefed* you?"

"Yes, sir. He wanted me to make sure we did everything thoroughly and by the book."

"By *we,* I assume he meant me. Am I right, Constable McEwan?"

The use of Alisdair's rank rather than his first name had a visible effect on the young officer. He turned away from Guthrie's stare and peered out the side window which was starting to fog up on the inside as the day turned colder with the rain outside.

"Well? C'mon, Alisdair. The camel's got his nose in the tent flap. You can't zip it up now. You might as well fill me in."

Alisdair kept staring out of the window. A middle-aged woman was hurrying up the hill, leaning forward into the rain, struggling with an umbrella in one hand and two bulging, plastic bags of shopping in the other. His gaze followed her along the road. "To be honest, sir, Inspector Buchanan didn't go into too much detail. He said he wanted to make sure you conducted the investigation as thoroughly as he would himself. If you know the inspector, then you know what that means."

Guthrie sniffed and rolled his eyes, "Aye, I sure do."

"That was really about it, sir."

The two men sat in silence again. Guthrie processed the tidbit of information, Alisdair picked up his sausage roll and took another bite. Guthrie's eyes narrowed as it occurred to him what Alisdair had not said.

"Let me get this right. Buchanan only told you to keep an eye on me to make sure everything was done by the book. Make sure I followed every lead, dotted every "i" and crossed every "t". That's all, correct?"

"Yes, sir."

"Why, then, did you say he told you that we are not on the best of terms from back in the day?" Guthrie's face was furrowed as he too followed the woman's progress up the hill against the weather.

"I didn't say that, sir. I said I knew that was the case."

"Okay, okay, Alisdair, I give up. How do you know?"

"I did a little digging. Pulled some old case files. You know, just some basic stuff. Found out that there were a couple of investigations that you and Inspector Buchanan were partnered on when he was a sergeant just before you retired a couple of years ago. Saw a couple of notes in the file where the inspector made an official complaint about your... methods of investigation."

Alisdair quickly filled his mouth with the last of his lunch and started chewing, head down. Guthrie slouched back in his seat again and wiped away the condensation on his side window with a napkin. Another silence filled the car, broken only by the noise of the rain hitting the roof and windshield.

"You did a little digging on me, did you?"

"Yes, sir."

"Found out that I'm not exactly on board with the way your Inspector Buchanan likes to do things, eh?"

"I think the phrase was, "modern policing methods," sir."

"And you gathered all this information when, exactly?"

"Between Inspector Buchanan's briefing and meeting you at the station yesterday, sir."

"What was that - an hour, hour and a half?"

"Forty-five minutes, sir. Give or take."

Guthrie let out an involuntary little chuckle. "You know, Alisdair, you're not as wet behind the ears as I had taken you for."

"Thank you, sir."

"And what's your opinion of my policing methods?"

"Actually, sir, I would hazard a guess that you think I'm another one of those new, young, university types who joined the service because he grew up on reruns of *The Bill* and regular doses of *Lewis* and decided he wanted to be the next *DS Hathaway*."

"It had crossed my mind."

"Well, I'm sorry to disappoint. I wanted to be a copper because my dad was one. He was a PC his entire career and I admired the way he just went about his job, day in, day out until he retired. But he did it the old-fashioned way - no Twitter accounts or Facebook pages, just getting to know his beat, getting to know the characters - the good and the bad. I know the service has changed since he first started out and changed for the better overall, but I'm not convinced we're any better when it comes to *policing* in a community. I know I've only been out in the real world for a short time and I totally understand the need to do things by the book, but where's the real coppering?"

Guthrie tilted his head back onto the headrest and puffed out his cheeks in a long sigh. "What exactly are you looking for, Alisdair? I mean, you're right, one of the reasons, the main reason, I retired was because I felt my time had come and gone. I wasn't able, or willing, perhaps, to change my ways. The system was getting to me and I thought I'd better quit before I did something that would get me the sack. You should know better than me how things have changed with Police Scotland, even over the last year." Guthrie looked at Alisdair. "Why are you telling me this?"

Alisdair flicked the windshield wiper. The view across the street consisted almost entirely of various shades of grey. The dark sky reflected in the drenched road as the traffic sprayed the water up from the surface of the road in a fine mist, the sound muffled from inside the car. "I want to be a cop. A real cop, not some anaemic police officer."

"I'm sure Inspector Buchanan would find that very commendable, Alisdair."

"Ha!" Guthrie turned, not expecting the outburst from Alisdair. "Look, sir, you and I both know Inspector Buchanan is a very competent police officer, but he's more concerned with budgets, cleanliness, and timeliness, than with getting his hands dirty and actually nabbing the bad guys, and *that's* why I joined. I've got the paperwork, the computer work down pat. What I want is the police work."

Guthrie smiled. "You want me to teach you a few tricks of the trade they don't teach you at Tulliallan, eh?" Alisdair nodded. "And what's in it for me?"

"I thought I could keep you on the right side of your favourite inspector."

Guthrie took another mouthful of pie and washed it down with the last of his drink. "I'll be buggered if I'm going to get my own coffee, though."

"Yes, sir."

"It's Tom."

TWELVE

Just as Guthrie and Alisdair were finishing up their lunch, a call came through from the incident room that Gant's parents were available for an interview.

The pair made their way to the small bungalow on the north side of the town, not too far from where they were.

The interview with the parents, however, brought nothing new to light. The father had sat stoically throughout and had offered up very little in the way of information. The mother managed to speak through a constant flow of tears. She blew her nose using a handkerchief she folded, unfolded, and refolded in her shaky hands. They had been driven down to Dundee by Family Services to identify the body first thing that morning, and the shock of the news of their son's death and the experience of seeing him lying lifeless on the examination table was obvious to Guthrie and Alisdair as they went through the normal list of questions.

When the interview was over the two detectives offered their condolences and quietly made their way out of the front room of the Gant's modest house and saw themselves out. Just before closing the front door Guthrie heard Mrs. Gant let out a mournful wail. Guthrie paused for a second then pulled the door closed as quietly as he could. Hand still on the door knob, he closed his eyes. He could feel his heart pounding inside his chest.

Thirty minutes later they arrived in Montrose. Gant's flat was still occupied by a SOCO officer and two young uniforms who quickly briefed Guthrie.

Gant's computer had already been taken to Dundee where I.T. forensics were looking through emails and various files. A digital camera had also made the trip with the desktop.

The flat was immaculate. Clean like its owner. There was one framed photograph of Gant with his parents, and no other personal touches. It was as if he lived in an IKEA showroom.

Frustrated, Guthrie told the two uniforms to box up every last scrap of paper they could find, before taking a quick look in the bathroom on his way out. He saw nothing that would lead him to think he was anything other than what everyone had said. He hoped something in the paper-work would provide an answer.

Guthrie said precious little on the drive back to the station. By the time they entered the incident room, the preliminary post mortem results were waiting for them. Guthrie read through the report and then handed it to Alisdair who walked over to an empty desk, sat down and slowly read each page.

"Nothing new from what we thought back at the scene," Guthrie said once Alisdair had shuffled the papers back in order and leaned back in his chair, stretching his arms towards the ceiling.

"Yup," Alisdair said. "Preliminary cause of death,

drowning. Beaten then tied up to wait on the tide to come in and drown him." He rubbed his eyes. "What are we missing? Who do we need to talk to? Someone must know something. I mean, this kind of thing doesn't happen unless something really ugly is going on. Right?"

"Right." Guthrie stood up and paced back and forth between their two desks. "My money is on the assumption that Gant knew his assailant."

"Or at least the assailant knew Gant," added Alisdair.

"Point taken. But it's still only an assumption, not fact. What facts do we have?" He looked at Alisdair, eyebrows raised questioningly.

"Okay, let's go through this logically. Robert "Bobby" Gant, male, thirty-four years of age. Resident of Montrose, employed at Ogilvy Outerwear as head of Research and Development. Initial interviews suggest a man of good character, well liked, with no obvious bad habits." Alisdair picked up the post mortem report. "PM indicates he was healthy, non-smoker, probably didn't drink alcohol often or so infrequently that he might as well have been a teetotaller. Had no old injuries or medical issues."

Guthrie picked up Alisdair's train of thought. "Suffered multiple blunt force injuries, consistent with a beating over an extended period of time - several hours, according to the PM report of the bruising. Dislocated shoulder, several cuts. Marks on his body suggest that his attacker, or attackers," Guthrie raised an index finger, conceding the possibility before Alisdair had a chance to correct him, "never actually laid a hand on him, but rather whipped him with various items."

Alisdair rose from the desk and continued. "He was still alive when tied up at the cliffs, albeit barely. Very little evidence of a struggle once tied up, consistent with the rope marks on his wrists, suggesting he was very weak. Cause of death, drowning, as corroborated by the physical evidence, and so on."

"Right."

Guthrie stood with his hands in his pockets. Neither said anything, lost in his own thoughts. A telephone rang. Two uniformed officers were talking to people who had responded to the news reports of the death. Guthrie stared at one of the officers then said, "Besides the people we've talked to today, who else did he hang out with that they don't know about?"

Alisdair shrugged.

Guthrie answered his own question. "We need to look at his phone records, bank statements, emails -- work and personal. Get one of the uniforms here to arrange that and go through them. You know what we're looking for. Brief them to note anything that will give us someone to talk to, something to look at. Anything out of the ordinary. Also, anything that may be regular, but doesn't fit with the picture we have of him, so make sure they know what would look unusual for Gant."

"Like regular payments to a bookie kind of thing?" Alisdair asked.

"You got it. There'll be something, Alisdair, there always is. And it's probably not going to be something as obvious as a bookie account, or an email addressed to hitman at killers dot co dot UK."

Alisdair looked at his watch. It had just gone five. "What next for us?"

Guthrie rubbed his face with his hands and took a deep breath, exhaling loudly.

"Alisdair, I know it's only the second day, but I feel like we're going to have to get lucky." He walked over to the windows and leaned on the sill. Outside, the rain was still coming down. The sun didn't really have a chance all day and it seemed as though it had just given up early. The evening gloom was taking over, the yellow glow from the street lights reflected by the hundreds of rain drops on the window. The coffee pots were almost empty, and the smell of burned coffee brought Guthrie back into the office from the scene outside.

"The SOCO report."

"Sir?"

"The Scene of Crime report. Do we have it back from Dundee yet?"

"Well, no, sir. They normally take a few days to process the forensics"

"What forensics? Don't you remember the SOCO telling us the scene was clean because it had been under water for several hours?"

"Of course," Alisdair stammered, "but they still have to go through the motions just in case, right?"

"Aye, aye. I know. My point is we can't just let them take their own sweet time though, can we? Look. It's time to call it a day. Give them a call and see if there's anyone still there. If there is, tell them not to go anywhere until I arrive and that I'll be expecting a preliminary report. Before you leave, make whoever we have working for us on nights get onto their task with Gant's records. I'll call you later if I manage to catch forensics and they have anything interesting for us. Got it?"

"Yes, sir. But do you think they'll have anything so quickly?"

"Probably not, but I have to feel like we're taking another step forward instead of going round in circles." Guthrie picked up a paper cup and was about to pour himself a coffee for the road, but thought twice about it, put the cup back on the table and headed for the door.

"Tell them to call both of us immediately if they find something useful in Gant's records... like the name and address of a known Arbroath thug. And call forensics."

Alisdair smiled as Guthrie shouted the last instruction as the door closed behind him.

THIRTEEN

Guthrie pushed the MG hard almost all the way from Arbroath back along the main road to Dundee. His mind was going as fast as the car as he travelled the thirty minutes to the SOCO lab.

Visions of dead-end leads and interviews that brought nothing new to light filled his thinking. He just couldn't let this case get away from him.

It was not that long ago he was leading a murder inquiry, as part of the now defunct Tayside Police, when things bogged down, and the investigation stalled. Guthrie's frustration and pressure from the offices on the top floor of HQ led him to put his own form of pressure on some of the individuals he suspected knew more than they were letting on. It was this disregard for "modern policing methods" Alisdair had alluded to earlier in the day that spelled the start of his fast track to retirement.

He was ready to go, or at least that was what he kept telling himself at the time. After a while he began to believe his own self-propaganda and he felt more and more that leaving the force was in his best interest.

To his colleagues and superiors, they felt the same -- it was also in *their* best interests for him to clear out his desk and retire. In fact, they thought his head had not been in the game ever since his wife had walked out on him.

He realised he was on autopilot. When he focused on the road ahead, lit up in the dim headlights, he couldn't remember the last five minutes of the drive. He rolled the window down a little, just enough to feel the cold air on the side of his head.

His phone, sitting on the passenger seat, lit up. A text message. Guthrie picked it up and swiped the notification to unlock the screen. Alisdair.

Someone will be at Forensics. Ask for Dr. Macintosh. Night shift briefed. Off home. Will be in early.

Good, he thought. He knew it would be a long shot that anyone would still be there, but he was glad that at least one thing had worked out today. Even though it would probably be someone not involved on the Gant case, he could at least make sure they knew they needed to get on it.

He replied to Alisdair's text with a quickly typed, *Ta,* and pressed send.

FOURTEEN

The forensics lab was located on Dundee's West Victoria Docks. Once the bustling home to the city's whaling fleet it had been in steady decline and underuse for decades until developers recently turned it into one of those up-market areas populated by hi-tech companies and high net worth individuals who, just twenty years ago, would never have dreamt of setting foot in this part of town.

Guthrie drove around the old harbour and found the nearest parking spot three buildings away from the lab. He backed the MG between a new Jaguar and a light grey AMG Mercedes. As he locked the door he wondered if the owner of the Jag would appear and offer to swap it for the MG. There was about as much chance of that as the forensics lab telling him the name and address of Gant's killers.

After checking in with the building's reception desk he climbed one flight of stairs and found the door marked Scottish Police Association Forensics Laboratory.

Unlike the science fiction portrayed by television, the office looked like a university chemistry lab. There were several workstations supporting microscopes and computers, machines that looked like they would be at home in a hospital, and an assortment of mini fridges with glass doors through which various test tubes and containers could be seen. The entire scene was a sterile mix of white walls and equipment, and chrome furniture.

Several smaller offices flanked both sides of the main room. Some were regular offices, many of them housed complicated looking machines. All were empty.

One office, however, was occupied by a woman in a lab coat. Guthrie approached the open door and knocked.

The woman was writing in a notebook. She looked up and smiled.

"Hello, there. What can I do for you?"

The accent was from the Highlands. The words sounded more like lyrics than a plain sentence — soft and less hurried than the typical Scots English. The "t" in "what" was actually pronounced rather than glossed over and dropped. Guthrie smiled inwardly.

"I'm Tom Guthrie. I believe someone from Arbroath called to say I was coming over. It's about the body found at the cliffs there yesterday morning."

"Ah, Mr Guthrie, yes. I was told you were on the way. Please have a seat." The lab-coated highlander closed her notebook and picked up a file folder from a tray on the desk. She held out her free hand. "I'm Jacquie Macintosh."

"Dr. Macintosh. Yes, I'm sorry it's so late in the day."

They shook hands and took their respective seats.

Guthrie studied the head of the forensics lab. He figured she was in her mid-forties. She was of average height, mousy, straight, brown hair which was tied back in a pony tail which she wore low. Her skin was tanned, and her eyes were highlighted by laughter lines. She didn't have to try very hard to be pretty.

"I assume you want to know everything we've been able to find out about your victim, Mr Guthrie."

"Your assumption is correct, Dr. Macintosh."

"Please, call me Jacquie."

"Jacquie. Tom"

Jacquie smiled. "Well, I'm afraid nothing much more than the preliminary report indicated. The victim was alive, albeit barely, when submerged, therefore the cause of death is drowning. The scene was literally washed clean by the incoming tide. This includes the body and the surrounding area."

"Any chance at all that you might find something on his clothing?"

"There is a remote chance, yes, but it's going to take a little while longer than normal you understand."

Guthrie slumped back into his chair, screwed his eyes shut and pinched the bridge of his nose between his thumb and forefinger.

"We will, of course, be looking in all the areas where the water doesn't have such a dramatic effect. The inside of pockets, for example. Perhaps we'll come up with something for you over the next couple of days."

"Thanks, Jacquie. I'd love to find a note with the killer's name in a pocket, but I understand what we're working with here."

Jacquie smiled and leaned forward. "I'll have the team on it as much as I can." She paused before saying, "Well if we're going to be working together for a while, and you've kept me waiting here for you, what say we go for a drink and talk shop?"

Guthrie couldn't help but react automatically with a frown. Before he realised it and raised his eyebrows instead, his face had already betrayed him.

"You're not opposed to the idea, are you, Mr Guthrie?"

Guthrie could feel the blood rush to redden his cheeks and the back of his neck. "Eh, no. No. I just, eh...," he stuttered.

"I'm sorry, Tom. A little forward of me perhaps? I shouldn't have put you on the spot like that."

Guthrie stuck a finger between his neck and his shirt collar, pulling the material away from his skin, conscious of showing the physical signs of being flustered and completely blindsided by the question. "No, Jacquie, it's fine. I'd love to. I guess I'm not used to being asked out for a drink by, by..."

"By a relative stranger — and a woman at that?"

"Well... yes. But how did you know...? I mean, what made you think...?"

"How did I know I could ask you, and what made me think you would say yes?"

Guthrie shifted his weight in the chair, "In a word, yes."

"No wedding ring for a start." Jacquie paused.

"And..?"

"And that you would say yes was a guess. Listen, Tom, you'll find working with me that I don't waste your time. You'll also find that I don't waste my time. I can be a little pushy and I know it, but I hope that doesn't put you off."

Guthrie cracked a nervous smile and running his fingers through his hair looked down at the desk in front of him.

"Well?"

"If you're half as good at the forensic stuff as you are a detective, Doctor Macintosh, I look forward to working with you. If I can regain my composure." Guthrie's obvious uncomfortableness in the situation brought out a smile and showed off the laughter lines on Jacquie's face, "I look forward to it very much."

"Then let's go!" Jacquie almost jumped out of her chair, walked around the desk and past Guthrie where she shed her lab coat and hung it on a hook fastened to the back of the door. Guthrie turned and saw the figure that was lurking behind the white coat.

He smiled.

FIFTEEN

Guthrie carried the drinks from the bar over to Jacquie. They had decided on the Invertay Hotel, a brand-new building just along the docks from the forensics lab. They walked the short distance to the hotel. When they entered the bar, Guthrie headed to fetch the drinks and Jacquie found a quiet booth in the corner. She had taken the high-backed double seat of the booth when Guthrie returned with a gin and tonic and a bottle of Corona. He took a seat across from her.

"Can't understand why I continue to buy these things," he said as they saluted each other by raising their drinks. "I mean, it's not the greatest beer in the world, from what I hear it costs next to nothing to produce, and it costs so much more than a pint of good old Scottish lager."

"Perhaps you like the exotic?" Jacquie responded with a raised eyebrow.

"I don't think Mexican beer falls into that category. I guess it comes from a trip I took to Florida a couple of years ago. I was on holiday and this was the beer I drank."

" Where in Florida?"

"Miami. I had always wanted to go there since seeing it on one of the Bond movies, years ago."

"I don't remember Double-Oh-Seven ever being in Florida," said Jacquie. She leaned back against the booth, took a pillow, laid it in her lap and took another drink. "Tell me more."

"It was at the start of Goldfinger. The scene where the girl is in the hotel room..."

"The one that ends up covered in gold paint?"

"That's her. She's watching a card game through binoculars and telling one of the players, via radio, what the other guy has in his hand..." Guthrie felt a little blood colour his cheeks in embarrassment. "I must sound like a complete teenage film geek."

"No! You go right ahead."

"Sorry, Jacquie. I spend a lot of my time watching films of an evening. Don't get out and about much these days — beyond work that is."

"Why not?"

"Ach, just not my thing anymore. Actually, not sure it ever was my thing, to be honest."

"What *is* your thing?"

Guthrie looked at Jacquie and took a swig from the beer bottle. Jacquie smiled and this time both eyebrows were raised questioningly.

"I lead a pretty quiet life. I fill my non-work hours cleaning house, doing the shopping, washing and ironing."

"Wow, you'd make someone a wonderful wife some day."

Guthrie shifted his weight in the chair. "Well, needs must I suppose."

"Sounds like you need a friend or two to get you out of the house."

"I like to keep myself to myself too much now for that, I'm afraid."

"So, all work and no play, huh? Hobbies?"

"For the last little while I've been working on my car."

"Oh, yes? What kind?"

"An old MG. Got it to where it's my daily driver."

"Well, I can see how that would keep you busy." Jacquie took another sip of her gin and tonic and brought her left leg up onto the seat, sliding her ankle under her right thigh. Guthrie was staring at the small table between them as if he was trying to burn a hole through the dark, varnished top. Jacquie let the silence linger for just a few seconds.

"Hello? You still with me? Tom?"

Guthrie almost jumped when he heard his name. "Sorry, Jacquie. I was miles away there."

"Well, that was obvious. I must be scintillating company if you can wander off so quickly in a conversation." She stuck out her bottom lip and effected an exaggerated pout.

"Ach, it's just work, you know?

"Oh, I know."

"Sorry. I'm probably not great company, am I?"

Jacquie leaned forward and put her glass on the table, then placed her hand on Guthrie's arm in a gesture of understanding. Without thinking he sat back, leaving Jacquie's arm resting on the table. Jacquie felt a tinge of embarrassment for what was obviously a move that made Guthrie uncomfortable. "Look. This was my idea. I said we should go for a drink and talk shop. Why don't we do just that? Talk shop."

Guthrie smiled. "Jacquie, I appreciate the thoughtfulness, but I feel like a bit of a git, sitting here, almost crying into my beer because of my pitiful troubles at work." Jacquie smiled at his self-deprecating assessment of his mood.

"No, really. I want to hear about it. Sometimes I get into the same kind of funk, especially when we're trying to work potential evidence at the lab, and nothing gels with the case. The police are calling us every five minutes, asking if we have anything, any fibre, strand of hair, minute spot of blood, that will positively link them to their prime suspect, and we're coming up blank. I know what you might be going through. If it's going to get you to open up and relax a little, let's hear it."

Her face was stern. Guthrie finally looked up from the table. "Come on, Mr Guthrie. I told you I don't waste time. Out with it."

Then she smiled.

He looked up to the ceiling, shook his head and smiled back at the head of forensics.

"Dr. Macintosh, you are very hard to resist."

"What can I say? It's my subtle charm that wins every time."

Guthrie laughed. "Why don't I fetch another round and we can start again?" He got up and picked up both glasses. "Same again?"

"Why not."

Guthrie nodded his agreement and walked over to the bar, catching the eye of the young girl standing at the far end, rearranging the bottles of spirits under the optics.

"Same again?" she asked. Guthrie nodded and looked back to the booth where Jacquie was watching a couple of girls, pouring over a mobile phone and sharing some in-joke. After a few seconds she looked over to the bar and made eye contact with Guthrie and smiled. He returned the emotion and then turned his attention to the girl behind the bar.

There was something about that smile, he thought to himself, that made him feel like a thirteen-year-old boy looking at the covers of the *questionable* magazines at the newsagents.

The drinks arrived and he handed over the cash. When he turned, Jacquie was still smiling at him. Okay, now he was flustered. He took a deep breath and told himself, *Get it together, you idiot.*

SIXTEEN

Friday, 28th March, 2014

The evening had, in the end, been a pleasant experience as Jacquie managed to peel away the layers of reticence Guthrie had put in place after his divorce. It was obvious he was uncomfortable in a one-on-one social situation with a woman, but she smartly kept to subjects surrounding police work, and if the conversation did stray from issues regarding the ones who got away, or comparing notes on cases they didn't realise they had both worked on through the years, she was quick to sense Guthrie's unease and unwillingness to open up about more personal topics and steered them back on course -- serious assaults, rape cases and murders. It had felt good to vent his frustrations about the Gant case and Jacquie was a patient listener.

It had turned nine o'clock when Guthrie and Jacquie had walked back to his car swapping stories about mutual acquaintances from the days of Tayside Police and complaining about the power struggles going on between the Chief Constable of Police Scotland and the Chairman

of the Scottish Police Services Authority who was in charge
of the forensic labs across the country.

When Guthrie offered to give Jacquie a lift home, she
politely refused, explaining that she lived in one of the
apartments in the Victoria Docks area and the short walk
was hardly worth the bother for Guthrie. He accepted the
explanation and tried to hide his disappointment, but when
she had given him a little kiss on the cheek and said thanks
for the company, his mood swung completely.

He had gone to bed soon after getting back to his flat
and picking out his clothes for the next day. His bed felt
warm and he sank underneath the duvet, falling asleep
quickly.

He was out the door early that morning, feeling
refreshed and energised after two slices of toast with jam,
washed down by a large glass of orange juice.

The drive to Arbroath was a pleasant one, with the sun
making an appearance, bathing the countryside in a warm,
orange hue. The trees bordering the road cast long shadows.
Guthrie thought about pulling over and taking a picture on
his phone, but decided instead to just enjoy the beauty in
the moment.

Arriving at the station he took the stairs up to the incident room two at a time. He entered and found a lone,
female uniformed officer manning a desk. She sat typing on
the keyboard of a desktop computer and was wearing a
wireless headset connected to the phone. Guthrie nodded a
greeting as she looked up from her screen, wondering if she
had been there all night.

It was early enough even Alisdair hadn't made it in, and
the coffee pots sat empty. At least someone had cleaned
them from the day before. He waved his travel mug towards
the WPC, who smiled and nodded, so Guthrie set about

trying to find the packets of coffee and filters, then filled the coffee pot from the water cooler in the corner. As he poured the water into the machine, he heard the door open and Alisdair entered.

"Jeez, you really do live here, don't you," Guthrie called across the room. Alisdair just shrugged. He walked over to a desk that, through default, had become his, and tossed the local newspaper onto it.

"Coffee?" Guthrie asked.

"No thanks. What did *you* have for breakfast this morning that you're here so early?"

"Early to bed, early to rise, I guess. Had an early night and decided that we needed to get going this morning." Guthrie was conscious of not giving anything away that would reveal to Alisdair his meeting at forensics was something other than purely business.

"I hear you," responded Alisdair with a yawn. "Actually, I didn't sleep well at all last night. I can't help but think we've missed something. Something obvious."

"Now, don't get too critical, Alisdair, but I'm with you -- to a degree." Alisdair sat down heavily in his chair and yawned again. "You and I both know that murders are typically solved within the first couple of days, but that's partly to do with evidence at the scene, forensics, witnesses, right?" Alisdair nodded. "But our scene was literally washed clean and the locus was well away from witnesses, to say the least."

"I know, Tom, but..."

"No *buts*, Alisdair. You said yourself you wanted to get down to *real* policing. Policing your beat. Policing *people*. Well, here's your chance, son."

"Meaning?"

"Meaning, we have no physical evidence from the

scene, unless forensics comes up with something, and the chance of that will probably be a bit of a miracle. We're going to have to do some old-fashioned legwork."

"Your meeting with forensics came up with nothing then, huh?"

Guthrie couldn't help but look up to the ceiling. "They may still come up with something, but we can't depend on it." He turned back to the coffee pot and filled his mug, masking any tell-tale facial expression that would give away the real meaning of his last comment.

"We need to talk to everyone we've interviewed, again. Dig deeper this time. We need to look at everything we have again and again until we find something. We need to find the one person who knows something."

Alisdair exhaled noisily and pushed himself to his feet. "On second thought, I'll take that coffee after all."

Thirty minutes went by and they had put together a list of interviewees to whom they wanted the team to talk for a second time. Top of the list was John Ogilvy.

"I felt he was a little reserved," Alisdair remarked. "But I'm not the expert here. I could be off."

"No, Alisdair, I had the same gut feeling about him. Nice enough, seemed to be straight up, but I got the impression he was holding back."

"Yup. I'm not exactly sure what it was though. There was something else."

"Oh, aye?"

I wasn't sure of it at the time -- whether it meant anything, or whatever -- but..."

"Well, c'mon, son. Spit it out." Guthrie frowned at Alisdair's unwillingness to share.

"Well, it's just that when we were waiting to see Ogilvy

the other day, I couldn't help but notice the car park outside their building."

"The car park? What about it?" Guthrie was curious. He was expecting something to do with Ogilvy. Alisdair tapped his pen on the desk with a nervousness Guthrie hadn't seen since he had first met him and had reminded him of the Labrador puppy.

"Well... apart from ours, there were just a handful of cars outside Ogilvy's facility."

"Seemed to me that we were their only visitors at the time."

"No, I'm talking about the cars of everyone in the building, not just visitors."

"Employees too, you mean?"

"Yes. Look, here's what I looked at last night when I couldn't sleep." Alisdair gave the mouse on his desk a little shake, waking up the monitor. The screen came to life displaying the Police Scotland logo and a login dialogue box. He entered his username and password, opened a web browser, navigating to Google Maps. Guthrie leaned over his right shoulder, one hand on the desk the other on the back of Alisdair's chair. Alisdair zoomed into a satellite image of Arbroath and further still to the industrial park on the edge of town and the Ogilvy Outerwear building. Taking his pen, he pointed at the screen.

"See? Where we parked is the only area for the Ogilvy building. There's no separate visitor and employee parking. Nothing round the back -- the building just backs onto farm land -- and parking for the next closest building is, what, at least two hundred yards away."

Guthrie took a step back and folded his arms. "You sure that's all they have?"

"I am, yes. Do you remember the receptionist?"

"Oh, I remember her, and I'm not surprised you do too." It was Alisdair's turn to hope his face didn't give away anything, but it quickly reddened, giving Guthrie all the evidence he needed to convict the young officer. "I thought so."

Guthrie smirked.

"Okay, Okay. I called and left a message last night- "

"Boy, you work quickly."

"-at the factory, and she called me back. Their phone system sends emails out when they get a voice message and she picks those up on her mobile. I asked her if there was any additional parking other than the spaces in front of the building -- there's not -- and roughly how many cars are normally there on a typical weekday -- less than a dozen. A couple of the employees take turns carpooling, a couple get dropped off, or get the bus to the stop at the entrance to the industrial estate on the main road, but that's it."

"All right. Where are you going with this?"

"I just figured that a successful company like Ogilvy Outerwear would be employing more people. It would be busier than it was. Might be me, but when we were in Ogilvy's office you could see the shop floor. It wasn't exactly a hive of activity."

"Alisdair, you're right. I didn't notice it at the time. I'm no expert on how to make foul weather jackets and what-not, but at the time I was impressed that everyone we talked to was available with almost no notice. I understand that people would be naturally happy to help when one of their friends or co-workers has been killed, and Ogilvy had spread the word to be available, but it was like no one needed to rearrange their schedule, or get someone to cover while they talked to us."

Alisdair clicked the web browser to close the program and looked at Guthrie.

"Something or nothing?" he asked.

Guthrie thought for a second. "To tell you the truth, I don't know, but it's the only something we have -- even if it turns out to be nothing."

"I agree. I'm also glad you didn't think I was thinking too much."

"Alisdair, if there's something we can't do right now it's not think too much. Why don't we top up our coffee and head over to Ogilvy's place? Perhaps you can grill the receptionist some more?"

It was as if someone flicked a switch.

That's how quickly Alisdair's face went from pink to bright red.

WHEN THEY PULLED up in front of Ogilvy Outerwear and got out of the car, they both took a few seconds to count vehicles.

"I got nine, not including ours, of course. What did you get?"

Alisdair nodded, "Same. Nine."

There were no signs indicating assigned parking spaces, but it didn't take a dyed in the wool detective to guess that the Jaguar nearest the door probably belonged to Ogilvy.

"How much you want to bet the red Fiesta is your receptionist friend's?" Guthrie grinned from ear to ear as he wandered over to the little hatchback and peered inside the passenger window, shading his eyes with both hands to get a better look.

"Nice and tidy. A wee sprig o' heather hanging from the rear-view mirror. How Bonnie," Guthrie said, without looking up.

Alisdair pretended not to listen and took his phone out of his inside jacket pocket. He opened up a notes app and quickly typed '9 vehicles' and hit save. He then started to make his way to the entrance, turning back to see Guthrie now looking through the Jaguar's driver's side window.

"Eh, sir?" Said Alisdair, looking around like Guthrie was committing a crime.

"Sorry. Always liked those. Never been able to justify owning one though. Ah, well."

He stepped backwards, admiring the lines of the car for a second longer then turned and strode over to Alisdair who was waiting at the entrance to the building, right hand grasping the large, chrome handle. When Guthrie was a couple of paces away he opened the door then followed him into the foyer.

The receptionist looked up from her computer when she heard the door open. "Oh, hello again gentlemen," she said. "What can I do for you?"

"We'd like to see Mr Ogilvy again, if he's available," Guthrie said. He leaned on the receptionist's countertop, arms folded. "Tom Guthrie and Alisdair McEwan. Probably don't remember me, but I think you know young Alisdair here." He nodded in the direction of Alisdair who was trying to do anything but catch Guthrie's eye.

"Mr Guthrie, I certainly do remember you. It was just a couple of days ago after all." She smiled politely. "If you'd like to take a seat, I'll call Mr Ogilvy and let him know you're here." She picked up the phone and dialled.

Guthrie went over to the large armchair he sat in on his first visit, but this time stood beside it, looking out of the glass wall and to the car park.

"Mr Ogilvy will be through in just a second, gentlemen. Can I have a tea or coffee made for you?"

Alisdair shook his head. Guthrie did likewise then asked, "Is that your Fiesta outside?" Alisdair visibly stiffened.

"Yes, it is."

"Do you like it?"

"Yeah, it's a great little car, just what I need."

"Had it long?"

"A couple of years. Why?"

"Oh, nothing. It's just in great nick that's all. Looks brand new. You must take a lot of pride in it."

"Well, I don't have to drive it much through the week, you know. Just from the house to work and back."

"Oh, aye? Where in town do you live?"

"I actually live out in Arbirlot."

"Arbirlot? Sorry, I live in Broughty Ferry, I'm not familiar with the local area. You are though, Alisdair, being a local boy and all?"

Alisdair could tell exactly what Guthrie was doing. "Eh, yes. Arbirlot. It's a little village a couple of miles to the west of town. Not too far from here, in fact. There's a nice little spot at the head of a nature trail. Has a little waterfall. I used to play there as a kid. Haven't been there for years though."

"Is that so? Well, you two have something in common then. Perhaps Miss..."

"Donaldson."

"...Donaldson could show you around, see if anything's changed."

It was the receptionist's turn to avoid eye contact with both men. She tucked a stray strand of hair behind her ear. The action was not missed by Guthrie, and Alisdair was about to respond but John Ogilvy entered the reception area before he had a chance to say anything.

"Mr Guthrie, Constable McEwan." Ogilvy stood at the door to the hallway leading down to his office. "Please, come through." He held the door open, smiling politely. Guthrie nodding and Alisdair returning the smile as they walked past him. Ogilvy's smile weakened slightly as his gaze switched to the receptionist. He turned and quickly caught up with the two men.

"Have you found out anything about Bobby's death?" he asked as he moved in front of them as they reached the door to his office. He opened it. "Please," he said, indicating for them to enter. "It's obviously dominating the conversation around here. I think it'll be a while before any of us will be able to think of anything else." He stretched an arm out towards the chairs. All three men had sat down before Guthrie answered the question.

"I'm afraid we still don't have much more to tell you, Mr Ogilvy. Of course, we're waiting on the forensics report, which may provide some more information, and we're pursuing several normal lines of inquiry."

"Yes, of course. I'm sorry if I'm asking about things I've no right to ask about, only..." Ogilvy interlaced his fingers and placed his hands on the desk in front of him.

"That's quite understandable, Mr Ogilvy," Alisdair chimed in. "It's only natural to be curious about what happened to an employee, someone you worked closely with through the week."

Guthrie quickly took the opportunity to follow up on Alisdair's comment. "Mr Ogilvy, during our last visit you described how Mr Gant more or less worked on his own, but how closely did *you* work with him on a daily basis?"

Ogilvy leaned back in his chair. "Closely, I suppose. We're a small company, therefore, you can't work in your own silo. We have regular staff meetings, once a week, to make sure everyone's up to date on projects, see if we need to allocate resources, et cetera."

"How often did you talk with Mr Gant, or have meetings he was part of?"

"Every day. Like I said, we're a small company and we all understand what everyone else is doing to a degree. It makes it easier to see where you can fit in with someone else's problems on a project or get stuck in with ideas for new products or processes."

"Mr Ogilvy," Guthrie paused before going on. "I know it seems like we're repeating ourselves, but was there anything that would lead you to believe Mr Gant was under any kind of stress or there was something going on outside of work that would result in his death?"

Ogilvy leaned forward, elbows on the desk, his arms folded. "You're right, Mr Guthrie, I have thought about that very thing many times. I really can't say I know of anything that could help."

Alisdair uncrossed his legs and sat up. "Mr Ogilvy, I have to admit that I had no idea what to expect when we came here the other day. I've never been in a factory that produces clothing before. I had all these images of rows of machines and lots of people, but was quite surprised when I saw your facility."

"Well, we invest heavily in some pretty high-tech equipment that automates most of what we do. It allows us to be very efficient."

"I appreciate that now, sir, yes. I was also wondering

how business was going, in fact. We're all very familiar with your foul weather jackets you produce for the police service, but I'm interested in how the other product lines were doing? That's an impressive display in reception."

"Oh, our product showcase? Just a tangible way to indicate what we do here. Of course, here in Scotland we're probably best known for our foul weather clothing for the emergency services, but our other lines, the sportier lines are what we're known for overseas."

"How has the economy affected you, Mr Ogilvy?"

"I would say we're surviving. We were not unlike every other business over the last six years. We've had to become very aggressive on pricing and marketing to keep our product competitive and our name in the consciousness of the consumer."

"Has it paid off, though?" Alisdair asked.

Ogilvy looked through the window that provided the view of the factory floor. He answered without turning away. "It's been hard. We laid off a few people and had to discontinue some product lines, but we've made some changes. We'll be fine."

Alisdair looked at Guthrie and indicated that he was finished.

Guthrie wound up the time with Ogilvy asking for opportunities to talk to his employees again if and when it was needed. Ogilvy agreed and once again offered any help he could as he escorted them back to the main door.

Outside, Guthrie closed his eyes and looked up towards the sun. "Ach, Alisdair. What were we thinking this was going to give us, eh?"

"Honestly, I don't know. Probably nothing, I guess."

"Then remind me why we even came here? What did we think Ogilvy was going to say? 'Yes, it's a fair cop. Young

Bobby was in cahoots with my finance director and they ran off with all our profits and we had to scale back the company so much I killed him.'"

"Well... We said coming over here was probably nothing."

"I know, I know. We're grasping at straws, Alisdair. We've absolutely nothing to go on and we're grasping at straws."

Guthrie walked over to their car, but Alisdair was rooted to the spot, head down and shoulders slumped like a child who had been told off by a parent.

"Come on, son. Let's think this through over a coffee. They do sell coffee here as well as Smokies, don't they?"

Alisdair cracked a hint of a smile. He fished the keys out of his jacket pocket and pointed the remote at the car, making the horn chirp as the doors unlocked.

"I know just the place."

SEVENTEEN

Nayte's Coffee Shop was tucked down a small close off the High Street. Along one side of the room was the counter, a mix of display cases housing an assortment of cakes and pastries, and chest-high storage units. Behind the counter and along the wall two people were making sandwiches and dishing out homemade soup from large pots.

Lining the opposite wall were several high-top tables each with four chairs. The majority of them were occupied almost exclusively by women, most of them looked to Guthrie like they were well past retirement age. Alisdair headed to the table in the far corner. He took off his jacket and hung it on the back of the chair. Guthrie had a smile on his face as he sat down.

"What?" was all Alisdair could say. He too was smiling.

"You know, Alisdair, you are turning out to be a bit of a mystery to me."

"In what way?"

"Well, the first time we met I thought, 'here we go, another one of these young kids who wants to make a name for himself in the Force, climb the promotion ladder and just be a right, royal brown nose,'" Alisdair's smile changed to a frown. "But then you tell me you couldn't care for all that stuff and really want to be a copper. On top of that you know the best place to get pies and now, *now*, you bring me to a place filled with old grannies talking about their knitting circles."

Alisdair chuckled, "I take that as a compliment."

"I'm not sure it was meant as one, but okay. What do they serve here, anyway? Denture-friendly quiche? Horlicks?"

"Now, now."

Just then one of the waitresses came over. Guthrie figured she was probably an art student, based on her age, clothes and number of piercings. "Hello, Alisdair. How are you?"

Guthrie physically jerked back a little. He wasn't expecting the familiarity.

"Oh, hi, Elaine. Just the usual for me, please."

"All righty. And you, sir?" She turned to Guthrie.

"I, eh, would just like a white coffee, please."

"A large one?"

"Sure, thanks."

"No problem," replied the young waitress. She flashed a smile to Alisdair who mouthed a *thank you* in return.

Guthrie tilted his head to one side and bobbed his head up and down. "What is it with you and the young ladies?"

"She's a friend of my sister. It's why I tried the place. Just like you I thought it was for the blue hair crowd, but they kept pestering me to give it a go. I'm glad I did, because the drinks are great, and the coffee towers are incredible."

"Coffee towers? What are they?"

"They're this coffee flavoured, cream-filled pastry with a small square of chocolate on top."

"Sounds a little too frou-frou for me," Guthrie wrinkled his nose.

"Try one and you'll thank me."

"Aye, well maybe next time, eh?"

Alisdair looked around at the activity in the shop. All the customers were engaged in animated conversations with their table mates. The staff were scurrying around making and delivering orders.

"Where do we go from here, Tom? You're the expert. I have no experience of murder investigations, but it really does seem that we have absolutely nothing to go on."

Guthrie put both elbows on the table and rested his head between his hands. He sighed.

"I know, I know."

"It seems to me we have one basic problem," Alisdair went on. "What did Gant say, do, or know that would cause someone to kill him?" He took out a notebook and pen from his inside jacket pocket, opened the notebook to a fresh page and wrote Gant's name in the middle of it. He circled the word.

Guthrie stared at the page but said nothing. His eyes felt dry.

Elaine the waitress returned carrying a tray with one large mug, a plain white demitasse on a saucer, a bowl of sugar and a small, pottery pitcher of milk.

"Here we go, gents," she said as she placed the coffees on the table along with the other bits and pieces. "Can I get you anything else?"

"No, thanks for now, Elaine," Alisdair said.

Elaine smartly turned on her heel and headed back to the counter.

Alisdair started writing on the page, around Gant's name. *Work. Friends. Family.* Each word he circled and connected to Gant's name with a line. He then added more words around each of those. Around *Work* he added *Ogilvy*, *Daily Colleagues*, *Vendors*. Around *Friends* he wrote *Work* and a question mark on its own. *Family* was given the same treatment until the page looked like an airline route structure map.

Alisdair swapped his pen for the demitasse cup and sampled the double shot of espresso without removing his gaze from the page. After a few seconds of savouring the pure coffee and golden crema he picked up the pen and tapped at the question mark on the page.

"Here's the blank in our information," he said as he continued to punctuate the page.

"I agree," was the only thing Guthrie could think to say.

"So?"

"Okay." Guthrie noisily put the mug down on the table. "Let's think about this logically. We know Gant didn't hang out with anyone from work -- not on a regular basis anyway. It's not like he went out for a pint after work with a bunch of the lads."

Alisdair nodded.

"Unless he kept to himself and peed in bottles like Howard Hughes, he had to associate with at least a couple of people regularly."

"But no-one can give us a single name. Not even his parents could give us a name."

"All right. Who might be holding out on us? Who have we talked to that may give us one name? Who have we talked to that knows him better than his parents?"

Guthrie looked around at the other customers in the coffee shop. They were all engaged in animated discussions. They all looked like they were sharing secrets and swapping tidbits of gossip. Their faces were a mix of knowing smiles, concerned frowns and shocked gasps.

Then it suddenly dawned on Guthrie.

"Coffee tower you say, eh?"

"Sorry, what?"

"Coffee tower. Good is it?"

"Y... yes," Alisdair stuttered. "They're... they're fantastic."

"Right, order us two. I'm going to make a quick call." Guthrie stood up. He took his phone from his pocket and squeezed his way past the other tables and out the front door of the coffee shop.

EIGHTEEN

When Guthrie came back into the cafe the coffee towers were already on the table. He sat down and immediately picked up the dessert fork and scooped up a generous portion.

"Mm-mmm. These are good," he said through a mouthful of coffee-flavoured cream.

Alisdair sat with his mouth open slightly and a puzzled look on his face.

"What?"

"Oh, you know what," Alisdair answered.

"Oh. You mean the phone call?"

"Aye, the phone call."

Guthrie took another bite, "Umm, these really are good."

"Tom!"

"Oh, aye. Gossip."

"Gossip?"

"Yup. Gossip."

"Sorry. You've lost me."

"Look around, Alisdair." Guthrie swung his fork around

in a wide arc, taking in the entire room and sending a tiny piece of pastry flying off. "What do you see?"

Alisdair surveyed the sights of a normal coffee shop.

"A coffee shop."

Guthrie rolled his eyes. "Stories, Alisdair. Tales of the neighbours. Who's going out with who. Young Jimmy up to no good again. Gossip."

"And that helps us how?"

"We're after our missing link, our friends of Gant. Our *why*."

"Yes, but- "

"Listen, you know what it's like, at the station. Do something, no matter how small or insignificant, and in no time at all, everyone knows about it. Am I right?"

"Yes. So?"

"So, how come, in such as small firm as Ogilvy's no-one could give us anything on Gant. I mean nothing. Not a single thing?"

"He was a loner. A nice guy, but he kept to himself."

"Oh, come on, Alisdair. You think that in a small group like that there wasn't one person who could put their finger on *something*?"

Alisdair gave the question some thought.

"So? The phone call?"

"Ah." Guthrie gulped a mouthful of the coffee, swilling down the last of the pastry. "Who is the least noticed person in a company like Ogilvy's? Who is the one person who probably sees more, hears more than any other single person, but yet is so obvious, no-one pays them that much attention?"

Alisdair sipped his espresso. Guthrie tutted and tried again.

"Who would know the comings and goings of all of the

important people in the company? Who fields all the incoming phone calls?"

Alisdair looked up to the ceiling when the answer finally came to him.

"The receptionist."

"Exactly. Miss Donaldson"

"And that's who you called?"

"Yes. We're going to have a chat with her as soon as she gets off work."

"Okay. And do you have a line you think we need to follow with her?"

"No. Let's just play it as it comes."

Guthrie eyed Alisdair's coffee tower, sitting untouched on its plate.

"You going to eat that?"

Alisdair smirked and pushed the plate across the table.

"You're a good man, Charlie Brown."

NINETEEN

"Thank you, Miss Donaldson, for taking the time to chat with us."

Guthrie and Alisdair were sitting beside each other on a couch in the front room of a Victorian era cottage in the tiny village of Arbirlot, just west of Arbroath. Teri Donaldson sat on the edge of an overstuffed faux-leather armchair positioned in the corner of the room, affording a view through the front window.

"No problem. I'm happy to do anything I can to help."

Guthrie smiled and looked down at his notebook. The page had his notes from one of the interviews they had conducted earlier at the factory, but the act of looking at it was a ruse. It was part of his plan to ease the young woman into the interview. To make her think this was just a chat, rather than part of a murder inquiry. He made a show of putting the notebook back in his inside jacket pocket. He clicked the top on his silver pen, and it followed the notebook. He sat back and crossed his legs. His plan included getting Teri Donaldson away from work and into her own environment.

"Pretty house, Miss Donaldson. Very cosy."

"Thanks. I always wanted to live in the village and when I saw this one come up for sale, I jumped at the chance. Have to stretch to make the mortgage payments, but it's my dream home." She gave a nervous smile to the two men.

"No, I understand. I have a place in Broughty Ferry. It's down on Beach Crescent, you know, by the harbour. I always wanted something on that street and when something becomes available you just have to go for it."

Teri nodded nervously.

"How long have you lived here, Miss Donaldson?" asked Alisdair.

"Four years."

"And how long have you been with Ogilvy Outerwear?"

"A little over five."

"You know everyone pretty well, huh?"

"Yes. Most everyone has been there longer than me, though. There were some that were let go when business started to dry up."

Guthrie followed up, "How many were laid off?"

"I'd say about half a dozen, all on the manufacturing floor."

"None on the management or research and development side?"

"No. In such as small company you still need those people. It's always the ones who make the product."

"Or *aren't* making the product, in this case?"

"Yes, I guess you could say that."

"But things are looking better," Alisdair said, "according to Mr Ogilvy."

"Yes. We had a meeting about a week ago. We were told

about some changes to our supply chain, and some other technical things."

"What changes?" Guthrie asked.

"Oh, I'm not sure really. It was all a bit technical, like I said."

"We understand, Miss Donaldson," Alisdair reassured her, "but we are, to be perfectly honest, looking at every possible thing that Mr Gant may have been involved in that would give us some clue as to why he was murdered."

The word hung in the air of the small room. Teri Donaldson had her hands on her lap. She started to rub one with the other. Alisdair looked at Guthrie and knew he understood why. A *tell*.

Guthrie pushed a little harder.

"Miss Donaldson, if you know something, heard something, saw something that could help, you must tell us. No matter how small you think it is. If something is niggling away at you, it's probably for a very good reason."

Teri kept her gaze focused on her hands. She was now fiddling with a ring on the index finger of her right hand.

"Well, there was one thing..."

"Yes?" Guthrie leaned forward.

"About a week ago... Bobby, Mr Gant, came out into the lobby from the factory floor. He was on his mobile talking about something that wasn't right about a supplier or something."

"Do you remember who the supplier was?" Alisdair had already taken out his notebook and was turning to a new page.

Teri thought for a second. Her brow furrowed as she replayed the scene in her mind. "No. No, sorry. I wasn't paying much attention. People often come out into reception to make calls. I'm not sure why, they just do."

Guthrie moved forward, sitting on the edge of the cushion and placed his hands in a prayer-like fashion between his knees. Quietly, he said, "Miss Donaldson, it is very important that you try and remember as much about who he was talking to. Again, it may not be significant at all, but then again it could be. Can you remember anything about what the issue was perhaps?"

Teri stood up and walked over to the window leaving the two men to look at each other. Her back was towards them. Alisdair was about to say something when Guthrie waved him off with an upheld finger. When Teri did speak again her voice was hesitant.

"I really don't know exactly, but it was definitely with a supplier."

"Which one, Miss Donaldson? Do you remember which one?"

Teri still stood with her back to them. "No. No, I don't."

Guthrie stood up and nodded towards the door. Alisdair took his cue from him.

"Thanks, Miss Donaldson. I know this is not an easy time, but we must figure out everything that went on leading up to Mr Gant's death. I hope you understand."

Teri turned to face them. Her eyes, however, were focused on the carpet.

"I do. Sorry if I haven't been much help."

"Miss Donaldson," Guthrie took a step forward and gently touched her on the arm, "everything, no matter how insignificant, helps."

"We'll just see ourselves out," said Alisdair. He was standing closest to the door into the tiny hall by the front door, so he opened it and, looking back, said, "Thank you."

"Please, Miss Donaldson. If there is anything else that you think might help us, just call the station at Arbroath. I think you might already have Alisdair's number, so please phone."

He walked out of the living room but just before he was about to close the door behind him, he turned.

"Just one more question, Miss Donaldson. When exactly did that phone conversation happen? You said it was about a week ago. Do you remember exactly?"

Teri pulled her cardigan tightly across her chest and folded her arms. "I, eh, think it was the day the announcement was made about the upcoming changes." She paused. "Yes, it was that morning."

"And what day was that? Do you remember?"

"Er... the announcement was made on Monday afternoon. It would have been Monday morning."

"This past Monday? The... twenty-fourth?"

"Yes."

"Thanks again, Miss Donaldson."

Guthrie made his way onto the stone slab path outside, closing both doors behind him as he went.

Alisdair was already standing by the driver's side of the car which they had parked a few yards away from the house in a church car park. The evening was still. A few birds could be heard in the trees, then the crunch of the gravel underfoot as Guthrie walked around to the passenger side of the car.

Alisdair wanted to say something but for the second time, Guthrie cut him off.

"Get in, Alisdair. If she's watching I don't want her to see us talking."

Alisdair obliged and, as soon as Guthrie had closed his door, started the car and made a three-point turn to escape the confines of the small parking area, turning right onto the road and heading back towards Arbroath.

After a minute he couldn't stand the silence. "Well?"

"Well indeed."

"Something or nothing?"

"Oh, very definitely something, Alisdair. Very definitely something this time."

"I assume you saw the body language? The hands, not wanting to be face-to-face, looking out the window."

"Oh, yes, I cottoned on to that."

"So, we have something?"

"Aye. But now we have to narrow it down."

"Who, exactly, was Gant talking to?"

"Right. And what was the issue? It's the only positive thing we have so far. The only thing that we know Gant wasn't happy about before he died."

"And get you, Mister Touchy-Feely."

Guthrie looked at Alisdair, who was smiling. Guthrie wasn't.

"What does that mean?"

"You being all comforting to Miss Donaldson. I saw the little tap on the arm. What happened to the unconventional policing methods I read about?"

"Ach, you're full o' shi- "

"It must be those coffee towers you had this afternoon. Turning you into a wee granny."

"You're about to step over the line, young man. How dare- "

"Oh, Tom, I'm just pulling your chain."

Alisdair started to laugh. Guthrie's scowl softened, but only slightly.

"Just get us back to the station, eh. I'm dying for a pee."

"Uh-oh. Another sign of old age. Constant urination."

This time Guthrie couldn't hold a straight face. "You young bugger. Just drive."

"Okay, okay."

"Wee granny, indeed. I should report you to your inspector."

"No need for that." Alisdair kept his eyes on the road. "If you look in the glove box there might be some humbugs though."

"Alisdair!"

They both laughed. The first time they had felt they could since starting the case. Without saying as much to one another they both felt they finally had something to work on.

TWENTY

By the time they had returned to the station at Gravesend, Guthrie had tasked Alisdair with obtaining the complete vendors list from Ogilvy Outerwear. They had agreed upon a time to meet the next morning when they would make sure the personnel in the incident room were going through the list and contacting the people with whom Gant had dealings.

Guthrie had driven home listening to classical music. He parked the car feeling relaxed. Once inside his flat he pulled out a frozen meal and microwaved it for the required four minutes, before sitting down in his armchair and eating the low calorie mix of vegetables, rice and chicken without bothering to transfer it from the plastic container. No need to dirty a real plate.

As he sat in the semi-darkness, his flat illuminated only by the light coming from two small recessed fixtures in the kitchen, he thought about the day. *Finally, something to go on... perhaps*.

He didn't want to get himself too worked up about the possibility of a lead. He had felt impotent since the first meeting with Buchanan at Gravesend. Here in Dundee he knew people. He knew who to pressure, who to push to get the information he needed. Alisdair knew Arbroath, but he didn't know the people. At least not the right ones. Not yet. Art students, grannies and pie shop owners. That wasn't going to get them very far. The door-to-door inquiries and the incoming calls to the incident room were yielding nothing.

He got up and scrunched the plastic plate into the bin which needed to be taken out, cleaned the fork, put it back in the drawer, then fetched a glass. He contemplated a whisky, but decided he needed a water.

Retreating back to his chair, he pointed the remote at the flat screen in the corner of the room. After a couple of seconds, it came to life. The news was on. Something about the run up to the Commonwealth Games in Glasgow. He flicked through a few channels before stopping at a film. Black and white. He always gave them a chance. It looked like something from the States and the 1940s. A couple were talking to one another across a small table in a smoky bar. The dialogue was sharp, but just below the surface there was an obvious attraction between the two characters.

It wasn't too long, however, before his attention turned from the film back to the events of the day. Alisdair's touchy-feely comment still didn't sit right with him. He tried to focus again on the screen, but there was something inside him that wouldn't let that comment go.

It had been innocent enough, but it had, somehow, hurt.

Hurt. Was that the right word? Probably not.

His mind then switched back to the conversation with Teri Donaldson that prompted Alisdair's comment. It wasn't that long ago that he had been questioning a woman about a case, and that ended up in a fist to his gut, a bloody lip — not his — and suspension. And retirement.

Had he mellowed over the last couple of years since being away from the everyday stress of the job? Perhaps. Perhaps not. He hadn't been in that same situation since then, so it was impossible to tell. He did know he was just as committed to finding the answers. Perhaps today they had taken one step towards the answers they were looking for in the death of Bobby Gant.

Then, suddenly, the face of Dr. Jacquie Macintosh appeared in his mind's eye. Forensics. They hadn't heard from the lab at all today. But that was normal. Still, wouldn't hurt to check in with them.

He made a mental note to do that in the morning. It would be nice to have a quick update.

It would be nice to talk to Jacquie again.

"Ach, Tom, you old fart!" he said out loud. He grabbed the remote and pressed the channel up button until he came to something a little less... touchy-feely.

TWENTY-ONE

Saturday, 29th March, 2014

The rear door was in shadow. It was all he needed to see if he could force the lock and gain entry to the warehouse. If he could break in, he would be warm tonight.

It took almost forty-five minutes, but that was okay. It passed the time.

Once inside he found just what he hoped for — an empty space. Even though he was used to the dark outside, it still took several minutes for his eyes to adjust to the almost total blackness in the windowless space.

He had lost count of the times he had been asked to move on from this place or that. Doorways, alleys, even half-finished houses on building sites. All they had to do was provide some form of shelter from the rain or wind. One of the positives, of course, was sometimes, just sometimes, those doing the moving on would take pity on him and let him sleep in a cell for the night. This place, however, could be perfect.

His eyes slowly acclimatised to the quiet darkness. The

place was almost empty, save for empty cardboard boxes that had been broken down flat and stacked up in the corner in half a dozen piles roughly a foot tall. He found some large pieces of white material that looked like they could have been drop cloths used by painters, alongside a collection of wiring, lumber off-cuts, and other left-overs from a building site.

Arranging the cardboard to make a mattress, he had the luxury of taking off his long, wool coat. With the material doubled up over him, and being indoors, he didn't need to protect himself from the elements. He would be more than comfortable here tonight.

Reaching into his tattered backpack, he rummaged around until he found a small, plastic lighter and a packet of cigarettes. He lit one and inhaled deeply. Trying to peer through the darkness all he could see was emptiness. It would seem that this was not a place people would be showing up in the morning. Perhaps he could sleep a little longer than normal. He'd take the chance. So what if someone kicked him out. It wouldn't be the first time and it wouldn't be the last.

He could feel his toes starting to warm up. He laid his head back and closed his eyes. No hard doorstep tonight. No soaking rain. No cold wind. He could sleep all night. Nothing was going to wake him.

TWENTY-TWO

Guthrie and Alisdair were at Gravesend by seven a.m. Not long after they arrived, Buchanan called them into his office.

"I have another task for the two of you." Buchanan rearranged the paperwork on his desk.

"Oh, aye? What makes you think we can take time away from a murder case to do you a favour?" Guthrie was ready for a verbal fight with his former colleague. He was in no mood to let him hijack his investigation. Buchanan bristled at the response.

"*I* don't think anything of the sort, Tom. And I'll thank you for exercising a little respect for my authority over your work. Don't forget, you are a civilian, working under the auspices of Police Scotland and I am ultimately in charge of everything you do here."

Alisdair looked at his shoes. He didn't want to make eye contact with either man. Guthrie said nothing. He stood, hands in pockets, daring Buchanan to break eye contact.

Buchanan looked at a notebook. "There was a fire on the north side of town in the early hours of the morning."

"What does that have to do with us?"

Buchanan's neck, above the crisp, white collar of his shirt, was turning red. Guthrie sensed the man's anger beginning to boil. Alisdair felt the atmosphere in the room turning and didn't dare look up. All three men experiencing completely different emotions. Buchanan took a couple of seconds to compose himself before answering.

"The fire was in a warehouse building. The damage was relatively minor in nature. The fire service managed to contain the blaze quite quickly and extinguished it before it consumed much of the structure. In fact, only one corner was involved. Once the fire had been extinguished, a quick search of the premises confirmed that the building was empty, bar a few odds and ends. The fire service investigator is pretty sure it was started by accident. We're trying to contact the owner as we speak. However..."

Buchanan closed the notebook. "However, when the fire service carried out their examination, they found a body."

Alisdair finally looked up.

"From the initial survey of the scene, it seems the body was most likely that of a homeless man..."

"Let me guess," Guthrie said, folding his arms. "While we're piddling around with this other case, what is it again? Oh yes, a *murder*, we might as well take on this one too. Am I right?"

Buchanan was trying not to let Guthrie's attitude rub him the wrong way. He needed to try harder.

"Look, Tom, you know how short-handed we are in Serious Crimes. Dundee told us to put you on it. As in the Gant case, we're to contribute in every way possible and assist with resources."

"Oh, that's just fine." Guthrie almost spat out the last

word. "Now we're going to be dividing our time between two cases."

"Tom, you, of all people, should know that we're spread thin. Dundee, Arbroath, the lot of us. I've had to put all my available resources into the Gant case, again, as you very well know. Door-to-door inquiries, background checks, phone records, everything you've asked for and then some. I am painfully aware that this second case will take time and effort away from the Gant murder, but that's how it's going to be. You had better get your brain wrapped around the concept and do it quickly. You're not the only one this affects."

Guthrie backed off. "Aye. Of course," but he couldn't keep his mouth from verbalising what he was thinking. "So, we have an accident? Why then do we- "

Buchanan, interrupted. "The death still needs to be investigated in order to rule out foul play."

"Or rule in foul play, sir." Alisdair said.

"Well, yes, Alisdair, you're quite right. We should never assume, but regardless, you need to find out the appropriate details and determine exactly what happened. Hopefully, the fire investigator is correct, and we can get back to Mr Gant full-time."

Guthrie and Alisdair shared a quick glance but said nothing. Guthrie felt like the office walls were squeezing the air out of the room. This was the last thing he needed, and just when they had an encouraging lead the day before.

"Now then," Buchanan continued, "while we're on the subject of Mr Gant, how about an update before you meet with you team?"

Guthrie and Alisdair gave him a short update, including the interview with Teri Donaldson. By the time they left

Buchanan's office and were heading down the corridor to the incident room, Guthrie was fit to be tied.

"Alisdair?"

"Yes."

"This fire thing is only going to distract us if what your inspector said is true."

"What? About it being an accident?"

"Aye."

"How do you figure?"

"I know the fire investigator. He's been in the business for donkey's years. If he says it's an accident, then it's an accident. I've never known the guy to get it wrong."

"Yeah, but."

"No. No 'buts', Alisdair. Trust me on this. This is what you need to do. Get two people working on this fire. One on identifying the body, the other liaising with the fire service to make sure the scene report is completed A.S.A.P. You and I need to concentrate on the Gant case. I'll make sure the fire investigation is doing the right things, asking the right questions, all right?"

Alisdair nodded.

"We'll make an appearance at the scene later. If questions come up from the team, have them funnelled back to me and we'll take them as they come, otherwise we'll check in regularly just to make sure. Got it?"

Alisdair nodded again. "Okay."

TWENTY-THREE

Back in the incident room, Guthrie headed straight for the coffee pots. Alisdair checked with one of the female uniformed constables. He wanted to know if they had received a list of Ogilvy Outerwear's vendors. They had. The company had sent it over just as Guthrie and Alisdair were called into Buchanan's office.

He then cornered a couple of uniforms who looked like they needed something to do and briefed them on the fire, before telling them what Guthrie wanted done. He then joined Guthrie, who was stirring a spoonful of sugar into a disposable cup.

"The vendor list arrived just a few minutes ago. I have Sal printing out a couple of copies for us. Also found a couple of lads to do the legwork you needed doing on the fire."

"Good." Guthrie blew across the surface of the coffee. "No bloody milk this morning."

It was obvious to Alisdair that the news of the fire investigation was not sitting well with Guthrie, but he decided to poke the bear anyway.

"I take it from your reaction in the Inspector's office that you're not overly happy with the addition of the fire investigation."

Guthrie laughed.

"Aye, well, just when we're beginning to get somewhere, when we finally get a lead worth digging into."

"I understand," Alisdair responded, "but if we do what you said, leave the grunt work to the folks here, and if what you say about the fire investigator is true, then we can just carry on, pretty much as we were, right?"

"Oh, I suppose so, Alisdair."

Sal walked over with the printouts of the Ogilvy Outerwear vendor list. She gave one copy to each of them.

"Thanks, Sal." Alisdair said. Guthrie smiled his thanks.

"Okay. Why don't we start here, then, Alisdair?" Guthrie waved the list.

"Sounds like a plan to me."

Guthrie picked up his coffee and walked over to an empty desk, leaving the chair in front of the computer for Alisdair. He put the cup on the desk and sat, crossing his legs. He took a pen from his inside pocket and started to go down the list. It was two pages of company names, addresses, telephone numbers and primary contacts, and stapled together in the top left-hand corner. Under each company listing was a short description of what they supplied to Ogilvy.

After thirty seconds of silence he looked over the top of the computer monitor at Alisdair who looked up and raised his eyebrows.

"Are you thinking what I'm thinking?"

"Where do we start?" Alisdair responded.

"Spot on." Guthrie sipped his coffee. "Well, think about

it. What is more likely? Gant having an issue with a larger supplier, or a smaller one?"

"A larger supplier."

"Agreed."

"I have no idea about any of these companies."

"We need a little more information on each one, otherwise we're just going through the list alphabetically, hoping to get lucky. Bugger."

"Let's do both. I'll have Sal call Ogilvy for the information. In the meantime, I'll start calling the contacts on the list. I'll take a guess at which ones would be most likely to be the more important vendors, then, when I get the information back from Ogilvy, I'll double back to the ones I missed."

"All right. Seems like a reasonable plan. I think I'll... eh. I'll give forensics a call."

Guthrie quickly rose from his chair and headed for the door. He took his mobile phone from his pocket and pressed the button bringing the screen to life. He didn't give Alisdair time to say anything, plus he wanted to make his exit before his face gave him away.

Out in the corridor he scrolled through his contacts until he found Jacquie's number. He had made sure he saved it the other evening. He clicked on the entry and held the phone to his ear, waiting for the connection to be made. As he did so, he walked slowly along the corridor, heading for the stairs and the exit.

Hello. You've reached Jacquie Macintosh. I'm sorry I can't answer your call, but please leave a message and I'll get back to you as soon as I can.

"Bugger."

The beep came and in a split-second Guthrie almost hung up, but then decided to leave a message anyway.

"Ah, Jacquie. Hi. This is Tom Guthrie. I, eh, I wanted to just check in and see if you had any news for me on the Gant case. Sorry to bother you. Anyway, eh, just give me a call at your convenience."

He rattled off his number and ended the call. Walking back into the incident room he saw that Alisdair was on his phone. He was propping up his head with one hand, the other held the phone to his ear. Both elbows were resting on the table either side of the vendor list. Every few seconds he would write a note on the paper and assume the head-in-hand position. Alisdair ended the call.

"Any idea when Ogilvy will get the information to us?"

"Sal just made the call out there and they told her they hope to get the details to us round about lunch time."

Guthrie nodded his head.

"Forensics?"

Guthrie picked up the coffee cup from the corner of the desk and thought better of it. He put it back down.

"Left a message."

Alisdair wasn't sure what Guthrie was thinking or feeling. The only noise came from two uniformed officers talking on their wireless headsets.

"I told Sal to make a couple more copies of the list and have the boys make some calls. I told them to ask what they supply, how often they fulfil orders, if they worked with Gant, and if they did, whether they had any social connections beyond business, that kind of thing."

"Thanks, Alisdair." Guthrie sat down heavily. "I guess we can keep going until we get the information from Ogilvy or we get through the list ourselves."

"I don't see why we shouldn't." Alisdair picked up Guthrie's copy of the list. "I'm starting at the top. The boys are taking the second page, so why don't you start from the bottom of page one and we'll meet in the middle?"

"Fine plan, young Alisdair."

Alisdair smiled. He heard the complete lack of enthusiasm in Guthrie's voice. He didn't know exactly how to take it. It seemed like one minute Guthrie was charged up about the fact that they now had a lead, but when it came down to the slog of following through, of doing the tedious job of making calls, the drive disappeared from Guthrie as quickly as a snowflake on a barbecue.

"What's wrong, Tom?"

"Ach, nothing. Just thinking."

"About?"

"It's still going to be a long shot: finding a connection — if there is one."

Alisdair sat back and folded his arms. "Are you looking for a short-cut?"

Guthrie rubbed his face. "Of course not, Alisdair. I'm just a little impatient."

"And?"

"And... I just wish I knew the town better. Knew the people better."

Alisdair suppressed the desire to say, *so you can pressure them into giving up information*, but instead he said, "I can understand that." He looked at Guthrie who was staring into his lap.

"Okay. Then we need to get on with the calls, don't you think?"

Guthrie took a deep breath. "Yes, you're right, Alisdair. No point in hoping the answer will come any other way." He picked up the vendor list. "Where did you want me to start again?"

"Bottom of the first page. Make your way backwards."

"Got it."

Guthrie got up and walked over to another empty desk. He flattened the paper on the desk and picked up the receiver of the phone, dialling the first of the numbers.

TWENTY-FOUR

After two hours of calls, Guthrie had had enough. He had sat at the desk the entire time without getting up for a coffee or even to stretch. After an hour and a half, he had asked Alisdair where he was on the list, counting down to the point where they met.

"Bloody hell. That was fun."

"Good old-fashioned detective work, I would have thought," Alisdair said, not without a hint of sarcasm in his voice.

"I've never been one for the mundane paperwork, Alisdair. I thought you would have picked up on that by now."

"Oh, I figured that alright. Just think, though. All this work will confirm one way or another our thinking about a link to a supplier."

"Alisdair, son, I've been at this a long time. Far longer than you." Alisdair started to blush, embarrassed that he had told Guthrie what investigative work entailed. "I know exactly what this means."

"Sorry, Tom. I just- "

"Och, don't worry. I'm still a bit pissed off from earlier. And these chairs must be the most uncomfortable..."

"Coffee break?" Alisdair walked around the desk towards the pots.

"Aye. But let's get out of here before something else happens and we get lumbered with it."

"What do you suggest?"

"We might as well take a look at this fire. We need to anyway. You know Buchanan will be all over us if we don't. At least we can say we've been out there."

"Okay. Let me check with the others working the list and see where they are. Perhaps we can look over what we have at lunch?"

"Good. Then rustle up a pool car. I'm off to the loo. I'll meet you downstairs at the car park door."

With that, Guthrie strode out of the incident room, arching his back, trying to rid himself of the stiffness, and rubbing his rear end. Alisdair watched him go. He smiled and shook his head.

TWENTY-FIVE

Guthrie's mobile had started to buzz in his jacket pocket while he was still standing, staring at the wall above the urinal.

"Ach!"

He quickly finished up and washed his hands. The phone had stopped buzzing a full minute before he could retrieve it. He clicked the screen into life before walking into the corridor.

The number was Jacquie's. He touched the number to call back.

"Jacquie Macintosh."

"Jacquie. Tom Guthrie."

"Tom, hello. How are you?"

Over the phone, her west highland accent seemed more pronounced than when face-to-face. Guthrie liked it. It was a far cry from the east coast sounds he had grown up with.

"I'm well, thanks. You?"

"Fine, yes."

"I'm sorry I missed your call. I was a bit busy,"

"You don't have to apologise, Tom. I know you're busy."

"All the same."

There was a moment of dead air, broken by both of them beginning to talk at the same time.

"Sorry, Jacquie, go ahead."

"I just wanted to let you know that we're working up a draft report on your Mr Gant."

"That's great, Jacquie. Fast too."

"I'm sure not as fast as you would have liked, though."

"That's probably true."

"I thought so." There was a smile in her voice.

"Anything of interest?"

"Wow. No small talk. No, 'how are you doing? I enjoyed the other night.' Straight to the bottom line, huh, Tom?"

"Sorry, I-"

Jacquie laughed. "Oh, come on, Tom. Surely you can put up with more banter than that?"

Guthrie felt the beads of sweat forming on his brow.

"Tom?"

"Eh, sorry, Jacquie. I was... Never mind. No, you're right. Of course I enjoyed the other night. Thanks for suggesting it."

Jacquie laughed again. "*Suggest*? I practically twisted your arm off."

"It was fun..."

"But..."

"But nothing."

"But you're working and you're after forensics, right?"

Another silence answered Jacquie's question.

"Okay. No time wasting. We completed a normal PM on the body. Nothing new from the preliminary report you saw the other day. The bruising on the victim's wrists was consistent with the rope used to tie him down. Injuries inflicted or suffered before death included a dislocated shoulder and several cuts on his face. The analysis of the victim's clothing revealed no major revelations. The trace elements we found included a grass stain on his trousers, sand and other small particulate matter, consistent with the victim's location, in his pockets, et cetera."

Guthrie listened for anything new or out of the ordinary. He heard nothing.

"You want me to go deeper?"

"Jacquie, was there anything that caught your eye. Anything at all?"

"Tom, if I knew you better, I would say you sound a little desperate."

Guthrie sighed. "I guess you know me well enough. Yes, I am desperate. So far we have practically nothing to go on."

"There was nothing I saw that I thought you might find useful. The scene was under water for several hours, as was the victim, obviously. He was washed clean."

"I understand. I was hoping for something."

Jacquie could hear the frustration. "Tom, this is preliminary. You know we'll pour over every part of the body and every millimetre of clothing before we finalise the report. Right now, we see nothing either out of the ordinary or unexplained, but that doesn't mean we won't come up with something that gives you what you need."

"I know."

"I wanted to give you a call anyway. Even if it was just to say we had nothing. Sorry."

Guthrie shifted his weight from foot to foot and pinched the bridge of his nose. His stomach started to churn. Something that he hadn't felt for months -- not since leaving the force.

"Tom?"

"Aye, sorry, Jacquie."

"You okay?"

"Ach, it's nothing. Dead ends, you know? I hate them."

There was a short pause before Jacquie spoke again. "You want to talk about it? Perhaps over dinner?"

Guthrie's immediate reaction was to say, *Yes. Absolutely. I'd want that more than anything right now,* but his sensible brain kicked in and before he could argue with himself, he heard himself say, "That's very kind of you, Jacquie, but I can't."

"No. Of course. I shouldn't have asked." She closed her eyes and shook her head. She mentally kicked herself. What was she thinking?

"Thanks, Jacquie. I mean it."

"That's me. No time wasting."

"I'll call you later, eh? Thanks again for the call and update. I really appreciate it."

Jacquie screwed her eyes shut even tighter than they were already. This was shaping up to be the usual mess. Trying to keep her tone light, she responded, "Sure, Tom. Any time. If anything comes up, I'll give you a shout."

"Thanks, Jacquie."

Guthrie looked at the ceiling. Putting his phone back in his jacket pocket he headed to the car park where Alisdair would be waiting. The last thing he wanted to do was fool around with the fire investigation.

Jacquie looked at her phone. When the screen darkened, she hit herself on the head with it.

"Idiot."

TWENTY-SIX

"Nice."

Guthrie took in the leather seats of the Jaguar Alisdair had signed out for their trip to the warehouse fire.

"Not bad, huh?"

"Who did you have to bribe to get this thing? Or did you just have to flash that boyish smile at the young lady at the front desk?"

Alisdair shot Tom a frown but didn't answer either question. "It's a loaner from Dundee. Inspector Buchanan is the only one who uses it, but there was nothing else available, so..."

At the mention of the inspector's name Guthrie visibly shrunk into the seat and grunted.

"I should have known. The thing is cleaner than the inside of a Dettol bottle." He folded his arms and watched the buildings go by. Alisdair smirked, but again refused to comment.

"Been seeing a lot of these things recently," Guthrie said as he inspected the interior. "You think I should trade in my MG?"

"I'm not sure they take cars that old," Alisdair answered.

"Cheeky bugger!"

After a couple of minutes, they were already nearing the north side of the town. Semi-detached houses built in the seventies gave way to fields. A garden centre on the right stood opposite the entrance to an area of lock-ups, garages and storage buildings.

"It's down, through here," Alisdair said, turning the car off the main road and onto the gravel access drive.

Making their way past smaller buildings they saw a larger steel construction. It had grey brickwork for the first five feet, then metal siding up to a corrugated roof. A police vehicle parked at the far corner confirmed this was the building they were looking for.

As they approached, Guthrie said, "You can hardly tell there was a fire from this angle."

Alisdair nodded silently.

Another car was parked beside the police car. Alisdair made the total three.

The ground around the building was mostly dirt. There was some gravel, but not enough to make a difference. The water from the fire hoses had turned the area around this end of the building into a thick, soupy mud. The dark brown goop squelched underfoot as if walking through inch deep chocolate pudding.

"Oh, this is just what we need," complained Guthrie.

The two men made their way around the parked cars to the corner of the building where a metal door was propped open with a piece of wood.

Guthrie pointed to the vehicle next to the police car. "That's the fire investigator's."

Guthrie went inside. There were no lights on except for some at the far end of the building, opposite from where they had just come in. Work lights that had been set up on tall stands. A hole in the ceiling, no larger than six feet by six feet also helped dispel the ambient darkness. The fire had indeed been confined to one corner. The hole in the roof appeared to be where two corrugated sheets had fallen in, most likely from the fire itself, but perhaps helped along by the fire service while fighting the blaze.

Had the roof been intact, you would be hard pressed to even notice the damage caused by the fire.

A lone uniform stood in the gloom.

"Good morning, sir." He then spotted Alisdair as he followed Guthrie into the warehouse. "Oh, hullo, Alisdair. What's up with the civvies? You taken a dislike to our finely tailored uniforms?"

For the third time in fifteen minutes, Alisdair ignored the question. Guthrie smiled, but felt sorry that Alisdair was getting flak from his fresh-faced colleague. He coughed and put on what he hoped was a sufficiently authoritative tone. "Constable McEwan has been assigned to the investigation of this fire and associated death. I'm sure his choice of clothing is of no concern to you, son, and makes no difference to proper procedure. I would appreciate very much, therefore, if you would inform the fire investigator we're here. My name's Guthrie."

The constable looked a little flustered. The tone must have been spot on, thought Guthrie.

"Yes, sir. If you would like to stay here, please. There's a single entry to the scene. If you wouldn't mind putting these booties on, I'll let the fire investigator know you're here." He pointed to a box containing packs of crime scene overshoes.

"Thanks, Mark." Alisdair gave him a thumbs up as the young man strode quickly towards the far corner of the building. He picked up a small package containing a pair of baby blue overshoes and handed it to Guthrie, then opened another for himself.

"You didn't have to put it on so thick with Mark, but I did like the look on his face."

"I know. It was funny though. He probably thinks I'm Buchanan's sarcastic cousin. You could see the blood drain from his face even in this light."

"Any idea what this place is, or was, used for?"

"They're working on it back at the station. They're trying to track down the owner. Doesn't look like much of anything though, huh?"

"No, Alisdair, you're right. It seems to be a fairly new building, if the landscaping outside is anything to go by." Guthrie lifted a foot and shook it, the blue bootie hiding the mud-covered shoe underneath. "Another good pair of shoes ruined in the line of duty."

By the time Constable Mark returned, Guthrie's eyes had acclimatised to the darkness of the building's interior. The place was essentially empty. There were a couple of piles of lumber along one of the walls. There was no interior office space. The entire building looked as new and unused as the exterior suggested.

Alisdair offered a quick thanks to his colleague and started towards the work lights on the far side of the building. Guthrie kept up the good cop, bad cop routine by not even bothering to look up as he passed the young officer. They both stayed close to the wall on their right, following the standard forensics protocol of a single entry point to the scene. When they reached the scene of the fire the stark, white light seemed to almost wash out any colour, in contrast to the lack of colour they had quickly grown accustomed to in the dimness.

In the corner was what was left of a pile of flattened

cardboard boxes. Almost the entire lot had been burned, but some of the material around the edges was still intact. The majority of it, however, was now a sodden pile of ash. To the left and up against the wall were a couple of plastic crates. An overcoat was draped over them. Bits of building site left-overs were scattered around this corner of the building. Scaffolding, lumber, paint tins, buckets. Four or five fluorescent tubes were leaning up against the wall.

In the middle of it all was a man in a blue over-suit and mask. When he saw the visitors, he stood up and walked over, careful not to disturb his worksite. He pulled the mask from his face.

"Well, well, well. Look what the cat dragged in. If it isn't ol' Isla Guthrie." Alisdair raised an eyebrow at the nickname. "I haven't seen you in donkey's. They didn't tell me you were coming here. In fact, why are you here?" He removed a latex glove and shook Guthrie's hand.

"Richard, how are you?" Guthrie's expression was the same as someone shaking hands with a pickpocket.

Seeing the look on Guthrie's face, the fire investigator protested. "What!"

"Oh, nothing, you old fart. I never know what you have up your sleeve." Guthrie turned to Alisdair who was standing slightly behind him, hands behind his back. "Richard Fisher, this is Constable Alisdair McEwan."

Alisdair took a step forward and raised his hand in greeting. "Hello."

"Hello, constable. Pleased to meet you. What brings the two of you here? Surely not work, Tom?"

"Actually, yes. I'm working this case with Alisdair, here."

"But I thought you'd retired?"

"I have. From the Force, that is. I'm here as a consultant."

Fisher whistled. "A consultant, eh? Isn't that code for 'can't get a real job'?"

Guthrie replied with a disapproving look. Fisher laughed.

"I could always get a rise out of you, Tom."

"Alisdair," Guthrie said turning to his colleague, "something you must always remember when dealing with our Mr Fisher is that he is, without question, the best at what he does. However, be careful not to get on the wrong side of him, or even the right side with your back turned. He has a habit of playing practical jokes."

"Now, now, Tom. I have apologised I don't know how many times."

Alisdair frowned questioningly.

"Alisdair," said Fisher, "when you get a chance, ask Mr Guthrie about the time when -"

"Richard," Guthrie interrupted, "I think we can spare young Alisdair the history lesson."

"Oh, I'd rather like to hear," Alisdair protested.

"No, you wouldn't," Guthrie said matter-of-factly. Fisher winked at Alisdair. "I think we should get on with the business at hand. We can catch up later."

"Och, Tom, you spoil-sport. If you insist."

Guthrie sniffed and said, "Okay, Richard, we're assigned to take care of this investigation from our side of things. What can you tell us? We've already heard that your preliminary assessment is an accidental death. Is that still the case?"

Fisher's tone changed to a monotone voice as if he was describing a cube of tofu. He reviewed, in detail, the method used to determine the source of the ignition, spread, evidence, and a myriad of details as if he were checking items on a mental list, no doubt perfected over years.

Guthrie had heard the spiel before and followed along, nodding occasionally. Alisdair scribbled in his notebook, trying his best to keep up.

When Fisher had finished, he folded his arms and looked at Guthrie with a crooked smile.

"Definitely accidental death caused by a lit cigarette?"

"Yup. Wouldn't be surprised if the PM shows that he'd had a skinful of cheap vodka before bedding down and lighting up his cigarette."

"Why do you say that?" Alisdair asked. He was still writing in his notebook.

Guthrie and Fisher looked at one another, then at Alisdair.

"What? Did I miss something?"

Guthrie pointed to an empty bottle lying beside the charred cardboard.

"Ach, sorry." His face reddened.

"That's alright, son," said Fisher. "Isla here wouldn't have spotted it either, if it wasn't for all the training I've given him over the years." Fisher slapped Guthrie on the back.

"I'm surprised you can stand yourself, sometimes," Guthrie responded.

"Well, you know I have to get out among the common folk every once in a while to make sure I don't get too caught up in my own brilliance."

"Ah, Shite, Richard," was all Guthrie could manage.

Fisher surveyed their corner of the building. "I suppose you'll want the report on all this yesterday?"

"You suppose correctly. Alisdair will give you a call later and make sure you have the contacts at the incident room." Alisdair nodded and made another note.

"Perhaps we can get together for a pint? Haven't done that in a long time."

"Aye. That'll be fine." Guthrie took his phone from his pocket and looked to see if he had Fisher in his contacts list. "Still at the same number?"

"Aye. Just give me a shout. Maybe we can go for a curry?"

"Now you're talking."

They shook hands. Fisher walked back over to the pile of cardboard. "Mind, Alisdair, you don't forget to ask him about that time-"

"Okay, okay, Richard. I'll call you sometime."

TWENTY-SEVEN

Guthrie led Alisdair out of the warehouse, having tossed their protective coveralls in a bin beside the door. Guthrie had scowled at the uniform again for good measure. Alisdair just shrugged his shoulders as he walked past.

"Bloody waste of time," Guthrie complained. He was leaning on the roof of the Jaguar, looking at his muddy shoes.

"What do you say to us going for that coffee?" Alisdair asked, hoping to get Guthrie off topic and into a more positive frame of mind. "We can ride in luxury for a while longer." He unlocked the doors and waited for a response. Guthrie screwed up his face in an even larger look of disgust, which Alisdair thought was physically impossible.

"We should get back to the station and see if the guys have found anything from the vendor list."

Alisdair nodded.

"Still. It would be a shame to not enjoy ourselves for just a wee while, eh? Coffee it is. Lead on young Alisdair."

Guthrie got into the car. A smile spread on Alisdair's

face, then he exhaled satisfied that he had averted a miser-
ably quiet ride, however short, back to Gravesend.

TWENTY-EIGHT

Fifteen minutes later they were sitting in a corner booth of the *Old Brewhouse* near the harbour at the foot of the town, having ordered a filter coffee, a latte, and a couple of shortbread biscuits.

On the way, Alisdair had called the station and spoken to Sal who told him they had finished going through Ogilvy's vendor list. He'd asked her to email him a bullet point summary. A sound like a tap on a wine glass told Alisdair the email had arrived on his phone. He swiped the screen and opened the email application.

"All right. Let's see what we have." He tapped the message and put the phone on the table so Guthrie could read the screen.

Rather than a short summary, Sal had compiled a spreadsheet of the results, including all the vendors Guthrie and Alisdair had contacted. Almost all of the rows were void of detail beyond the name of the contact person at the company, what the company supplied Ogilvy Outerwear, and the annual sales attributed to the contract.

"What do you think?"

Guthrie studied the list intently. "Nothing stands out, but then again, what are we expecting to see?"

"Okay," Alisdair responded, "what about prioritising? Largest contracts to smallest, like we said earlier, or local to furthest away?"

"That's the only thing I can think of. I assume the lack of any kind of notes indicates that whoever made the call found nothing worth reporting."

"That's the way I would take it."

Guthrie blew out his cheeks and exhaled noisily.

Thirty minutes later the pair had the list rewritten in a way that they could hand out to uniforms for more detailed follow-up.

Guthrie sat back in his chair. "Our biggest lead at this point is the phone call between Gant and the mystery supplier Teri Donaldson told us about. I was hoping we would get a little more out of that from this list."

"Perhaps I could pay her another visit." Alisdair kept his gaze on his drink.

"Well, well, young Alisdair. You do have a little crush on her." Alisdair blushed and shifted his stare to a spot above Guthrie's head. "All right, why don't you give her a call and see if you can set up a meeting this afternoon."

"What about you?"

"I think I'll take a little drive."

TWENTY-NINE

Guthrie sat across from the entrance to the industrial estate that was the home of Ogilvy Outerwear. The light was beginning to fade as the sun disappeared behind a thick layer of grey cloud. The heat had long dissipated from the MG. Guthrie turned up his collar and sunk down in the seat.

The fact that he was in a forty-year-old sports car and about to follow someone was not lost on Guthrie. It was not going to be easy blending in to the traffic in a classic car. He hoped Ogilvy left late enough the fading evening light would make it more difficult to spot that a particularly uncommon car was following him.

No such luck.

Ogilvy's Jaguar appeared at the junction and turned right, heading north, away from town. Guthrie sat up in the seat, turning the ignition key and firing up the MG.

A couple of cars passed before he could pull out onto the main road, but Guthrie was happy with the buffer between him and his quarry. They drove a couple of miles into the countryside. Ogilvy turned right at the village of

Colliston onto a country road. The cars between the Jaguar and the MG continued straight. Guthrie hoped that Ogilvy would not be paying much attention to the traffic and since there were no cars behind him, Guthrie slowed, increasing the gap before he too had to turn.

The road brought them to a gated entrance of an up-market housing development. The Jaguar's indicator blinked confirming Guthrie's suspicion that Ogilvy would live here.

The Jaguar wound between well-manicured lawns and driveways. In the fading light Guthrie caught glimpses of what looked like long stretches of grass. A golf course? Every house had at least a single garage and those cars on display in drives were all out of Guthrie's price range.

Ogilvy turned his car onto the gravel drive of one of the larger homes. Guthrie slowed to a stop two houses back. He watched as Ogilvy got out and walked towards the front door, which opened, spilling a warm, yellow light onto the path.

Guthrie expected Mrs. Ogilvy to greet her husband. Instead, a tall man, hands in pockets, filled the doorway.

Guthrie rolled the window down to try to get a clearer view of the stranger. The two men shook hands and went into the house.

Guthrie sat and asked himself what he thought he would accomplish by tailing Ogilvy. He drummed his fingers on the steering wheel while considering his options. For all he knew, Ogilvy was visiting a friend. It didn't always have to be a clandestine meeting of some local gang of thugs.

As soon as the thought had formed in his mind, Guthrie dismissed it. Probably just some golfing and drinking pal.

He put the car into first gear and, executing a U-turn, headed back the way he had come.

His mobile phone was lying on the passenger seat. He picked it up and checked to see if he had any missed calls or texts. There was one text from Alisdair wondering if he was coming back to the station. There was also a missed call and voicemail from Buchanan.

Guthrie pulled over and pressed the voicemail icon on his phone. Buchanan.

Tom. I need an update. I won't accept being kept in the dark, and I want regular briefings each morning. I know you technically don't have to follow protocol, but it's not what I'm used to or expect. Briefing tomorrow with me at seven-thirty, and with the entire team at eight.

Guthrie breathed in deeply. He closed his eyes and leaned back on the headrest. He really couldn't be bothered with Buchanan. They were like chalk and cheese and Buchanan was right, he didn't have to follow protocol. That was for them. He just had to stay, approximately, within the lines.

He opened his eyes again and switched screens on his phone, going back to the text page. He clicked on the contact details for Alisdair and called him.

THIRTY

Guthrie walked back from the bar to the corner table he had secured while waiting for Alisdair. They had decided to meet for dinner at the Colliston Inn, just a few minutes from Ogilvy. Guthrie almost hoped Ogilvy and his mystery companion would decide to visit the local pub for a pint, allowing him to innocently bump into him.

"Cheers." Alisdair took his pint as Guthrie sat down.

"What did Miss Donaldson have to say?"

"She doesn't know who the supplier was Gant was talking to -- or at least that's what she said."

Guthrie ran his fingers through his hair, "Bugger."

But she did say that it had something to do with tests on one of the materials."

"Really?" Guthrie slapped the table. "Well, that's something at least. Perhaps we can cross-reference the vendor list with whatever product testing that has taken place recently."

"I can have Sal ask for any records and go through them to see if there are any possible links."

"Sure. Get them on that first thing."

"I'll call Sal this evening and give her a heads-up."

"Thanks."

"By the way, Buchanan was not too happy today. He was asking all sorts of questions about where you were, why he couldn't get hold of you."

"So, Buchanan is on my case is he?"

"I would say that's a fair description. He's livid that we're not getting anywhere, and you've been a little less than free with the information updates."

Guthrie almost slammed his pint glass on the table, some of the head spilling out over his fingers. "What information, Alisdair?"

Alisdair held up his hands in mock surrender. "Hey, I'm on your side. I'm just telling you what I'm hearing back at the station."

"I know, I know."

"What's your plan to get him back onside? You know you have to, otherwise it's going to be a nightmare. You've known him longer than me, but I obviously know what kind of shop he runs and what he expects of his officers."

Guthrie took a long swallow of his beer, wiping the foam from his top lip. "Well, let's get on the front foot with him -- take the initiative on the morning's briefing."

"What do you mean?"

Guthrie took out his notebook and opened to a fresh page. He found his pen, wrote *BRIEFING* at the top of the page and underlined it.

"He wants daily briefings with him at half past seven, and the team at eight."

"He also mentioned four," Added Alisdair.

Guthrie rolled his eyes but continued. "Okay. Then let's give him what he wants."

THIRTY-ONE

Sunday, 30th March, 2014

Buchanan stood at one end of the incident room. Guthrie sat at a desk to his left, nursing a bottled water. He had to cut down on caffeine.

It had been ten the night before when he and Alisdair parted company having drawn up the briefing summary, downing a couple of pints in the process. By the time Guthrie got back to his flat, it was almost eleven.

Even with the alcohol in his system, the long day behind him, and a slow drive home, he couldn't fall asleep. His mind went through the case then wandered to thinking about Jacquie and how he owed her a call. He couldn't believe he let the entire day go by without calling her. Another Guthrie fail. He had finally fallen asleep around two.

The room was filled with officers from Arbroath, a couple from Montrose, and a few new faces Guthrie had not seen before. He wondered if they had been drafted in that morning, or he had just failed to notice them over the last couple of days. Around thirty men and women in total. There was a general buzz about the room as officers talked in their small groups. A couple stood by the coffee pots, the noise of spoons rattling around the inside of mugs as heaps of sugar were stirred in to help kickstart their day.

Buchanan began the briefing.

"All right. Settle down." The room fell silent. "As I communicated yesterday, we shall be having regular briefings. Eight and four. Most of you will be expected to attend the morning briefing. The afternoon briefing will be for those working the two 'til ten shift and carrying out tasks assigned by the main team. I shall also be talking with Mr Guthrie prior to that, in order to keep up to speed on any progress through the day."

Guthrie could feel his neck turning red as Buchanan called him "mister". He tried not to let his face betray him and smiled to the assembly.

Alisdair, who was sitting on the corner of a desk at the back of the room, caught Guthrie's eye. He turned up one corner of his mouth in a half smile, letting Guthrie know he had caught the epithet.

"Mr Guthrie has provided a summary of the facts so far. Everyone should have been given a copy when they came in. If you didn't, please raise your hand and Constable McEwan will get a copy to you."

A couple of the later arrivals raised their hands and Alisdair snaked his way between the tables and chairs, an occasional *excuse me* as he stepped over outstretched legs of those who were either too lazy or uncaring to move.

"Please review the summary completely at the end of this briefing," Buchanan continued, "and ask Mr Guthrie or McEwan if you have any questions. However, Mr Guthrie, if you would run through the highlights of both cases and provide the teams with their tasks?"

Guthrie had his head tipped back slightly as he polished off the last mouthful of water. He placed the plastic bottle on the table and stood up.

"Good morning, everyone. Thank you, first of all, for your work on both cases." Buchanan stood with his arms folded surveying the room. His expression was stone-faced. *Prat*, thought Guthrie. "Let's start with the fire victim, since that's pretty much an open and shut case, apart from the official report from the Fire Service investigator."

Guthrie went over the salient points of the case. They were just waiting on Richard Fisher's report along with the usual paperwork, including the SOCO's final report.

There was a small group of officers who had been dedicated to the case. Alisdair made sure they had their marching orders for the day, to include chasing up the reports and clearing the case in order to free them up to be reassigned to the Gant investigation.

Guthrie picked up the lead from Alisdair and switched to the murder case.

"Right. The Gant murder." He looked around the room. The briefing summary that he and Alisdair had worked on looked impressive at first glance, but when you took time to digest it properly, it didn't take long to see the lack of potential credible suspects.

Every officer was staring back at him. Guthrie thought one of the more senior sergeants looked like he was waiting for Guthrie to crumble. *Bloody, jumped up, ex-cop. Thinks he can just swan around acting like some big-time private investigator.*

Bugger it, he thought. He had to go on the offensive.

"Here's where we stand. We've got a couple of leads, but

as of yet, nothing solid. We don't have anyone in particular in the frame for the murder, and, quite frankly, I feel like we're spinning our wheels, waiting for the answers to fall into our lap."

His mouth was dry, despite the water. "I'm sure Inspector Buchanan will agree with me when I say that this is unacceptable." He looked at Buchanan who kept his gaze towards the body of the room. Arms still folded across his chest, Buchanan nodded slowly.

Guthrie continued. "That's why I want us to go over everything we've done — again." There was an audible groan from everyone. Officers shifted in their seats and a few leaned towards their neighbour and whispered their obvious disapproval.

"Okay. Quiet," Buchanan said. He walked slowly towards the other end of the room where two sergeants were talking to one another, their briefing sheets held up to their faces, covering their mouths, as if that would hide what they were doing.

"Continue, Mr Guthrie."

Guthrie picked up the water bottle, saw that it was empty and set it back down on the table. He could murder another one.

"As you can see from the briefing notes, our only lead is this phone call between Gant and one of the Ogilvy Outerwear suppliers. Constable McEwan has been following up with Miss Donaldson, the receptionist-"

The younger of the two officers from Montrose let out a wolf whistle. The locals from Arbroath visibly cringed, and Buchanan made his way over to stand between them, causing one or two smiles.

"Miss Donaldson, the receptionist," repeated Guthrie, "but we still need to nail down who this was. Alisdair has assigned two of you the task of calling the suppliers to find out who Gant was talking to."

Alisdair pointed to the pair from Montrose, who raised their hands. Guthrie half nodded towards them in response.

"I don't want to hear you couldn't find out who this was. I want an answer by the end of the day."

"Sir," Wolf Whistle said, looking serious for the first time in the briefing. Buchanan folded his arms again and settled a death stare on his partner who sheepishly began flicking through the vendor list Alisdair had given to them.

"The biggest hole in our information is Gant himself. He's a mystery. He's clean, and that in itself is suspicious to me. The majority of you have been assigned to the task of digging up everything there is to know about Bobby Gant. We're going to interview his colleagues at work *again* as well as his parents. I want you to go through every piece of paper we secured from his flat. Call every name you find, every connection he had, no matter how insignificant you think it is."

Guthrie closed his eyes and pinched the bridge of his nose. He put the briefing sheet on the table.

"Look, I know many of you have never been involved with this kind of investigation before," his voice was quiet, "and I realise only a handful of you have had any formal training for this work, but I am counting on you to do your very best. Bobby Gant was beaten up and left to watch the tide come in and drown him.

"I know it's a cliché, but we owe it to him, his parents, to find who did this."

Guthrie sat down.

Buchanan walked towards the door. "Right. You heard Mr Guthrie. Let's get to it."

The room thinned out. Alisdair took a seat beside Guthrie just as Buchanan joined them at the table.

"I appreciate the prep work for the briefing, Tom." Buchanan picked up the summary sheet, emphasising his point, before tossing it back on the table.

"No problem, Ian." Guthrie nodded at Alisdair. "You have young Alisdair to thank for that. He's the one keeping my paperwork straight — and you know how I love my paperwork."

Buchanan smiled, but it had no warmth. "Perhaps PC McEwan can keep reminding you about the policies we have in place during an investigation?" He looked at Alisdair. "Remember, you have been given quite a bit of leeway while working with Mr Guthrie," There was that *mister* again, "but I will not allow you both to just do as you please."

Guthrie leaned back in the chair. Beads of sweat beginning to form on his forehead. He was about to fire back at Buchanan when Alisdair saved him.

"Sir, I apologise if I have not followed proper procedure as a serving officer. As you know, I have very little experience in this kind of investigation, but I also appreciate the nature of Mr Guthrie's remit with us."

Buchanan's brow furrowed.

"During our work for this morning's briefing we resolved to make sure you and the team are briefed per your expectations."

"I'm glad to hear that, McEwan."

Guthrie felt he needed to dive in. "Look, Ian, Alisdair's taking his cues from me. If you have any heartburn with him, it's my fault."

"Oh, I am fully aware of your M.O., Tom." Buchanan closed his eyes and leaned his head back. Opening his eyes again, he focused on the ceiling, "My issue is that I am the one who's career can be affected by your actions. I've waited long enough — probably too long — in this investigation to reel you in and get you acting like an officer and not a civilian."

Guthrie's chin fell to his chest. *Here we go*, he thought. He knew it was only a matter of time before Buchanan puffed out his chest and started to lay down his law. For the second time this morning, Guthrie could feel the heat beneath his collar.

"I was assigned to this investigation because of my experience and track record when I was with the force," Guthrie said quietly.

"You were assigned to this investigation because we are under-manned and had no other resources to pull from," Buchanan responded. Guthrie pushed his chair back and stood up. He placed two fists on the table and leaned towards Buchanan.

"My arrest record was one of the highest in the force." His voice was quieter still. "You're just jealous that neither you, nor anyone from Arbroath, was deemed capable of taking on this case in your own back yard."

Buchanan's face was turning red. He was barely able to contain the anger welling up inside. The two of them stood, staring at one another like two boxers before a fight. Alisdair didn't know what to think, other than at some point a punch was going to be thrown.

"Get on with your work, Mr Guthrie. I expect you to be here at three-thirty to brief me." Buchanan slowly turned and walked out of the room.

Alisdair slumped heavily into the nearest chair. "Jeez, Tom, what was all that?"

Guthrie spun around. His face was red and a bead of

sweat rolled down his face from his right temple. "Bloody prick."

Alisdair raised both hands. "Now, wait a minute, Tom. Let's calm down and look at this from the inspector's point of view."

"Must we?"

"Yes, we must. He does have more at stake here. He has to answer for your actions, for *our* actions."

"Are you saying I'm treating this as a game?"

"Certainly not. I'm saying you need to be careful. Buchanan has the ability to recommend resources, argue the budget requirements. He has the power to have you kicked off this case, if you get right down to it."

Silence.

"Look, why don't we just play his game?"

Guthrie tutted.

"I know that's the last thing you want to hear, but the realities are just what I explained."

Guthrie let Alisdair's words roll around in his head. "I was a bit of an arse," he said eventually.

"Aye, you were."

"Notice, though, he couldn't come back at me when I said no-one here could handle the case?" Guthrie flashed a wry smile at Alisdair.

"Yeah, thanks for that, by the way."

Guthrie caught the look on Alisdair's face. "Oh. Sorry. No offence."

"None taken. Just be a little more cautious when it comes to picking a fight with Buchanan. It may not be his game, but it's his ball we're playing with."

"Don't forget, young Alisdair, that I have been playing ball with Buchanan since before you were out of school, never mind a police officer."

Alisdair blushed slightly realising he had stepped in it again.

"Thanks for that image, though," added Guthrie. "I'm going to be thinking about playing with Buchanan's ball for the rest of the day."

THIRTY-TWO

The balance of the morning was spent coordinating the teams dispatched around the town and elsewhere. Alisdair concentrated his efforts helping the pair of uniforms from Montrose who were assigned the task of tracking down the mystery supplier. It was almost one o'clock when he reported to Guthrie.

"Any luck?" Questioned Guthrie as Alisdair approached his desk.

"Actually, yes."

Guthrie sat back and put his hands behind his head. "Oh, aye? Do tell."

"We have two decent leads. First one is a company that provided Ogilvy with zips and fasteners, Fassentec." Alisdair spelled it out for Guthrie. "Everything from heavy duty plastic ones for coats, to small ones for cycling shorts." Alisdair flicked the page of his notebook and continued.

"You said 'provided'," Guthrie said, leaning forward, elbows on the desk.

"They were recently replaced by another company, based in China."

"A cost saving measure no doubt?"

"Absolutely. And not the only company that were either replaced or had their costs cut by Ogilvy."

"Really? Tell me more." Guthrie took out his notebook and turned to a fresh page, clicking his pen and writing the word 'Suppliers' at the top of the page. He underlined it twice.

Alisdair turned back a couple of pages in his notes. "Okay. Let me rewind a little. The Montrose boys did a pretty good job. They quickly made a connection during the calls that Ogilvy had been pressuring their suppliers on cost."

"Ogilvy the company, or Ogilvy himself?"

"Ogilvy the company. The one doing the pressuring was Ogilvy's brother-in-law," Alisdair looked at his notes again, "Douglas Mitchell."

"Shite! Why haven't we heard of this guy?"

Alisdair shrugged, "I know. As soon as we found out I started digging."

"Well?"

"In short, Mitchell was head of procurement at Ogilvy. Last conversation any of them had with the guy was roughly a week ago."

"Or about the time Gant had his mystery phone call?"

"Right."

"Did you ask whether Gant's call was related or not?"

"We did, yes."

Guthrie now sitting up straight. "And?"

"None of the suppliers said they had any contact with Gant."

Guthrie slapped the desk. "Bugger!"

"That's what I thought. So, we went back and looked for any of the suppliers who indicated they had a harder time with Mitchell. Fassentec was one. Advanced Fabrics was the other."

"And what do they do?" Guthrie didn't look up but continued taking notes.

"They supplied the liner material for the foul weather jackets."

"Past tense again, Alisdair."

Alisdair smiled. "Who said you weren't one for the details?"

"Bugger off!"

"Ha! Yes, they *used* to supply the material. for the jackets. They were dropped in favour of another vendor about a month after the contract renewal on the Police foul weather jackets."

"And that's the contract keeping Ogilvy afloat, right?"

"For all intents and purposes, yes, but not long after they were dropped their contract was renewed. They're still a supplier."

Guthrie rattled his pen between his teeth, looking at Alisdair. "So?"

"So, we have two more avenues to head down. Fassentec and Advanced Fabrics."

Guthrie stopped rattling his teeth and started to tap his notebook with the pen. "*And* we have to talk to Ogilvy again. Why didn't he tell us about Mitchell? The bugger had plenty of opportunity to let us know he was involved, but not a peep." He wrote the name in his notebook and underlined it. Three times.

"Smells a little fishy to me. Time to pay our friend, Mr Ogilvy, another visit."

THIRTY-THREE

Despite the time, Guthrie made no mention of either coffee or lunch before Alisdair signed out a pool car for the trip to Ogilvy's office. No Jaguar this time. Instead, a rather worn out hatchback was their conveyance.

"Back to slumming it." Guthrie said clocking the crisp packets stuffed into the ashtray in the centre of the dashboard. An empty Red Bull can rolled around his feet.

"They weren't too pleased with the state of the Jag when we brought it back. All that mud from the warehouse fire. Should've seen the looks I got when I asked for a car."

"Nothing we could've done. All part of doing our duty, right?"

"Yes, but probably another reason we're not in Buchanan's good books."

"It *was* a bit of a disaster zone when we handed it in." Guthrie's face lit up in a satisfied grin, looking like a toddler who had just eaten the biggest bar of chocolate on the planet.

Alisdair shook his head. "You really love to put one over on Buchanan, don't you?"

"Every chance I get."

They pulled into Ogilvy Outerwear, parked opposite the main entrance and walked across the small, still relatively empty car park. Inside they were greeted not by Miss Donaldson, but by another woman, much older and certainly not as attractive. She looked up and greeted them as they approached the reception desk.

"Can I help you?" It was not the normal, refined telephone voice you would expect from a receptionist, but a smoke-deepened, rasping local accent.

Alisdair pulled out his warrant card and held it up. "PC McEwan and Mr Guthrie from Police Scotland. We'd like to see Mr Ogilvy, please."

The receptionist's eyes opened a little wider. "Oh, of course. I'll just call through and see if he's in his office. I know he's here." She lifted the handset and punched a couple of numbers.

"Mr Ogilvy? Two gentlemen from Police Scotland are here to see you. Yes. Of course. Thank you." She hung up the phone and stood.

"If you would like to follow me, please."

The receptionist led them across the lobby and down the familiar hallway to Ogilvy's office. Ogilvy was sitting at his desk and motioned for them to take a seat opposite. The woman smiled, backing out of the room, quietly closing the door.

"Gentlemen. What can I do for you today?"

Guthrie thumbed over his shoulder, "No Miss Donaldson today?"

"No. She had to take a day off. She says she might be coming down with a bit of a cold."

"I hear it's going around. Hope she gets better quickly."

Ogilvy shuffled a few papers lying on his desk. "Yes. Good temps are life-savers, but it's never the same when you lose one of your regular employees."

"Quite."

Guthrie looked at Alisdair, who took out his notebook. He then looked around the room before bringing his gaze back to Ogilvy. "Why didn't you tell us about your brother-in-law's involvement with the company?"

Ogilvy picked up a mug from his desk and sat back. Guthrie had smelled the coffee as he came into the room. His empty stomach had growled the moment his brain had registered the aroma. Ogilvy took a mouthful, keeping his eyes focused on Guthrie.

"Mr Ogilvy," Guthrie continued, "I should not have to remind you that we are investigating the murder of one of your employees. Didn't you think that piece of information may have been helpful to us?"

Ogilvy cupped the mug between both hands. He turned to look at the shop floor through the large windows.

"Douglas was, until recently, our head of procurement."

"Did he have regular dealings with your suppliers?"

"Yes, of course. He arranged for all the raw materials we use in our products. He no longer works for the company."

Guthrie felt his jaw tighten. He shifted in his chair. "Mr Ogilvy, why is he no longer part of your company?"

"We had a disagreement about a decision he made regarding a vendor."

"What exactly was the disagreement about?" Guthrie pressed.

"I didn't particularly agree with a change he made affecting one of our major suppliers."

Again, a curt answer. He's trying to avoid something.

Guthrie's aggravation level was rising with every second he wasn't getting the full story. The more he thought about it, the more he wanted to jump across the desk and grab Ogilvy.

"Look, Mr Ogilvy, I'll get straight to the point here." He paused, making a show of getting out his notebook and turning a few pages. "We know Mr Gant was in an animated discussion with one of your suppliers a week before he was murdered."

Ogilvy took another swallow of coffee. He kept the mug in front of his face. Alisdair immediately thought, *a tell*. He made a note.

Guthrie went on. "You conveniently forgot to mention that your brother-in-law was the head of procurement at the time. He no longer works for the company, and Bobby Gant ends up dead. I'm sure you can appreciate why that would look a little suspicious to us."

It was Ogilvy's turn to move slightly in his chair.

"I didn't think the fact that Douglas was no longer working for us was of any relevance to Bobby's death. The fact that he's my brother-in-law is irrelevant."

"Mr Ogilvy, please let us decide what is, or is not, relevant to this investigation."

Ogilvy put the mug down on the desk. "Sorry. I obviously made a mistake."

Guthrie looked down at his notebook and clicked his pen several times before making some notes. After an empty half minute, he looked over to Alisdair. He raised an eyebrow - Alisdair's signal to ask his questions.

"Mr Ogilvy, you say you let Mr Mitchell go because of a disagreement about a decision regarding a vendor?"

"Yes."

"Could you tell us more about that, please?"

"Not sure there's much to tell. We disagreed-"

Guthrie stood up, taking both Ogilvy and Alisdair by surprise. He walked around his chair, turning to face Ogilvy. "Mr Ogilvy," Guthrie's voice seemed to fill the office, almost on the brink of shouting, "You fired Mr Mitchell, *your brother-in-law*, from a key position within the company. From what we've found out, your company has been in the middle of some serious cut-backs. You did mention that to us before, but we understand that a couple of your suppliers were not too pleased about the whole deal."

Ogilvy closed his eyes. He breathed noisily. Opening his eyes, he focused on Guthrie. "It wasn't an easy process. Our business had gone through a steady decline in sales since 2009. We were struggling with the economy going down the drain, and cheap competition from overseas, particularly China. By late last year we were having a hard time keeping anything on the order books. Many of our contracts had gone elsewhere."

"What exactly did you do to stay afloat?" Alisdair asked.

"We cut some manufacturing personnel."

"The people on the factory floor?"

"Exactly. We also contacted all of our suppliers and negotiated better pricing."

Guthrie was leaning against the far wall. "What about those who didn't give you a better deal?"

"Most did. After all, most were in a similar position as us. They didn't want to lose our business. Some we agreed to keep the pricing the same as we didn't want to lose them. Others we cut loose and found new suppliers that would give us the pricing we needed."

"And Mr Mitchell was the one leading this project?"

"Yes."

"What about Mr Gant?" Guthrie folded his arms.

"Bobby was not involved in the negotiations with suppliers..." Ogilvy trailed off. He took another sip of coffee and looked blankly at the door to his office.

Guthrie was getting fed up with having to drag the facts out of Ogilvy. He walked over to the large desk and leaned on it, getting close to Ogilvy, the smell of coffee making his stomach rumble again. "Mr Ogilvy, we do not have time to play games here. I feel there is a *but* in your explanation. If you would like to tell us now, I would very much appreciate it so we can get on with solving a murder!" Guthrie slapped the desk causing Ogilvy to blink. "If you keep up this game, we'll take a trip to the station and we can discuss the matter of wasting police time."

"Okay. All right." Ogilvy returned the mug to its coaster and pushed his chair back, more to get away from Guthrie than anything else.

"Bobby also had an issue with Douglas about one of the suppliers we replaced."

Alisdair flicked back a few pages in his notebook. "Fassentec, or Advanced Fabrics, by chance?"

Ogilvy looked up at him. "Advanced, yes. How did you know?"

"Alisdair, here, is very good at digging up information," said Guthrie. He sat down again and stared at Ogilvy. "Was this the company you were referring to that led you to fire Mr Mitchell?"

"Yes."

"And Mr Gant's only real involvement in the whole process with your suppliers was with this same company, and he had an issue with what was going on?"

Ogilvy sighed, "Yes."

"Alisdair?"

"Yes?"

"I think we need to have Mr Ogilvy come down to the station and continue this conversation on the record. And get someone to bring in Mitchell."

THIRTY-FOUR

Ogilvy was made to wait in the interview room having gone over all the information for little over an hour, a digital voice recorder running this time.

Back in the incident room, Guthrie was paging through his notebook when Buchanan appeared like a silent assassin beside him. "Tom."

Guthrie jumped. "Jeez, Ian! You'll give someone a heart attack sneaking up on them like that."

"I didn't exactly sneak up on you, Tom. Looked to me like you were in your own little world there."

Guthrie flipped his notebook shut. "I suppose you want your update?"

"That's the plan, yes."

Guthrie slowly got up and picked up some loose papers from a stack on the desk. "Okay. You want to do this in your office?"

"No. Here is fine."

Guthrie scrunched his face into something he hoped looked like disgust. He turned, "Alisdair! Over here, please." Back to Buchanan, "Take a seat then."

Buchanan took the seat Guthrie had just vacated, leaving Guthrie to sit on the edge of the desk, papers held in his lap. Alisdair joined them and stood beside Guthrie.

"Sir," he acknowledged the inspector, who nodded.

"Well? Dazzle me with your brilliance."

Guthrie just wanted to sock him between the eyes. "Okay. Well, the teams have been out going over the interviews we've already conducted. Door-to-doors are slow going, just as they were first time around. The one good piece of news is that we just finished a formal interviewed with Ogilvy."

Buchanan raised his eyebrows, "You brought him in? Is he a suspect?"

"No. At least not yet."

"What do you mean, not yet?"

"He didn't tell us that his brother-in-law, Douglas Mitchell, was their head of procurement right up until last week. He was fired after making a change to a supplier. The same supplier Bobby Gant was having a rather heated conversation with a week before he was murdered."

"We have Mitchell on the way in now," Alisdair added.

"What are your thoughts prior to interviewing him?"

"I'm not exactly sure at this point. I'm willing to listen, obviously, but there's something going on here. Ogilvy was hiding the fact about his brother-in-law from us, he fired a family member from the business..." He shook his head. "I'll put money on a connection."

"Fair enough, Tom, but don't go charging in there with just a gut feeling, trying to get a confession."

Guthrie gripped the paperwork tighter. "I'll be on my best behaviour, Ian. Alisdair will see to that."

THIRTY-FIVE

"Interview commenced at sixteen thirty-two hours. Present are Constable Alisdair McEwan, Mr Tom Guthrie, contracted special investigator for Police Scotland," Guthrie's pulse unexpectedly quickened as Alisdair verbalised the official description of his position, "Mr Douglas Mitchell, and Mr David Taft, representing Mr Mitchell." Alisdair looked over at Guthrie who sat facing Mitchell, leaving Alisdair to contend with the stare from Taft.

All four sat around a well-worn, wooden table, one end up against the wall. Windows above overlooked the station's rear car park. Various scores and scratches in the dark wood, indicating decades of use, made the table seem out of place in an otherwise spartan and utilitarian room. The digital recorder occupied the end of the table between Alisdair and Taft, a red light blinked indicating the machine was functioning.

Guthrie had rolled his eyes when he was told that Mitchell wanted his lawyer present during the interview. He protested, saying that they only wanted to speak with

Mitchell as part of their regular process, but the lawyer insisted otherwise.

Taft oozed apathy and sat, nonplussed, dressed in a dark suit, white shirt, and red tie.

"Mr Mitchell," Guthrie began, "as you are aware, we are investigating the murder of Bobby Gant who was employed at Ogilvy Outerwear."

Mitchell was a tall, athletic man in his fifties. Close cut salt and pepper hair topped a tanned, square face. He was dressed as if he had been on the golf course when the uniforms had picked him up, dark blue trousers and Pringle sweater with a light pink shirt, unbuttoned to show a hint of greying chest hair.

Just the type of guy Guthrie took an instant dislike to. So much for the open mind.

"Yes, of course. Terrible thing." Mitchell replied, his smooth tone and holier-than-though attitude confirming Guthrie's gut instinct about the man.

Ponce. "Mr Mitchell, tell us, please what your position was at the company."

"I was head of procurement."

"Meaning?"

"Meaning I was responsible for sourcing our raw materials, drawing up contracts with suppliers, maintaining those relationships."

"How long were you with Ogilvy Outerwear?"

"I started not long after John founded the company."

"But you were recently fired. Tell us how that came about?"

Mitchell's face turned into a frown. He pursed his lips as he chewed on the inside of his cheek. "I wouldn't say fired. John and I came to a mutual decision that we should part company, as it were."

Smarmy git. "In our discussions with your brother-in-law, the word fired was used to describe your departure from the company, but please tell us how you see it."

Mitchell huffed and folded his arms. He looked out of the window. "The company was under quite a bit of financial pressure. We had lost several contracts to foreign manufacturers and we needed to cut costs to compete. As head of procurement, I was tasked with coming up with the list of potential cuts, not only externally, but internally too. I started with the suppliers."

"Why? asked Alisdair.

"John didn't want to let anyone go. The goal was to try and reach the required savings through material cost cutting. Letting employees go was a last resort."

"Do you think that was a realistic expectation, considering people were laid off after it was all said and done anyway?" Guthrie leaned forward on the desk. He twirled his pen in his fingers.

"No, quite frankly, I didn't."

"What did you do? Did you throw up your hands and say it was impossible?"

"On the contrary, Mr Guthrie, I worked hard to reach our goals and was almost successful in achieving the target through external cuts only, but I couldn't close the gap, so we were forced to make several personnel reductions."

Smarmy, smarmy. Guthrie forced himself to maintain a neutral expression. "We'll get to the redundancies in a moment, but let's talk more about the cuts you made with the suppliers. A couple in particular interest us. Fassentec is one."

Mitchell made a show of checking his watch, an oversized, expensive looking number in gold. Guthrie couldn't decide if it was real, or one of those fake jobs Mitchell picked up, along with his tan, on some vacation to Turkey.

"They were unable to give us the break on pricing we had targeted. Other options were available to us and we cancelled their contract and switched to a new supplier."

"I'm sure they weren't too pleased with that decision."

"No, they weren't. But we had to do what was in the best interest of the company."

The line sounded like Mitchell had rehearsed and used it a time or two before. The words had not the slightest hint of sincerity behind them.

"Did they threaten any legal action because you cancelled the contract?" Alisdair asked without looking up from his notes.

"They did at first, yes, but their contract was coming up for renewal anyway. We worked it out and settled with them."

"Was Mr Gant involved at all in any of these negotiations or the discussions leading up to the cancelling of the contract?"

"No."

Alisdair looked at Mitchell. "There would be no cause for us to be concerned that someone from Fassentec would have any kind of grievance with him because of this decision?"

Mitchell looked almost shocked that Alisdair would ask such a question.

"Certainly not. Bobby rarely had any direct contact with suppliers. He was well liked by everyone."

"That's what we've heard, Mr Mitchell." Guthrie wanted to switch gears. "What about Advanced Fabrics? What gave Mr Ogilvy cause to fire you-"

"It was a mutual decision," Mitchell interrupted

"-Fire you from the company?" Guthrie leaned back and tossed his pen on the table.

Mitchell glanced at his lawyer who looked as though he would rather be packing up his work for the day and heading off to some expensive bar, than sitting in a police interview room.

"Advanced supplied us the raw material for the lining we use in a couple of our product lines."

"Which products exactly, Mr Mitchell, asked Guthrie.

"The Rockman Extreme Expedition jacket and the foul weather jackets for the Police Scotland contract."

Alisdair searched through a stack of papers on the desk in front of him. Picking out one he said, "The Rockman jacket is the company's current best seller on the retail side, yes?"

"Yes, it is."

"Why is that?"

"It's a high-quality product, priced right, and marketed well. We've had great reviews in both print and online arenas."

"It wouldn't have anything to do with the fact that its popularity is down to the weatherproofing technology Ogilvy Outerwear developed in-house and patented?"

Guthrie shifted his chair back from the desk. He was curious about where Alisdair was heading with this, but he thought he could see the potential.

"As I said, we marketed it very well. Yes, we did make full use of highlighting the technologies we incorporated into the product."

Guthrie stepped into the conversation. "Is this the same technology used in the Police jacket?" Guthrie saw Alisdair smile and knew they were on the same wavelength.

"Yes."

"And Advanced Fabrics was the key supplier in those technologies?" Guthrie continued.

Mitchell looked at Guthrie. "Yes."

"In what capacity, exactly?"

"At the risk of boring you with technical details-"

Prick.

"-both the Rockman Extreme and the Police Scotland foul weather jacket share the same patented, thermal and moisture wicking technology we developed in-house." Mitchell picked a hair from his trouser leg and let it fall to the floor. "In short, the Police Scotland contract requires a jacket design that can both protect the wearer from cold weather, but still be light enough to wear in warmer temperatures.

"This is, to say the least, a difficult problem to solve, since, in order to provide a suitable thermal protection, you need a certain thickness of insulating material. However, this comes at a price, namely moisture build-up."

Guthrie was quickly feeling like he was back in his high school physics class. Alisdair was still scribbling in his note-book. Mitchell's lawyer, Taft, looked like he was asleep.

Mitchell looked up at the florescent light fixture above the desk, a move that encouraged some more chest hair to escape from under the pink shirt. "We developed a system, if you like. A combination of jacket design and liner mate-rial that could handle both the desired moisture wicking requirements and thermal properties with a material that is half the thickness of material other manufacturers currently use."

Guthrie stood up and walked over to the window. He clasped his hands behind his back and stared at the pool cars parked outside. A seagull landed on the wall at the rear of the car park. Its repetitive squawking call muted by the double-glazed window.

"Let me make sure I am following you, Mr Mitchell. You made a decision to change the key supplier of material used in a patented form of lining used in a contract that is essentially keeping Ogilvy Outerwear afloat?"

Mitchell looked at his lawyer again, getting no response. "Yes."

"And would I be correct in assuming, Mr Mitchell," Alisdair chimed in, "that this patent is worth a considerable sum of money?"

Guthrie was, for the second time, impressed with the young officer's line of questioning.

Mitchell tilted his head back as he answered in an exasperated tone, "Yes. Yes, it is."

"In what way, exactly, Mr Mitchell?" said Guthrie.

Mitchell placed both hands, palm down, on the table in front of him. He drummed his fingers on the wooden surface.

"Ogilvy Outerwear has created a design that has the potential to revolutionise the industry. It doesn't take a sports clothing expert, Mr Guthrie, to see what the advantage is of this technology." He glared at Guthrie, who, again, wanted to rearrange Mitchell's features.

Alisdair picked up on the tension and decided to head off any potential paperwork resulting from Guthrie pounding on a member of the public by asking, "And as long as Ogilvy Outerwear holds the patent, they've cornered the market on this new design, thereby maximising their potential revenue?"

"Correct," answered Mitchell.

"A ton of money to be had from this, then?" asked Guthrie.

"Potentially, yes."

Guthrie paced around the room twice, stopping directly behind Mitchell. The lawyer, who apparently wasn't asleep, moved his chair to keep an eye on Guthrie, who leaned on the back of Mitchell's chair.

"Thank you, Mr Mitchell, for your explanation. I do have one question that's niggling away at the back of my mind, though."

Mitchell shifted his weight in the chair. "Yes?"

"Why would Mr Gant, head of research and development for Ogilvy Outerwear, be in conversation with Advanced Fabrics, a company no longer supplying material for Ogilvy, just a week before he was murdered, when you say he had little or nothing to do with suppliers?"

"I'm sure I have no idea."

"You're sure, huh?"

"Since I am no longer working for the company, I don't think I can possibly speculate." Mitchell interlaced his fingers and placed his hands in his lap.

Taft sat up. He opened a file folder and started to write something on a blank piece of paper.

Guthrie pushed himself up from Mitchell's chair. "Alisdair. Let's you and I have a little talk."

Alisdair reached for the stop button on the recorder. Checking his watch, he said, "Interview paused at sixteen fifty-seven hours." He pressed the button.

THIRTY-SIX

"Bloody hell, Alisdair! Do you think he just gave us a reason to suspect him for Gant's murder?" Guthrie sat at a desk with his hands clasped behind his head.

"I don't know, Tom. Did he?"

"Come on, Alisdair, you're smarter than that. You followed a path that's the root cause for how many crimes, huh? Follow the money, right?"

"It seemed logical to me, but where's the evidence Mitchell had anything to do with Gant's murder?"

"Ach! Evidence!" Guthrie said, rocking forward to reach a sheet of paper and a pen. He looked at Alisdair and smiled. "I know, I know. Just joking."

"Jeez, Tom. Sometimes I really don't know when to take you seriously."

Guthrie squared the paper in front of him. He scribbled a bullet point list as he talked. "Look, the way I see it, Mitchell screwed with the major supplier for a product - two products - Ogilvy Outerwear needed to stay in business. Changing the supplier was a big enough deal that Ogilvy fired him because of it. The guy, I assume, who designed the product was Gant. He normally has no contact with suppliers yet gets into a major discussion with Advanced Fabrics. A week later he's under water at the foot of the cliffs."

Guthrie tapped the paper with the pen. The two men looked at the list.

"Surely Mitchell should have been the one bumped off," said Alisdair.

"Eh?"

"Well, look at it. By replacing the liner company, Mitchell could have potentially sunk the company. Motive number one to Ogilvy." Alisdair held up the index finger on his right hand. "Advanced Fabrics is now out of a deal that could be a financial windfall for them. Motive number two to Advanced." Two fingers held up. "If Gant was still alive, he had reason to harm Mitchell for changing up suppliers of a hugely important raw material he was using in his work. Motive three to Gant." Three fingers.

Guthrie rubbed his face. "Ach!"

"Where do we go from here?" asked Alisdair.

Guthrie felt bile rise in his stomach. He stood up. "We need to talk to Advanced, that's for sure."

"What about Mitchell? And we still have Ogilvy in the other interview room."

"Bugger! I had forgotten about him." Guthrie slowly shook his head. "As much as I hate to do this -- let's get Buchanan in here."

"'Tom, I'm surprised at you." Alisdair picked up the phone from the desk and dialled Buchanan's office number. "Last thing I would have said you would come up with."

"Sod off, cheeky beggar! Let him deal with Mitchell and Ogilvy. We can't hold them, but perhaps Buchanan can warn them that we're looking closely at the circumstances around the deal with Advanced."

Alisdair held up a hand in a wait gesture. "Sir? McEwan. Could you come to the incident room, please? We need to bring you up to speed on the interview with Mr Mitchell." A slight pause. "Yes, sir. Thanks." Turning to Guthrie, "He's on his way."

THIRTY-SEVEN

"You still have no evidence and no real suspect for Gant's murder. That's really what you're telling me?" His brow was furrowed and had been all through the quick briefing. He stared at Guthrie.

Guthrie's blood pressure went up a notch. "Ian, that's not entirely true."

"I didn't hear much that would convince me otherwise. Do you have anyone in the frame at this point?"

"I think Mitchell has to be our prime suspect." Guthrie shot a glance towards Alisdair who remained non-committal.

"Okay. Why?" asked Buchanan.

"Seems to me that he has more of a motive than anyone. He lost his job. Lost face with people around him because of that. Certainly damaged his relationship with his brother-in-law."

"Seems to *me* that Ogilvy would have a better case against Mitchell, rather than Mitchell against Gant," Buchanan countered. Alisdair's face betrayed his thoughts. "He stood to lose his company, not just his job."

"Aye. Well, Alisdair thought the same thing."

"Glad to see you're at least thinking beyond one possible solution," Buchanan said as he shifted his weight from one leg to the other. Alisdair lowered his head but looked to Guthrie from under his eyebrows.

Slightly exasperated, Guthrie continued, "The working hypothesis is that Mitchell did a little paying back by nailing Gant, or more precisely, having Gant murdered."

"A bit of an extreme reaction to losing your job, don't you think?"

Guthrie threw his hands up. "Oh, come on, Ian. You know as well as I do that people will kill just because they want someone's trainers. It doesn't take some major reason before someone tops someone else."

"Okay, Tom, I'll give you that. Let's just say you're right, or at least have the right suspect. What evidence do you have?"

Guthrie shrugged. "Nothing."

"Then I suggest you start digging a little deeper, because until you can come up with something that will justify Mitchell's stay in our facility, I have to let him leave. Unless you have some more questions for him?"

Guthrie shook his head.

"And the same goes for Mr Ogilvy."

"We have nothing for him at this time, sir," Alisdair responded.

"Very well. I'll take care of Ogilvy and Mitchell. You," pointing at Guthrie, "need to get me some evidence that connects someone with this murder."

"We don't have much to go on. You know that, don't you?"

"I'm painfully aware of the fact. Dundee is too." Buchanan marched towards the door. He stopped and turned. "Why would Mitchell murder Gant if he had a beef with Ogilvy? Seems a bit of a stretch." He looked at the floor. "And don't forget to wrap up the fire investigation." He opened the door and stepped halfway into the hall. Without turning around, he shouted, "I'd like the paperwork on my desk by the end of the day tomorrow," before closing the door behind him.

THIRTY-EIGHT

"Bloody fire! I still can't believe I've had to deal with that in the middle of a murder inquiry." Guthrie sipped a milky coffee waiting for Alisdair to agree.

Nayte's coffee shop was a short walk from the station. The pair had finally broken down and decided they needed food. They made it just before the place closed for the day. There were only two other customers, both old men reading newspapers. The staff were busy cleaning the countertops and packing away food.

"*We've* had to deal with it." Alisdair's tone was one of correction, not concurrence.

"Aye, sorry. I keep going on about that though, don't I?"

"Yes, but I understand the frustration." Alisdair took a bite out of his cheese toastie. "The reports came in this afternoon. Why don't I get through the paperwork in the morning, then we can get up to Advanced Fabrics?" He brushed the crumbs from his fingers and washed the mouthful of warm bread and cheese down with a chaser of tea. "You can make sure it's all good when we get back and we're shot of it."

"Cheers, Alisdair. Sounds good. You'd make a good Detective Constable, you know?"

"Chance would be a fine thing," Alisdair snorted.

"What do you mean? You've got the smarts, heck, you certainly know how to use computers and stuff that I can barely figure out how to switch on. You should push for it."

Alisdair played with the teaspoon, mounding up the sugar in the bowl. "I can't see anything like that happening any time soon. I've barely begun my career, so they're not going to consider me for a DC position. And since the switch to Police Scotland, the whole force doesn't know which way is up. See exhibit A." He pointed the spoon at Guthrie.

"What d'you mean by that?"

"The force is still trying to work out how we all work together. Resources are being shifted, cut back, or eliminated altogether. That's why you're here right now. We don't have a clue how it's all going to shake out."

Guthrie could sympathise with the young officer. He left the force because he had turned into a dinosaur. The police service was changing. Not for the better, in his mind, and he and his old ways were certainly not in vogue.

Glad to escape when he did, he still had compassion for the likes of Alisdair who just wanted to do the job, rather than collate stats and write meaningless reports that would never help solve a crime.

"Still," he said, "never say die, right?"

Alisdair did his best to smile.

"I'll see what I can do, see who I can talk to, if you want. I can put in a good word. There are still some people that think I'm a good judge of character."

"Thanks. You don't have to, but I would appreciate it."

"Very well. Let's tie up the fire in the morning and get

back to real detective work. At least Buchanan will be out of our hair for a bit."

"You sound like some fifties cop show character now."

Guthrie picked up his coffee and tried not to smile. "Bugger off! Cheeky shite!"

"'That's better."

THIRTY-NINE

It was almost eight when Guthrie finally left the station and made his way west towards home. He had called Jacquie, but the call went straight to voicemail. He didn't leave a message, instead, opting to send a short text.

Fancy a drink - if it's not too late?

He pocketed his phone and climbed into the MG. Just past the football ground on the edge of town, as he was negotiating a roundabout, the phone started buzzing.

"Bugger it!" He changed down a gear and then switched hands on the steering wheel, trying to recover the phone from his right trouser pocket. Without looking at the caller ID, he answered.

"Hello, this is Tom."

"Tom. How are you? This is Jacquie."

"Oh, aye, hello Jacquie." Guthrie switched hands again for another gear change.

"Is this a good time? You sound like you're a little preoccupied."

Guthrie swore again, under his breath. "No, no. It's fine. How are you?"

"Great, thanks. You texted me about going for a drink. I'm game if you are."

"No, that's brilliant." Another roundabout.

"Are you sure?"

"Yes, absolutely. Sorry, I'm in the car outside Arbroath and these bloody roundabouts..."

"Mr Guthrie. Are you not on hands-free?" Jacquie's tone was the same as if she were scolding a child.

"Aye, well don't say I can't multitask."

Jacquie chuckled. Guthrie smiled to himself. "Where do you want to meet?" she asked.

"Would you mind coming over to Broughty? I feel bad asking, but I reckon it would be a little quicker since it's already quite late."

"Of course I don't mind, Tom. Where?"

Guthrie thought for a second. Somewhere casual, but quality. "Do you know The Fisherman's Tavern in Broughty?"

"No, sorry. Where is it?"

"It's on Fort Street, up from the lifeboat shed."

"I'll find it. When do you think you'll be there?"

Guthrie checked his watch. Just gone eight. "Eight-thirty?"

"Perfect. See you there."

FORTY

Jacquie was already at the Fisherman's when Guthrie
arrived. She was sitting in a booth across from a fireplace.
He saw she had a drink but motioned to her if she wanted
another. She shook her head. Guthrie walked over to the
small bar and ordered a lager.

As he waited, he looked back to Jacquie. "Shite," he said
to himself. The barman looked at him, quizzically. "Uh,
sorry," Guthrie said. "Talking to myself." The barman
returned his focus to pouring the pint.

Guthrie was mentally kicking himself for not going over
to Jacquie when he came in. She sat looking out the
window. Guthrie felt his stomach lurch with a mixture of
guilt and sickness. He paid for the drink and walked over to
Jacquie. He sat opposite her, a wooden table between them,
stained with circles from the bottom of various glasses.

"Sorry."

"For what?"

"For being a complete idiot."

"Okay. Again, why?"

"Coming in and heading straight for the bar. I didn't

even say hello before..." He trailed off. He put the pint glass down on the table with a thud. "I'm sorry. You must think I'm some kind of caveman." He looked at his hands in his lap.

Jacquie smiled. She placed her glass on the table, stood up and leaned over. She kissed Guthrie on the forehead.

Guthrie looked up, surprised. "What's that for?"

"I forgive you, Caveman Tom." She sat down, smoothing out her skirt. Guthrie turned red with embarrassment. "So," she continued, "tell me about your day."

"You don't want to know."

"Sure I do. Come on spill the beans." Her face lit up with a smile which she hid behind the glass as she took a drink.

Guthrie couldn't help himself. He smiled back. "Same old, same old," he said.

"Are you getting anywhere? Making any progress?"

"We're making some moves in the right direction. Thing is, we have this fire and associated death on our plate too. It's taking time and resources away from the Gant murder. Quite frankly, it's been a pain in the arse to have to deal with it. I think Buchanan's done it on purpose just to screw with me."

"Now, Tom. Surely you don't really think that, do you?"

"I wouldn't put it past him." He took a long draw from the lager.

"But am I right in saying he wouldn't have been the one assigning the resources? Wouldn't that come from Dundee?"

Guthrie didn't answer immediately, then admitted defeat. "Aye. But I know he gets a kick out of telling me what to do. Git!" Guthrie slumped back in his chair.

"I feel you have an issue with Inspector Buchanan, Mr

Guthrie." Jacquie's tone was serious, but her eyes betrayed her true thought.

"Now *you're* just trying to wind me up."

"Oh, come now, Tom. I thought you were one of those old school coppers who could take his fair shake of physical and verbal abuse -- not that I would call this conversation anything close to an assault on your ego. I'm surprised you let that stuff get to you. You've been at this game long enough to know the routine."

"Ach, Jacquie, you're right. There's just something about Buchanan that just gets my goat." He sat up and began adding to the circles on the table top from the condensation that had collected around the bottom of the pint glass.

"Don't let it. Don't feed it. Don't give him the opportunity to press your buttons."

"Aye, I know. It's just-"

"It's just nothing, Tom," Jacquie interrupted. Her voice was almost hushed. As she spoke, she leaned across the table and placed her hand on his, which was wrapped around his glass.

Guthrie looked up. There was that smile again -- warm, reassuring. Without thinking, he lifted the drink to his lips and took another swallow of the cold liquid. Jacquie sat back.

They sat and watched the others in the bar.

"Penny for them," Jacquie said.

"Sorry?" Guthrie turned to look at Jacquie, then shook his head. "Oh, sorry," he repeated. "Miles away."

"I know. Look, if you would rather call it a night-"

"No, no, Jacquie. I was just going over what we did today in Arbroath."

"And was it a productive day?"

Guthrie looked up at the ceiling. "I think so. We figured

we can get the fire off our desk tomorrow and we can concentrate on Gant."

"Well, there you go then. What do they say? How do you eat an elephant?"

"One bite at a time."

"Exactly. And by this time tomorrow you'll have taken quite a sizeable bite out of your elephant."

"Aye, I guess you're right, Jacquie."

"I know I'm right." She held up her glass. "Now, I think I'll take you up on that offer of a drink when you came in."

FORTY-ONE

The evening air was crisp. There was still a hint of blue in the sky to the west, a taste of the long days of summer to come. Guthrie and Jacquie walked around the corner from the pub to where Jacquie had parked her car. Neither one spoke, but walked, head down, along the pavement, the yellow glow from the street lamps accentuating the dark nooks and crannies of the shop doorways. Jacquie wasn't wearing a coat, just a sweater; she folded her arms and hunched her shoulders in an attempt to retain some of the warmth they had left in the bar.

When they reached her car, she dug around in her purse to find the keys. Pointing the fob at the car, the lights flashed as the doors unlocked. She turned to Guthrie.

"Thanks for the invite, Tom. I enjoyed the company."

"Thank you, Jacquie. I know I can be a bit of a selfish, unthinking-"

"Caveman?" She interrupted.

"Caveman," Guthrie laughed.

"That's okay. I'm fine with it, just as long as you don't get any ideas and beat me over the head with a club and drag me off to your cave."

"Not much chance of that."

Jacquie's smile immediately faded.

"I mean I would never dream of getting any ideas. What I mean is I wouldn't dream of-"

"Tom?"

Guthrie rubbed the top of his head as if the act would erase the words and rewind time about a minute.

"Yes?"

Jacquie took a step forward. She stood looking up at Guthrie.

"Tom, I would be okay with you getting ideas and dragging me off to your cave. I really hope you might feel the same."

"Look, Jacquie, I-"

Jacquie put her hand on Guthrie's chest and stopped him.

"Tom, you don't have to agree, or explain, or anything. I just want you to know I enjoy being with you. I think we get along well. I don't want you to feel you have to do or say anything to me, but I told you I'm not afraid of saying what I think — and that's what I think."

Guthrie looked at Jacquie as if she was talking in a foreign language. She started to pull her hand away, but he quickly covered it with his and pressed it back on his chest. Reaching down with his left hand he opened the car door. The white interior light in stark contrast to the muted colours of the street. He still held her hand in his right.

"From caveman to gallant knight." She said.

"I'm not one for sweeping ladies off their feet, I'm afraid. So..."

She squeezed his hand. "Don't worry. If I'm pushing you, just say so. Deal?"

"Deal."

Jacquie took a deep breath. "All right! Why don't you call me — whenever — and let's plan on dinner somewhere we can relax and not have to worry about work or what we need to say or not say." She paused. "Ah. There I go again."

"Jacquie?"

She looked up at him, eyebrows raised questioningly.

Guthrie hesitated and he could feel the beads of sweat starting to form on his forehead. As he thought about it, it made him self-aware and only served to make him sweat more.

"Yes?" She was smiling.

Guthrie swallowed hard. "Look, I appreciate what you're doing, but I..."

"You don't want to." It wasn't a question.

"Well, not exactly." Guthrie couldn't find the words. His stomach was churning and the shirt under his jacket was now sticking to his back.

"But?"

"Ach, Jacquie. I really don't know. Just a little out of my depth here."

"I understand."

"And what with this investigation and all, I'm not sure you and me getting too friendly is the right thing to be doing."

"I see." Jacquie stepped back and pulled her hand away from under his. She looked down at the car keys and started to fiddle with them. "I understand. I should have realised it wouldn't be the best thing."

"Look, I'll call you sometime, okay?"

Jacquie opened the door, almost pushing Guthrie out of

the way, and got behind the wheel. "Yes, sure. That'll be fine. Thanks again for the drink, Tom, I enjoyed it. I would like to do it again, so why don't you solve this murder quickly, huh?" She looked up. Her smile was not bright, but more of a pleasant, polite one normally used by shop assistants and hotel receptionists when dealing with total strangers.

"I'll try," was all Guthrie could say.

Jacquie reached over and pulled the door closed. Without looking up she started the car and pulled away from the kerb. Guthrie watched until the brake lights disappeared around a corner.

It was suddenly very cold.

FORTY-TWO

The barman smiled as Guthrie walked back into the Fisherman's.

"Same again?"

"Aye, please."

The barman poured a dark pint and handed it over to Guthrie who, in turn, handed him a ten pound note. Once he had pocketed his change, he took a seat at the same booth he and Jacquie had vacated just a few minutes before. This time, however, he was sitting where she had sat. The seat was still warm.

He looked around. An older man was at the far end of the bar, staring at a small television in the corner. The sound was down. Some kind of talent show. A young couple sat in another booth. They were in hushed conversation, sharing a joke or funny story, large smiles, animated faces.

Guthrie flopped his head back onto the velvet fabric of the back of the booth and closed his eyes.

"Shite."

FORTY-THREE

Monday, 31st March, 2014

"Where the hell have you been, Tom?" Alisdair whispered when Guthrie slunk into the incident room. It was already half past nine. "Buchanan's been looking for you. I've been looking for you. I had to make up some excuse for you missing the briefing."

Guthrie walked past Alisdair without saying a word. He pulled out a chair and sat down heavily. He leaned forward, placed an elbow on the desk and sank his head into his hand.

"Jeez, Tom. You look like crap. Are you okay?"

"Can't say I'm in top shape this morning, Alisdair, no." The tone was sarcastic.

"Are you sick?"

"Let's just say I had a little too much of the self-pity at my local last night."

"Ah." Alisdair took a seat opposite. "Anything I can do to help?"

"You can solve this bloody murder."

Alisdair was silent. It was obvious Guthrie was not only hungover, but in a foul mood. He picked up a wad of papers from his in tray and shuffled them around.

"Not sure I know where to go next, Tom, I..."

"Oh, bugger it, Alisdair! If you want to be a bloody detective, then start detecting!" Guthrie's outburst had everyone in the incident room turn and face them. The normally quiet atmosphere of the station was well and truly broken. The Arbroath officers were not used to emotional outbursts in Buchanan's realm and they wondered who was getting the earful.

Alisdair looked around at his colleagues.

"Look, Tom, all I was trying to say was..."

"Alisdair, I don't want to hear it. Just get on with and file the fire paperwork and have it on Buchanan's desk as soon as you can. I'll call you if I need you."

With that, Guthrie stood up, scraping the chair across the polished floor, once again piercing the quiet of the room. He walked out of the room.

Alisdair's colleagues were looking at him. He caught the eye of a couple who were smiling.

"Lovers' tiff?" one of them said. Alisdair ignored the comment and turned his attention to the documents on the corner of his desk. It amounted to everything they had gathered on the fire. He took a deep breath and, exhaling, wiggled the mouse on the mousepad and opened up a report form.

He typed in a title on the first page then reached inside his jacket pocket for his notebook. Flicking to the day from his visit with Guthrie to the warehouse, he began typing a summary of the incident.

He had only typed a few words before he stopped and

sat back in his chair. The incident room door opened, and Guthrie strode back into the room.

"I want Teri Donaldson brought in for a wee chat."

"Okay. I'll ask her to come in."

"No," said Guthrie, "send a uniform to pick her up. Sooner rather than later. I'm fed up letting the lunatics run the asylum in this case."

"All right. Anything else?"

Guthrie thought for a moment. "No. Let's see if we can accomplish that before we try something a little more complicated shall we."

Guthrie disappeared again.

Alisdair sat, staring at the door. He didn't know what to think. He did know he was on the receiving end of whatever had ruined Guthrie's morning, or evening.

"Sal!"

Sal raised a finger in a *wait* gesture. She was on the phone. When she hung up, she removed her headset and walked over to Alisdair.

"Aye?"

"I expect you heard Mr Guthrie's request."

"I did hear something, but I was on the phone."

Alisdair narrowed his eyes. "You're just being nice, Sal."

"All right. I heard him. Everyone did. What's up with him today?"

"Not sure."

"*Are* you having a lovers' tiff?"

"Shut up, Sal!"

"Fair enough. Thought you two were getting on really chummy like."

"Sal," Alisdair rubbed his forehead, "I just need you to get a couple of uniforms to pick up Teri Donaldson and bring her in for an interview."

Sal folded her arms.

"You wanting to ask her out or something?"

Before Alisdair could say something, Sal had turned and was walking back to her desk. She looked over her shoulder as she sat down, a large grin on her face. Alisdair closed his eyes and shook his head.

Turning back to the computer screen he started to type. How he hated these reports. He didn't mind sitting in front of a computer screen and researching. That was as good as solving a puzzle. But, reports.

Slowly, he entered in the details of the investigation. As he did, he sorted the paperwork into a logical order that matched with the report. In the end he would print it out, attach it to the documents and send it to Buchanan for review.

One of the last documents was the inventory of the warehouse, or, to be more exact, the inventory of the area immediately surrounding the location of the fire and the body.

A rain coat, plastic lighter melted by the fire, a listing of the cardboard and material that was set alight by the cigarette and then eventually consumed the man's body. All the bits and pieces that were in the corner of the building.

Alisdair looked at the list of personal effects. Nothing to show for a life, he thought. He let his eyes go out of focus as his mind wandered, thinking about the man who had died. Who would miss him? Who saw him walking the streets? Probably no-one. Just another invisible, home-less person who had been somebody once, yet ended his life a nobody. He lived right under the noses of so many people every day, yet no one saw him. Hidden in plain sight.

He looked over at Sal who was giving him a thumbs up.

Presumably, she had dispatched the uniforms to bring in Teri Donaldson. He nodded.

Plain sight.

He looked again at the inventory. Something was niggling him. He traced down the list with his index finger. Next page. Three from the top, he stopped. He tapped the page.

FORTY-FOUR

Alisdair had found Guthrie in the canteen. He had been reading a newspaper and sipping from a bottled water. Alisdair told him that Teri Donaldson was waiting in the interview room and excused himself, saying that he had to finish up the fire paperwork for Buchanan. Guthrie didn't object. He was still in a mood and the hangover was hanging on.

All the preliminaries had been taken care of. Teri Donaldson had been asked, for the record, all the same questions she had been asked before. She gave the same answers. Her mood and body language suggested she was tired. She sat with a cup of milky tea from the canteen, cradling it in her hands, as if it was the only thing keeping her warm, even though the room was stuffy with no air moving at all.

"Miss Donaldson, I need to understand more about the phone call you had told us about, between Bobby Gant and the supplier." Guthrie sat across the table from her.

"I'm not sure I can tell you anything more. I just heard Bobby talking to one of the suppliers about a problem."

"Well, you see, Miss Donaldson, that's where I think you're wrong."

"What do you mean?"

"I mean, I think you know a whole lot more than what you're letting on."

"I don't understand."

"Oh, come on, Miss Donaldson!" Guthrie shouted at the young woman. She jumped, almost spilling the tea.

"You know who and what, don't you?" Guthrie continued in a soft voice. "You know just *exactly* who Mr Gant was talking to, and you know *exactly* what they were talking about."

"I... I don't know what you mean."

Guthrie slapped the desk. Teri looked up for the first time. Tears were welling up in her eyes. Guthrie knew he was close. *Keep pushing.*

"Who was Bobby Gant talking to?"

"One of our major suppliers."

"Which one?"

"I don't know."

"Of course you do!"

"No..."

"Yes, you do, Teri! You heard enough of the conversation to know that it was a supplier and there was an issue. That tells me you probably heard enough to know who it was and what the issue was. Not only that, you just told me that it was one of your major suppliers. How many major suppliers do you have? Not many." Guthrie was now leaning forward across the table, almost in Teri's face.

"You knew it was a problem. I bet you have a good idea of the problem, otherwise why would you say that? Why would you say it was a problem?"

"It... It was just the way he was talking." Teri backed

away from Guthrie.

"I don't believe you."

It was Guthrie's turn to sit back. He waited for Teri to say something.

"It was Advanced Fabrics," Teri said without looking up.

Guthrie took his pen and wrote in his notebook which was lying open on the table. His expression didn't change, it was still a look of annoyance.

"That didn't hurt, did it?"

Teri didn't answer.

"So. Let's keep going Teri." Guthrie's voice was now quiet. The use of her first name was also a ploy. "What were they discussing?"

Teri fidgeted. She put her tea on the table but said nothing.

"What were they talking about, Teri?"

Teri swallowed hard. "I'm not sure I can say."

"Teri," Guthrie leaned forward, reaching across the table with both hands, palms flat, "shortly after this call, Bobby Gant was beaten to within an inch of his life, taken to the cliffs, tied down, and left to drown." Teri shifted in her chair. "You owe it to him to tell me what you know. I don't understand why you can't tell me what they were talking about. I need your help, Teri."

"I don't know everything, but..." Teri picked up the tea and took a sip. "They were talking about something to do with the material Advanced supplies us."

Guthrie picked up his pen again. "Okay, Teri. Let me tell you what I know, all right? Perhaps that will help you help me."

Teri nodded. She was still looking down into her lap.

"I know Advanced Fabrics was dropped as part of a

cost-cutting measure. I know that they were reinstated shortly after. Mr Mitchell made the cut and Mr Ogilvy reinstated them. Am I correct?"

"Yes."

"What was Bobby talking to them about? This was after they had been reinstated, yes?"

"That's right. They were talking about some problem with the liner material."

"What kind of problem?"

"I'm not really sure. They were talking about quality, or specifications, or something."

Guthrie turned the page in his notebook and scribbled again.

"Do you remember any details? Did Bobby have issues with their product?"

"I think so. He was talking about not meeting specs." Teri looked at Guthrie. "Mr Guthrie, I really can't remember much. I was just sitting at my desk and Bobby came into the reception area. He was already on his phone. I just overheard snippets of the conversation. I wasn't listening."

"I know, Teri, but you're doing great. This could be a very important. I'll be honest, we don't have much to go on and this is, frankly, the only thing we see in Bobby's recent past that points toward anything."

Guthrie sighed. He folded his arms. He looked at Teri. She seemed younger than he knew she was. What was going on in her mind? What did she know and was holding on to? He knew he needed to get it out of her. His stomach started to churn, a sure sign that he was about to snap and let her have it. He didn't have time to waste being nice. He needed to get on and get whatever information she had out of her, and now.

Just as he was going to explode with frustration, Teri opened her mouth about to say something.

"Bobby and Mr Mitchell also had discussions about Advanced and the quality of the product." She looked up at him. Her face was expressionless, almost as if she was looking through Guthrie.

"Douglas Mitchell, Mr Ogilvy's brother-in-law?"

Teri's answer was a whisper. "Yes."

"Sorry, Teri, did you say yes?"

"Yes."

Guthrie thought for a moment. Another piece of information that was held back from them. Another fact the team had failed to unearth. The more he processed it, the angrier he became. Why were these people intent on keeping this stuff to themselves? He swallowed his anger and composed himself again.

"What did they talk about? Exactly?" He tapped his pen on the table to emphasise the word. No more teasing the information out this time.

"Bobby had an issue with the liner material Advanced was supplying after they were reinstated. He called Douglas and told him the material had failed a Q.C. check."

"Quality control?"

"Yes."

"Why did it fail? Do you know?"

Teri only nodded.

Guthrie screwed his eyes shut. He tried to think about a possible connection, but then something made his gut turn again. He opened his eyes.

"You called Mr Mitchell, Douglas."

Teri's face gave up a small smile.

"You've never referred to him that way. Why the change all of a sudden?"

"Douglas Mitchell is my step-father."

Before Guthrie could say anything, there was a knock and the door opened. Alisdair took one step inside the room.

"Alisdair," Guthrie said, barely able to keep his anger in check, "what do you want?"

"Sorry to barge in, Tom. I thought you would like to know just as soon as the word came in."

Guthrie didn't try to hide his disapproval of the interruption. "Oh, for crying out loud, Alisdair, what is it?"

"It's Mitchell."

Guthrie slumped back in his chair. "What now?"

"He's been taken to the infirmary. Hit and run."

Teri's head snapped up and a hand went to her mouth.

"When did this happen?" Guthrie stood.

"A couple of hours ago. One of the lads who responded recognised the name and called me."

Teri stood up and said, "I need to go. I need to get there!"

Alisdair looked at Guthrie. He held his hands out as if to say, *why?*

Guthrie turned and said, "Teri, why don't you go with Alisdair here. He'll make sure you get up there, okay?" Teri nodded. Then, turning to Alisdair, "Take her to reception and arrange for someone to drive her up to the infirmary."

"But I don't understand..."

"Just do it, Alisdair. Okay? I'll meet you out front in my car. We'll drive up there and I'll fill you in."

"Uh, fair enough."

Guthrie took Teri's arm and guided her around the table, handing her off to Alisdair. When the door had closed, he turned and picked up his notebook and pen, pocketing them. He felt a wave of sickness run through him.

"Buggering hell," he said out loud.

FORTY-FIVE

Guthrie didn't have to wait long before Alisdair appeared at the door. He jogged across to the car, opened the door and nestled into the passenger seat. He didn't give Guthrie time for small talk.

"What was all that about?"

"Teri Donaldson is Mitchell's step-daughter."

Alisdair turned in his seat. His mouth was open, and he had a look of disbelief on his face. "What?" he said.

"You heard me. Your Miss Donaldson is Douglas Mitchell's step-daughter."

Alisdair chose to ignore the *your* remark. "How...? Why...?" however, was all he could say.

"I know. I know. Believe me I've been sitting here asking myself the same question."

"Shite."

"Aye. And you know what else that means?"

"What?"

"She's John Ogilvy's niece."

"Shite!"

"Ah-huh."

Alisdair felt sick. "How did we miss that? How the hell did we not know that?"

"Alisdair, I can't believe it."

They sat in silence. Guthrie checked his map on his phone to make sure he was going the right way. Alisdair noticed.

"You'll want to go right at the roundabout."

Guthrie didn't answer.

They made their way up the hill towards the infirmary.

"Park anywhere in front," Alisdair offered.

Again, Guthrie said nothing. Alisdair's feeling of dread grew. He knew what this could mean for them. Buchanan would be mad; Dundee would be down on them. Then his life would be miserable, if Guthrie's current mood was anything to go by.

They pulled into a parking space close to the main entrance. Neither man said anything as they made their way to reception. Alisdair led the way, being familiar with the building.

They stopped at the main reception desk and asked for Mitchell's room. Alisdair showed his warrant card, and they were given the number. As they walked up the stairs to the first floor, Guthrie seemed to read Alisdair's mind.

"How did we miss the connection between Donaldson and Mitchell? Or Donaldson and Ogilvy?"

Alisdair rubbed his forehead then, subconsciously, pinched the bridge of his nose, a habit he seemed to have picked up from Guthrie. "I really don't know, Tom. I don't know what to say."

"Well, I do. Do you want to know why?"

Alisdair swallowed hard, expecting the worst. Expecting at least a bollocking for letting something like that get by.

"Eh, I suppose so."

"Lack of resources," Guthrie announced. Alisdair was caught off-guard. "Lack of bloody manpower. No help whatsoever from Dundee, never mind Arbroath and your friend and mine, Inspector Buchanan."

"Sorry, what?" was all Alisdair could say in response.

They reached the top of the stairs. Guthrie paused in the middle of the bright, white-tiled corridor. He turned to Alisdair. "You heard me. This whole thing has been just you and me doing most of the heavy lifting on this case."

"What about everyone involved with door-to-doors, re-interviewing people, calling suppliers?"

"I hear you, Alisdair, but think about it. That stuff had to be done, right?" Alisdair nodded. "But what were we supposed to do? We had to delegate that stuff to some-one. We don't have a dozen detectives on this case. We have you and me, and no offence, son, you're not a detective."

Alisdair couldn't help but feel like he was just kicked in the stomach, but he knew Guthrie was right. They had no real resources.

"And don't get me going again with this fire nonsense." Guthrie did a three-sixty. "Which way?"

Alisdair pointed to the right and they started down the corridor.

"All right," said Alisdair, "but how were we supposed to do the job?"

"That's just exactly what I'm going to ask Buchanan as soon as we get back to the station. And if I don't get an answer from him, I'm going to Brian Campbell in Dundee."

The Chief Inspector's name made Alisdair stop. Guthrie took a couple of paces before he realised Alisdair was no longer by his side.

"You think that's wise, going to Bell Street if Buchanan can't deliver?"

"Who do you think sent me here, Alisdair? Who do you think has the authority to get a civilian heading up a murder investigation? Who do you think realised right from the start, SCD didn't have the manpower in the first place?"

"I guess you've got a point."

"Too bloody right I do." He started walking again, checking room numbers as he did so. "And I'm not going to let us missing all this stuff we should have found out, get in the way of making that point. In fact, I need to make sure they don't think about it too long."

"Why?"

"'Cos they'll have our guts for garters. Aye, we're under-manned, but it's still no excuse for screwing up basic police work."

Alisdair thought the bollocking was coming now. Guthrie had been getting more and more agitated as he spoke.

"I'll be buggered if I let them dwell on that," Guthrie added. "I've been a bit of a pillock today, Alisdair, I know." Guthrie stopped again. "I'm sorry."

"That's okay."

"Balls! No, it's not. I did a bit of thinking in the canteen this morning. I've not exactly been focused on things, but that's going to stop. This latest revelation of Donaldson, Mitchell and Ogilvy came at the worst time, but I think we can use it to our advantage."

Alisdair shoved his hands in his pockets and listened.

"It's time to push these people a little harder, Alisdair. It's time to really shake the trees and see what falls to the ground."

"You're not going to do something silly, are you?"

"Alisdair! I'm shocked you would even think such a thing!" Guthrie smiled a wicked smile. He pointed to the door beside them. "One seventeen, right?"

Alisdair nodded. Guthrie knocked and entered without waiting for an answer.

Mitchell was lying on a bed, propped up by pillows. One leg was in a cast. An arm was in some kind of sling contraption. His face looked as though he'd gone ten rounds in a street fight. A machine, obligatory in these situations, was blinking away next to the bed, no doubt hooked up to record various vital statistics. Mitchell's good arm was hooked up to a drip. No-one else was in the room.

"Mr Mitchell." Guthrie wasn't quiet.

With that, Mitchell's eyes opened, but narrowed as he tried to turn his head towards the owner of the voice.

"Mr Guthrie." His voice was quiet and raspy. "Come to figure out who did this?"

"No, I only deal with dead people. You're still alive. But I wouldn't be surprised if I have to."

Mitchell's laugh turned into a cough.

Pulling up a chair, Guthrie sat down at the side of the bed, facing Mitchell. He leaned forward, forearms towards his knees, the fingers of both hands interlaced. Alisdair took up a position at the foot of the bed.

"Tell me what happened."

Mitchell grimaced. "I was coming out of a pub down at the harbour and crossing the road to my car. I heard a car coming. Didn't think anything of it. Next thing I know I'm lying on the street."

"Did you see the vehicle?"

"No. I wasn't paying any attention."

Alisdair was taking notes.

"What pub was it?"

"The, uh, Commercial."

Guthrie looked questioningly around at Alisdair.

"I know it." Alisdair responded.

"Why were you there?" Guthrie continued.

"I was having an early lunch." Mitchell closed his eyes.

"Were you alone? Just decided to have a quiet bite to eat on your own today? Or were you with some pals?"

"I was having a meeting."

"With?"

Mitchell's eyes remained shut. "I'm not sure that has anything to do with finding out who hit me with their car."

The pause before answering was like a red rag to a bull. Guthrie seized the opening.

"Mr Mitchell," Guthrie said, in a loud whispered voice, "that's for me to determine wouldn't you say? After all, I am the professional investigator, not you."

Mitchell didn't move.

"So. Who were you with?"

Again, no response.

"Mr Mitchell, I'm rather fed up with the runaround I seem to experience when I talk to you. Now, you are either going to tell me, or I'm going to break whatever appendage or extremity that isn't already broken." Mitchell's cheek twitched slightly. "Do I make myself clear?"

Mitchell paused before giving up a quiet, "Yes,"

Alisdair had stopped writing in his notebook as the tension rose, not sure if he'd have to stop Guthrie pounding on Mitchell. His mouth was open and dry. He realised and swallowed several times.

"All right. Let's try that last question again then shall we? Who were you with?"

Mitchell opened his eyes and stared at Guthrie. Guthrie raised an eyebrow, in effect, silently repeating the question.

"John."

"John? John Ogilvy?"

"Yes."

At first, Guthrie didn't know what to say. He wasn't expecting anyone in particular, but for some reason John Ogilvy wasn't on the list of potential answers. He sat back and put his hands behind his head.

"What were you talking about?"

"Nothing. We were just having lunch."

"Really? You just said you were having a meeting."

"Lunch, meeting, call it what you want. We just decided to get together."

"Huh. I would have thought that your brother-in-law would be one of the last people you would want to hang out with, considering recent events at Ogilvy Outerwear."

"Mr Guthrie, as I told you before, what happened there was a mutual decision."

Guthrie snorted.

"John is still my brother-in-law, after all."

"And you were just having a quiet... chat about nothing in particular."

"I'd say that's a fair comment."

Guthrie took a deep breath and exhaled through his mouth.

"Okay, okay. Let's talk about something else, eh? Something I came over here to talk to you about."

"We're done with figuring out who tried to kill me?"

"Like I said, right now I'm much more interested in the dead. If I'm unlucky to be assigned to the investigation of your little accident," it was Mitchell's turn to grunt his disgust, "then we'll dig a little deeper, okay? But until then, or until I think this is connected with my investigation, I'd like to stay focused on catching Mr Gant's killer or killers."

"You're full of compassion, aren't you?" Mitchell rearranged the pillow with his head, nestling into the oversized cushion.

"Oh, now, Mr Mitchell. You can't really say that. Here we are, Alisdair and I, paying a visit to you after your accident. I am sorry we didn't bring any grapes, or flowers, or a 'get well soon' balloon, but I thought it would be nice to stop by and see how you were doing."

Mitchell smirked and shook his head.

"You really are full of it, aren't you?"

"What can I say? How can I prove it? Oh, I know. What if I shared a little something with you? A little confession, as it were."

"Oh, yes?"

"Yes. I have to tell you that our investigation of Mr Gant's murder has been rather sub-par. And by sub-par I certainly don't mean in a good golfing way."

"I know what you mean, Mr Guthrie."

"Good. Then you'll perhaps appreciate the fact that this is also rather embarrassing."

Mitchell laughed again. "I can't imagine much embarrassing you, Mr Guthrie."

"Ah, well, you see, that's where you'd be wrong. I get embarrassed by a lot of things. Recently, it's been about certain facts in this case going, let's just say, undiscovered."

Mitchell said nothing. He closed his eyes again. Guthrie glanced at Alisdair. His look was a mix of disgust and annoyance.

"Who are you trying to protect?" Nothing. "Why is everyone tight-lipped?" Again, no reaction from Mitchell. "Are you trying to protect your step-daughter?" Guthrie thought he saw a twitch. It was enough for him to want to press further.

"We know Teri is your step-daughter, Mr Mitchell. One of those undiscovered facts I was telling you about." He paused. Still nothing from Mitchell. He looked down at his shoes. "Why did you, your brother-in-law, or your step-daughter fail to mention your relationships to us when we interviewed you?"

"Perhaps you failed to ask the right questions." Mitchell's answer was devoid of emotion, more a statement than anything else.

Guthrie jumped out of his chair and got to within an inch of Mitchell's face. "Look, you supercilious son of a…"

As soon as Alisdair saw Guthrie lunge, he moved too, around the bed, and grabbed Guthrie's arm, pulling him away from Mitchell. Guthrie shrugged off Alisdair's grip but remained standing. Alisdair stood close, just in case.

"Who do you think you are? This isn't a game. Someone died, murdered, and you are playing games. You, Teri, Ogilvy, you're all playing games!"

Just then the door opened. A nurse stood in the opening. "Mr Mitchell? You called for us?"

Alisdair saw the call button in Mitchell's left hand.

"I wonder if you could show these gentlemen the way out."

Guthrie couldn't help himself. "Douglas Mitchell, I will be recommending that a formal charge be made for this nonsense. You will be prosecuted for wasting our time…"

"Excuse me, sir," the nurse interrupted.

Guthrie raised a hand towards her and exclaimed, "Just a second!" He turned back to Mitchell.

"I'm going to get to the bottom of this, and you'd better start thinking about what you need to tell me." He turned to leave, but after a couple of steps turned back to Mitchell and said, "Just tell me one thing. Did you leave together?"

"Pardon?"

"Did you leave together, you and Mr Ogilvy? Did you leave the pub together?"

Mitchell pushed his head deeper into the pillow.

"Mr Mitchell? Was your brother-in-law with you when you were hit by the vehicle?"

"No. He left before me."

At last, a straight answer.

"How long before you did he leave?"

"I guess it was only five minutes."

"How do you reckon that?"

"I made a short phone call, then paid the bill. I figure it was five minutes. Certainly no more than ten."

Guthrie looked at Alisdair. Saying nothing, he walked past the nurse and out of the room.

Alisdair was about to do the same when Mitchell said, "Constable?"

"Yes?"

"It was a white van."

FORTY-SIX

Alisdair caught up with Guthrie in the car park. Guthrie was in full stride, heading to the MG.

"Tom!"

Guthrie stopped and turned around. "What?"

Alisdair trotted over to him before speaking. "Mitchell told me it was a white van."

"What?"

"A white van. That's the vehicle that knocked him over."

"Are you serious? He told us he didn't see the vehicle. Now he's telling us it was a van? A white one?" Guthrie scratched his head vigorously.

"Right after you walked out of the room."

Guthrie tried to find the words to express his confusion. He stuttered and failed.

"Wait a minute," he finally managed. "Are you telling me he didn't want to tell *me*? Is that what you're telling me?"

"I don't know, Tom."

"That bugger is screwing with us. With me!"

A car pulled into the car park. It was an unmarked pool car from the station. The two men moved back, out of the way. Alisdair recognised the driver and waved. The driver gave a thumbs up in return.

"That's Teri Donaldson," Alisdair said to Guthrie.

Guthrie was now pacing back and forth, like a tiger in a small enclosure.

"I've a good mind to go back up there and have it out with the two of them!"

"No, Tom. Let's leave them for a bit, eh?"

"Don't tell me what to do, Alisdair!"

Guthrie balled his fists. What on earth were they playing at? What is going on with this case? The only answer he had was, "Shite."

Alisdair couldn't tell if that was a good or a bad sign.

"Is that an 'okay'?"

The answer didn't come immediately. Guthrie paced some more then stopped to look out across the park opposite the infirmary. Beyond was the North Sea. The image of Gant's body, lying on the rocks, played on his mind's eye.

The pool car stopped at the main entrance. The passenger door opened, and Teri Donaldson got out. She glanced quickly towards the two men. The look was the only acknowledgment of recognition. She quickly disappeared inside.

Guthrie walked over to his car and unlocked the door.

"Let's get back to the station and tell Buchanan what we've found out this morning."

"I'm sure he'll appreciate that," Alisdair replied, sarcastically.

Guthrie tutted. Once inside, he reached over and unlocked the passenger door. Alisdair climbed in and buckled the lap belt.

"Do you think it's related, or just a coincidence?" he asked pointing up to the building.

"I'm not a believer in coincidences, Alisdair. I'm sure it's related."

"And Ogilvy?"

Guthrie took a deep breath. "Remember that conversation we had the other day about who had motive?"

"Yes." Alisdair's eyes narrowed.

"Ogilvy had motive, Advanced Fabrics had motive, even Gant had motive. All against Mitchell."

"Yes, I remember. What about it?"

"I think we can rule out Gant running over Mitchell."

"If it wasn't serious, I would laugh at that."

"We haven't talked to Advanced yet, and Ogilvy has always been in the frame for me."

"So?"

"I thought Mitchell was our best bet, especially after we interviewed him."

"But now you're not sure?"

Guthrie started the car. They were heading back down the hill to the roundabout before he spoke again.

"Why did he tell us what he did just now?"

"What? Now you're questioning him telling us things, where before you were on him for not?"

"No. Think about it Alisdair. He's been economical with information right from the start. Now he's telling us he was with Ogilvy and Ogilvy left with enough time to get into his car and run him over when he leaves the pub."

"Yes, but what does Ogilvy drive?"

The question was one to which Alisdair knew the answer, and Guthrie knew it.

"A Jag."

"Aye."

"Bugger it, Alisdair. Why do you make it difficult all the time?"

This time, Alisdair did laugh. "What? Me? I'm just reminding you of what we *do* know. I'm not the seasoned detective that's supposed to come up with all the stuff we don't."

Guthrie glared at Alisdair for a second before returning to the road.

"That wasn't meant in any way other than I don't know where to go with it, Tom."

"Aye, of course. Sorry."

They sat quietly as they made their way back past the harbour and towards the station. It was Guthrie who spoke first.

"I tell you what you're good at, though."

"Oh, aye? What's that?"

"You can connect the dots. You can think beyond what's in front of you. You need that to figure this stuff out."

Alisdair watched the scenery pass by but said nothing. Guthrie looked over a couple of times.

"Penny for your thoughts."

Alisdair kept his gaze away from Guthrie. "Ach, nothing. You know what I feel about the job. I appreciate the compliment, that's all."

"Well I didn't know it was going to turn you all introspective and serious. There are tissues in the glovebox if you..."

"Bugger off!" Alisdair exclaimed, but unable to do so without smiling.

Another pause, then Guthrie asked, "Do we know for sure Ogilvy doesn't have a white van?"

"No."

"There you go, then. Ogilvy. White van. Two dots you need to connect."

"What about Advanced Fabrics? We've still to get them on record, get their side of the story."

"True." Guthrie flicked the indicator on and swung the car into the car park at Gravesend. He spotted a visitor space immediately in front of the entrance and nosed the MG into the space.

"You know Buchanan will go mental if he sees you parking here?"

"Buchanan. I'd almost forgotten about having to update him. Thanks for reminding me." The insincerity in his voice was not difficult to spot. Taking the keys out of the ignition, Guthrie patted the steering wheel almost impatiently as he thought.

"Here's the plan. I'll go and brief Buchanan while you make a couple of calls."

"Okay."

"First, I want you to call Ogilvy. I want to chat with our smug friend about Mitchell's accident and what they were talking about. Things aren't quite adding up there. *He said, she said* kind o' thing."

Alisdair nodded. "And?"

"Call Advanced Fabrics and go see whoever you think you need to talk to. I don't care if it's the managing director or the cleaner, get their take on what happened when they were dropped and how they were re-established as a supplier."

"Will do." Alisdair reached for the door handle, but Guthrie grabbed his free arm. Alisdair turned.

"I'm trusting you to get everything out of Advanced. Do you understand? Don't take any kind of brush off. If you think they're stalling, or you sense any kind of hesitation, get stuck in. You hear me?"

"Sure." Alisdair's pulse was quickening. Was this a test? He didn't know, but he knew he had just been given the opportunity to go solo on the initial interview, and permission to go a little *Guthrie* if he had to.

"What are you smiling about?"

"Sorry. I was just thinking about getting all Tom Guthrie on the cleaning lady at Advanced Fabrics."

Guthrie's face turned grey. "You think I'm joking?"

"No..."

"Because I'm not, Alisdair. We've missed a lot of details here, and that stops now. Am I making myself clear?"

"Crystal, Tom"

"Right. Off you go. And you're on your own for transport. I'll drive this. Try and grab a pool car."

Alisdair got out of the car, but before he could close the door, Guthrie shouted, "And get someone to check on whether or not Ogilvy or his business has a white van!"

FORTY-SEVEN

"I got the report on the fire. Thank you," Buchanan said. He picked up a binder from his in-tray. Guthrie just nodded his head and kept his mouth shut. Let him believe he did something to get the paperwork to him. "I'll have one of the incident room personnel finish entering the details into the system," Buchanan continued, pointing at the computer screen on his desk, "but I saw that Alisdair logged in and submitted the summary forms."

"Yes, he said he would take care of it."

"How is he working out?"

"He's sharp. I think he's suited to this kind of work. I know he wants it."

Buchanan sat back and steepled his fingers. "I agree that he's sharp. I'm not sure he's quite ready for that sort of thing yet, Tom. He's still quite inexperienced."

Guthrie inwardly recoiled at Buchanan's superior inflection. He tried not to show it.

"So. Bring me up-to-date -- since you weren't available this morning."

Guthrie hoped he wouldn't have to deal with why he

missed the briefing, and he knew Buchanan was looking for an explanation. Guthrie had no intention of providing one -- as he had none. He had thought about how he could break the news that they had come up short on some aspects of their various interviews, but nothing presented itself as the perfect answer, therefore, he had decided to not sugarcoat it and just tell it like it was. Hopefully, this would also keep Buchanan away from digging into his tardiness.

"We found out that Teri Donaldson, the receptionist at Ogilvy Outerwear is Douglas Mitchell's step daughter, which, of course, makes her John Ogilvy's niece."

Buchanan shifted forward.

Guthrie continued. "That would explain why Donaldson was somewhat unwilling to share what she knew about Gant's telephone conversation with the supplier, and, as we found out, about another phone call with Mitchell."

Buchanan had screwed his eyes shut. "Sorry, you didn't know about the connection between Donaldson, Mitchell and Ogilvy until...?"

"Earlier today."

Buchanan processed the information. Pinching the bridge of his nose he said, "Normally I would expect that kind of information to come to light a little sooner during an investigation, if you thought there was reason that Miss Donaldson was being anything other than cooperative or had something to hide." He spoke quietly. He had relaxed his eyes, but they remained closed. Both index fingers of his steepled hands tapped against one another.

"I assume you have no reason to believe she has anything to hide." Now he stared, coldly, at Guthrie.

Guthrie weighed his options. He didn't necessarily want to say that his instinct was screaming that she was protecting someone, Mitchell, Ogilvy, someone. "I just think she's afraid of what we may be thinking about her step-father and uncle. Family's family after all."

"I appreciate that, Tom, but..."

"But you don't think we should be pussy-footing around during a murder investigation."

"No, I don't."

"You know me, Ian. Last thing I would do is let someone's feelings get in the way of me getting to the truth." Guthrie folded his arms and flashed a grin.

Buchanan rolled his eyes. "That's exactly what I'm afraid of."

Guthrie's grin melted away like butter on warm toast.

Buchanan continued. "Do you suspect any sort of obstruction from the three of them?"

"I do, but I have nothing solid to hang my hat on. Just a gut feeling."

"You know how much I like your gut feelings?"

"Yes, I do. That's why I've been a very nice boy and not embarrassed myself." He knew Buchanan was fishing, looking to get under his skin. He wasn't going to give him the satisfaction.

"But it's only a matter of time."

"Oh, bugger off, Ian." The time was shorter than he expected.

"Now, now." Buchanan wagged a finger. "I'll hear you out. What's this gut of yours telling you?"

Guthrie wanted to say that his gut was telling him to punch the inspector in the mouth. He settled for, "My money's on Ogilvy."

"Why?'

Guthrie stood up and walked slowly around the room. He had no real evidence. Who was he trying to fool? He had no evidence at all. Not for the first time, a doubt crept into his mind.

You've lost it, Tom. You're not the detective you used to be, and it's beginning to show. Some consulting detective you turned out to be.

He had read some Sherlock Holmes stories in the first few weeks of his retirement. He had tried several things to keep his mind occupied and off the reasons he was no longer employed as a police officer. He started by reading crime fiction. Probably not the best choice. He progressed to hacking golf balls around the local course and quickly found out that particular pastime gave him too much time to think about the things he was trying to keep from thinking about. Again, probably not the best choice. Mountain biking was next. That would get him into the countryside, keep the muscles working and perhaps reduce the middle-aged spread. That only served to get him mixed up with a death while out for a quiet weekend of fresh air, which, in turn, led to him researching how to set up a private investigation company. That was how he ended up working as Police Scotland's resident, consulting detective out of Dundee.

"Tom?"

Buchanan's voice brought Guthrie's mind back into the room.

"Huh? Oh, sorry. What?"

Buchanan sighed. "Why is your money on Ogilvy?"

Guthrie stopped his pacing and bent down, supporting his weight on the back of the chair across from Buchanan. "He has the most to lose. Therefore, he has the greatest motive."

"Continue."

Guthrie started his pacing again. "His company's in a financial meltdown. There are only a couple of products keeping him afloat, one of which is the foul weather jackets for Police Scotland. That was the source of the biggest issue within the company we've found recently."

"The liner contract."

"Yes. So, the guy who made the changes as part of the cuts was fired - Mitchell. The guy seen having a dust up with the key vendor is murdered within days. And Ogilvy has been plain obstinate about almost everything we've questioned him on." Guthrie looked up to the ceiling.

"Seems like Mitchell would be more in the frame. He lost more because of Ogilvy and, perhaps, Gant."

"Ah, Mitchell. Let's talk about Mitchell." Guthrie put his hands in his pockets, forcing his arms straight and raising his shoulders. "He's in the infirmary."

Buchanan almost recoiled from the words. "What?"

"He was involved in a hit and run earlier today."

"Is he all right? How bad is he? Why am I just hearing about this right now?" Each question was asked louder than the last, and the louder the inspector's voice became, the more his face turned red.

Guthrie coughed. "The uniform who responded to the call recognised the name from one of the briefings and called it in to the incident room. Alisdair relayed it to me."

"The obvious question, Tom -- is it connected?" Buchanan was still fuming about not knowing but tried to keep his focus on details.

"Not sure, but my gut..."

"Yes, I know about your gut," Buchanan shouted. He picked up a pen and threw it back down on the desk.

"Alisdair and I talked to him."

"*And?*" Buchanan's face now a solid red. Guthrie thought he was going to explode. He was certainly not going to tell him that they were nearly thrown out of the infirmary. "He did give us a couple of pieces of information. He was hit by a white van."

"Well, that's something at least. Did he recognise it?"

"He didn't say, but I'll tell you what else we found out."

"Well, spit it out, Tom." Buchanan was now in no mood to play Guthrie's games.

"He was having a meeting in a pub, close to the harbour. The Commercial?" Buchanan nodded. "He was with Ogilvy."

Buchanan cocked his head to one side. He knew what was coming.

Guthrie continued. "Ogilvy left the pub just before he did. When Mitchell left, he was hit by the van."

Buchanan took time to process the information, then stood up and grabbed his uniform jacket from a coat hook in the corner of the office.

"Right. You and I are going to have a chat with Ogilvy."

"Now, hold on, Ian!"

"No, Tom. This has gone on long enough." He walked back to his desk and picked up a sheet of paper from his in tray. He handed it to Guthrie.

It was a printout of an email from Dundee. It was from the Chief Inspector. The same Chief Inspector who assigned Guthrie to the investigation. It didn't leave room for interpretation. Dundee was not happy with the lack of evidence in the case, along with the fact they had no prime suspect. It also indicated that Buchanan needed to get his finger out and take control. After all, he was the senior officer, responsible for the day-to-day execution and the successful outcome of the investigation. Guthrie looked at Buchanan.

"Now. You and I are going to talk to Ogilvy."

"Oh, come off it, Ian! Shite."

"What's wrong, Tom? You now know how this is looking -- officially."

"Ach, they don't see everything we're doing. They don't see the roadblocks these people are throwing up in front of us."

"It doesn't matter. I have been told, in no uncertain terms, my rear end is the one that's going to be kicked up and down the High Street if we don't get a result and get one soon."

Guthrie spun on his heel and walked to the door. He could feel a tightness in his chest. A sign he was on the verge of exploding, never mind Buchanan. He stopped.

"Tell me what good it will do, having you talk to Ogilvy? You haven't had the-"

Buchanan cut him off. "Tom. Let me stop you there." He held up a hand. "I'm taking charge of this. From now on, you do nothing without getting my express approval."

"Ian..."

"No use protesting, Tom. The decision's already been made." He picked up the copy of the email and shook it in Guthrie's face. "I'll meet you in the car park in five minutes. I'll drive."

FORTY-EIGHT

Alisdair made his way along the A92 to the west. The Elliot
Industrial estate was almost the last thing you passed before
heading into the countryside.

He looked at the map on his phone. A couple of turns
and he should see the facility. Switching off the screen, he
slipped the phone into the inside pocket of his jacket which
was lying on the passenger seat.

The Advanced Fabrics factory was a typical big box
construction. There was no sign outside. No flag poles.
Nothing to suggest what the building was, or who owned it.

Alisdair found one remaining spot at the far end of the
car park and backed into it. After gathering his jacket, he
climbed out and locked the door. The air was getting colder,
as if the little warmth the sun had managed to produce for a
couple of hours that day was trying to escape back into
space. The wind was also picking up, coming in from the
North Sea. Cold. Damp. The kind of wind that made your
ears sting and turn red if you stayed out long enough. And
long enough was no time at all.

Alisdair tutted to himself as he remembered he'd left a

scarf back in the incident room. He turned up his collar and began walking smartly to the main door.

Inside was a reception desk, behind which was a woman in her early sixties. She looked up and smiled.

"May I help you?"

Alisdair showed her his warrant card. "Alisdair McEwan, Police Scotland. I'm investigating the murder of a Mr Bobby Gant who worked for Ogilvy Outerwear."

"Oh, yes. Such a terrible thing. Right here in Arbroath too."

"Yes. I understand Advanced Fabrics is a supplier to Ogilvy Outerwear. I'd like to talk to someone who worked with them, or who may have spoken to Mr Gant prior to his death."

The receptionist sat forward. "Oh, yes. Of course." She put a telephone headset on and continued, "Now let's see. I'll sure you would need to talk to... yes, Mr West is in, our managing director. Would you like me to see if you could talk with him?"

Alisdair smiled and said yes. "And if you think of anyone else who may be useful to talk to, I'd appreciate it."

The receptionist asked Alisdair to take a seat.

It was about five minutes later that a man walked through the door across from where Alisdair was sitting. He was dressed casually, in jeans and a long-sleeved white shirt. He approached the receptionist and bent over the desk in order to keep the conversation unheard by their guest. After a brief exchange he looked over at Alisdair, then back to the receptionist. He nodded as if in answer to a question she had asked, then straightened up and looked back to Alisdair.

"Devon West," he said, walking over.

"Constable Alisdair McEwan." The men shook hands.

"I understand you would like to talk to someone regarding Bobby Gant." The accent was from the northeast of England. Newcastle was Alisdair's guess.

"That's right. We know Advanced Fabrics is a major supplier to Ogilvy Outerwear and I was hoping to fill in some background, just to make sure we have a complete understanding of what Mr Gant's role was with respect to Ogilvy Outerwear and your company."

"I'm the company's M.D., head of sales, and I do a whole lot besides. I should be able to answer your questions." West indicated for Alisdair to follow him and started walking towards the door, through which he had appeared. "Of course, I'm not sure how exactly we can help you. Bobby had very little contact with us, and what he did have, was with me or my father. Please."

West held the door and Alisdair walked into an open plan office area. There were half a dozen cubicles down the middle of the room. On the right, windows looked out to the car park. On the left were four conference rooms behind floor to ceiling glass walls; one large one, and three smaller versions. It was to the nearest of these more intimate spaces that West guided Alisdair.

West closed the door. "Please," he pointed to one of the four chairs arranged around a small, round table. Alisdair took a seat affording him a view back out towards the main office. West sat across from him. Alisdair took out his notebook and a pen.

"Mr West, as I said, we are just piecing together additional information that will help us in the investigation of this crime."

"Of course." West's demeanour was relaxed. One leg crossed over the other, ankle on knee.

"We know that Mr Gant talked with someone here at

Advanced Fabrics shortly before his death. The conversation, from what we know, was rather heated. Do you know anything about that?"

West shifted slightly in his chair. "Well, as a matter of fact, I was the one Bobby was talking to."

Excellent, Alisdair thought. Guthrie will be pleased it wasn't the cleaner after all. "What were you discussing?" he asked.

"Oh, the usual kinds of things one normally talks about between a company and its clients."

"I'm sorry, Mr West, I'm not a businessman. Could you explain what that might be?"

West uncrossed his legs. "Sure. Shipment timing, product details, pricing. That sort of thing."

"Any particular product?"

"No."

"Any particular issue?"

"No. From what I recall it was a routine conversation."

Alisdair's eyes narrowed. "Mr West, we know the conversation was not a *routine conversation* as you put it. Why don't you just tell me exactly what you were talking about?"

A smile broke West's stare. He looked to his left, where he could see the office. Alisdair didn't know if he was going to hear a revelation, or yet another evasive line. Heaven knows, the investigation was full of them.

"Mr West?" he pressed.

Without look around, West responded, "We were discussing why we were dropped as a supplier."

"And why was that?"

"It was a price issue. Pure and simple."

"You were too expensive?"

"I wouldn't say that, exactly."

"What would you say, *exactly*?" Alisdair felt like it was Guthrie talking and not him. It was his turn to shift in his chair, uncomfortable about the prospect of Guthrie rubbing off on him.

"They were going through some cutbacks and we had been dropped."

"But you had been reinstated as their supplier by the time of this conversation, correct?"

"Yes."

"You're telling me you were revisiting that?"

West paused before answering. "It was about product quality."

Alisdair clicked the top of his pen and noted the response in his notebook. "What exactly was the issue?"

"There was a problem with a batch of product we had delivered. It was taken care of once they let us know."

"I see," said Alisdair.

"Look, it's not something we like to admit. We pride ourselves on our high standards and take it personally when we deliver something that is not up to the quality demanded, or expected, by the client." West stood up. "We're very proud of what we do, and we don't like it when we're called out for failing to deliver what we've promised."

Alisdair decided to change direction.

"We know that Mr Gant was not your normal contact at Ogilvy Outerwear. Who would that have been?"

"Douglas Mitchell."

"Were you surprised he was asked to leave the company?"

"Yes and no."

"Explain."

"Douglas is a good man. I like him."

"Do you keep in touch with him?"

"I guess you can say we do. I mean, we're not golfing buddies or drinking pals, but we still occasionally call one another, just to see how everything is. Nothing earth-shattering, though."

"If you were supplying a quality product and were on good terms with Mr Mitchell, it must have been hard for him to cancel your contract."

West laughed, "Yes it was. He had a job to do, and I can't hold that against him."

"What happened when the contract was reinstated? How did that come about and who made the decision?"

"John Ogilvy called my dad."

"Your dad? Why...?"

"It's my dad who owns Advanced Fabrics."

Great, thought Alisdair. *Another family business.* The last thing he needed was to be playing games with these guys, just like Ogilvy. He settled for, "I see," instead.

"Do they know each other well?"

"Not really. They've done business together for several years, what with the contract and all, but the relationship was purely professional. My dad's not one for the golf club, or the Rotary. He likes to keep himself to himself."

"Mr Ogilvy called your dad and asked him to consider supplying them again?"

"Pretty much. They needed our product, and we were more than happy to supply them."

Alisdair wrote again in his notebook, slowly, carefully. He wanted to make sure he could answer all of Guthrie's questions without having to decipher his own handwriting. When he looked up, West was standing, arms folded, watching him intently.

Alisdair stood up. "Thank you, Mr West. I'll let you know if we need to do a follow-up. In the meantime, if you think of anything at all that might help us, please just call the station and they'll put you through to the incident room."

"Of course, of course. Anything we can do. Such a shame about Bobby."

Alisdair nodded. West's expression reflected the concern.

"Let me show you out."

West led Alisdair back past the cubicles and into reception. He pushed the main door open for him.

"Thanks again," Alisdair said as he eased past him and into the cold, damp air of the afternoon.

FORTY-NINE

Guthrie was fuming.

His attitude was as dark as the weather. The rain was coming down steadily now, and the street lights were reflected in the wet road as Buchanan pulled the Jaguar into the car park at Gravesend.

The conversation in the car, from the moment they had left Ogilvy Outerwear to that point, was all about how Guthrie had failed to secure any solid evidence, allowed Ogilvy, Mitchell and the rest to lead him down dead ends, and why Buchanan's doubts about putting him in charge of the investigation were correct in the first instance.

"I *know* Ogilvy is mixed up in this," Guthrie snorted.

"He's mixed up in it because it was his employee who was murdered. That's where his involvement ends." Buchanan parked the Jag in the first available spot closest to the front door.

"Ach, shite, Ian!"

Buchanan killed the ignition and unbuckled his seat belt. He faced forward, hands in his lap. He didn't turn to Guthrie.

"Tom, we need results. We need them now. You're not getting anywhere."

"We're going to break them down. All we need is one little chink, and I'll unravel whatever it is they're covering up."

"I saw nothing during our conversation with Mr Ogilvy that led me to believe he was covering up anything. I think you're barking up the wrong tree."

"Ian, you're wrong. I know it."

Buchanan sighed loudly. "I'm going to step up our social media campaign. We're going to the mainstream media to ask for help. Get the word out to a larger number of people."

Guthrie's response was far from positive. "We're going to tweet something, asking for help. Do you think some little fifteen-word message to a bunch of teenagers, who are more interested in taking pictures of themselves and have absolutely nothing to do with this case, is going to net us a result?"

"I've been asked to give a comprehensive briefing for the television news as well as the papers."

"Great." Guthrie reached for the door handle.

"I'll let you know when it is, but I expect you to be there."

"Oh, come on..."

Buchanan raised a hand. "No arguments, Tom. This is coming from Dundee, but I agree and, quite frankly, I think it's long overdue. I'll let you know on the timing."

Buchanan got out of the car. Guthrie followed suit.

The inspector jogged to the cover of the overhang above the station's front door. It appeared the rain was settling in for the night. When Guthrie closed the passenger door, Buchanan locked the car with the remote and waited for Guthrie to catch up.

"I'm close, Ian."

"No. I don't think you are."

"I just need some time to put a little pressure on these people. I *know* they're hiding something."

"Pressure is the last thing you need to put on them. I know what your definition of pressure is."

Buchanan pulled on the door to go inside, but Guthrie pushed it shut again. He stood almost nose to nose with Buchanan. When he spoke, it was almost a whisper. "I just need some more time before you go back to Bell Street. That's all I'm asking. I promise to keep everything on the level."

"Why do I find that hard to believe?"

The two men stared at one another. Neither wanted to give in. Guthrie certainly wasn't going to give his former colleague the satisfaction.

"All right, Tom. You have twenty-four hours."

"What? I need more than a day to-"

"This time tomorrow, Tom. If there's not what I determine to be satisfactory progress, I'm calling Dundee and requesting resources from Serious Crimes."

Guthrie didn't know what to say, other than, "And where will that leave me?"

"I think you know."

Guthrie took his hand away from the door. Buchanan disappeared inside. Looking at his watch, Guthrie decided to call it a day. He could call Alisdair on his way home. For the moment, he didn't feel like doing anything but going back to Broughty Ferry and getting some sleep.

Twenty-four hours. How clichéd was that?

He rummaged around in his jacket pocket and found his car keys. At least the MG was only a few yards away and

Buchanan hadn't noticed it parked in the visitor spot. He walked over and unlocked the door.

Inside, he started it and turned the windshield wipers on. The defrost tried its best, but was notoriously weak. Guthrie retrieved a white cloth from behind the seat and used to quickly clear the glass. He checked his phone. No messages from Alisdair. No messages from anyone, for that matter.

He thought about calling Alisdair, then decided he could do it on the drive.

Food. He needed food. He hadn't eaten since breakfast. He wondered if he should call Alisdair anyway, see if he wanted to have dinner and go over his visit to Advanced Fabrics, but he quickly dismissed the thought. *Just go home. Pick up something on the way. Get to bed early and start again in the morning.*

His emotions were a mix of anger, tiredness, frustration, and a little self-pity thrown in for good measure.

Twenty-four hours.

"Bugger."

FIFTY

"Hello, Tom."

Guthrie's phone was on his kitchen countertop. Alisdair was on speaker so Guthrie could unwrap the fish supper he had picked up.

Once he got on the road, his mind started racing with everything he had gone through over the past week. Before he realised where he was, he was on the outskirts of Broughty Ferry.

The rain had also given up early and had eased to a drizzle by the time he arrived back at the flat. Since Murray's was just around the corner, he decided to park the car and walk to get a carry out. By the time he returned to the flat, the package was still hot.

"Alisdair. Tell me about your afternoon." He fiddled with the grease-proof paper. Steam rose as he opened it, the smell triggered loud rumblings from his stomach.

"Oh. Nothing much to report, Tom. I went over to Advanced Fabrics like you wanted me to."

"And?"

"I met with Devon West. He's the son of the owner,

Harry West. Devon is a director and head of sales, but like a lot of these family businesses, they tend to wear several hats."

"Tell me something I don't know. All we need is another keep-it-in-the-family deal." Guthrie remained standing at the kitchen counter. He wasn't going to take the time to transfer the unwrapped meal to a plate. He certainly wasn't going to fetch a fork. He stood, wolfing down the fat chips that had been doused in vinegar and loaded up with what was probably too much salt to be good for him, but if you didn't, the taste wasn't quite the same.

"Aye. That was my reaction when I found out. Not as bad as Ogilvy, though. There seemed to be a healthy staff in the office. Smart set-up too."

"But that's not telling me what you found out."

"Like I said, nothing much to report. Gant's phone call was to Devon. It appears Gant wasn't too pleased with the quality of the product Advanced was producing."

"Details?"

"None. They resolved it pretty quickly."

"Did you ask about why they were dropped?"

"Yes. Price. Just as we know."

Guthrie was picking the flakey white fish with his fingers. Between mouthfuls he said, "What about being reinstated?"

"Ogilvy called Harry West directly and they sorted it out. It was a case of needing what Advanced Fabrics could supply. Don't think they had much choice."

"Okay."

A pause, while Guthrie finished up the last of his chips, was broken by Alisdair. "I bumped into Inspector Buchanan when I got back."

"Oh, aye? What did he have to say?"

"He said they were having a press conference tomorrow."

Guthrie walked over to the sink. He tore off a paper towel and wiped his hands. Opening a cupboard, he took out a glass and poured himself a water.

"Tom?"

"I'm still here." He took a long drink before continuing. "Did he tell you he gave me twenty-four hours to get something more solid than a gut feeling?"

"Yes, he did." Another pause. "For what it's worth, Tom, I think it's not on."

"I appreciate it, Alisdair, but I really can't blame him. The pressure's coming from Dundee."

"What are you going to do?"

"I don't know." Guthrie picked up the phone. He deselected speakerphone and held it up to his ear as he walked over to the window. "I can't say I've never been in this situation before -- coming up blank on an investigation, but..."

"But you really want to put one over on Buchanan?"

Guthrie laughed. "Ha! I told you you'd make a good detective. No, for some reason, it's not just that."

"Then what?"

The scene outside was one Guthrie had grown used to over the years. The small harbour, the castle to the left, the hills of Fife barely visible as black shapes against the dark sky, directly across the Tay. He'd stared through this window on many evenings in the middle of an investigation, wondering where to go next, who to pressure. He just didn't feel it this night.

"I'm not sure I have it anymore, you know? Sometimes I just feel like I'm going through the motions to do what? Please myself, probably. Fool myself into thinking I'm still useful."

"Now, Tom. I'm not one to judge your personal performance on this case against your career, and I am certainly not experienced enough, even as a copper, let alone a pseudo-detective, to pronounce judgment on how you've handled this investigation, but I don't think you can be too hard on yourself."

"I appreciate the sympathy..."

"It's no sympathy," Alisdair interrupted. "I'm just saying."

Guthrie found himself staring, unfocused, at the scene outside. He shook himself and said, "Right! What are we going to do tomorrow? Whether I'm still on the case at the end of the day or not, is irrelevant. There's still a murder to be solved. Bobby Gant is still dead and that needs to be put right by nailing whoever did it." He walked over to the leather armchair and sat down.

"No matter what Buchanan says, my money is on Ogilvy."

"But, why, Tom? We have nothing on him."

"It just is. I don't know how to explain it. He just rubs me the wrong way."

"Not really a good argument to pin a murder on someone though?"

Guthrie thought for a second. "We just have to find something. If tomorrow is my last crack at this thing, I want to go down swinging."

"Why don't I pick up some breakfast for us, early? I can meet you at the station and we can plan out our day. It's late and we're probably not on the best of form right now."

Guthrie thought. "All right. I can't believe it's been six days already."

"Me neither."

"What about six in the morning?"

"Are you sure? You still have to drive to get here."

"I'm sure. I can sleep when I'm kicked off the case."

"You're such the optimist, Tom."

"Thanks. I'll see you in the morning."

Guthrie hung up. He let his head fall back onto the chair and closed his eyes. His stomach started to churn. He didn't know if that was as a result of eating late after having nothing for most of the day, or it was an ulcer, or nerves. The busyness of the day caught up with him. His head started to swim. Then he thought of the night before, and Jacquie.

What a mess.

That hadn't turned out the way he thought it might. She was far too pushy for his liking. Probably a good thing he had said what he did.

He looked at his watch. He needed to get to bed if they were to start at six in Arbroath.

FIFTY-ONE

Tuesday, 1st April, 2014

It was six on the nose when Guthrie walked into the incident room at Gravesend. Of course, Alisdair was already there.

"Do you ever sleep?"

"I've been known to, on occasion. Breakfast is over by the microwave if you need to heat it up."

Guthrie walked over to the counter and saw a plate with a carry out container siting on it. He opened it up and saw a complete fry up: eggs, fried tomatoes, beans, sausage, mushrooms, bacon, black pudding and toast.

"Where on earth did you get this?"

"A little transport cafe on the Montrose Road. I wasn't sure if you'd like the black pudding..."

"No. No, it's great. Thanks. What do I owe you?"

"Nothing. It's on me."

"I see. A little going away testimonial, huh?"

Alisdair shook his head.

Guthrie ignored him. "Well, thanks again. Coffee?"

"Got one," Alisdair responded.

Guthrie poured a cup and stirred in too much sugar and creamer. He picked up the plate with the container and joined Alisdair back at the desk.

"Cheers."

"Cheers. So? Thought about a plan?"

"Ogilvy, Alisdair. It's about Ogilvy today."

Alisdair couldn't help but roll his eyes.

"No, listen. If I'm going to be kicked off this investigation, what do I have to lose, huh?"

"Your reputation. Your chance to get back on another case down the road," Alisdair said.

"Aye, right. But, really, what if I'm right? What if we can get him to crack?"

"You're still assuming he *is* mixed up in the murder. We had Mitchell pegged the other day for giving us a motive, don't forget."

"I know, I know." Guthrie scooped up a mouthful of baked beans. Still chewing he asked, "What about yesterday? I completely forgot to ask. Did you get anywhere with the white van?"

Alisdair put his fork down and swallowed some coffee before answering. "Sal ran a check. You can imagine how many returns we got. I asked her to filter it to see, just on the off-chance, that Ogilvy, or their suppliers had white vans registered to them."

"And?"

"And, nothing yet. I asked Buchanan if we could assign some resources to following up on that today."

"What did he say?"

"We could have two uniforms."

"That's something at least. How many vehicles are we talking about?"

"Sixteen."

Guthrie rubbed his head. "I'm not sure if that's good or bad."

"Good, I think," said Alisdair. "A good chunk of them, about seven, belong to one company."

"I assume it's not Ogilvy Outerwear," Guthrie stated before scooping up some egg onto a piece of bacon.

"A leasing company, I'm afraid."

"Bugger! Knew it. That would be too easy, wouldn't it?"

"They're trying to find out who operates them."

The two of them ate without talking.

"Why would Mitchell tell us what he did? You know, say he saw nothing, then throw the white van out there for us?"

"Buggered if I know, Alisdair. Knowing him, it's probably a red herring. Something to throw us off what's really going on."

"Do you believe that, or are you just saying it to convince yourself?"

Guthrie looked up towards the ceiling. "Oh, I'm just venting. I still don't trust anything these guys tell us. I do believe that."

"Either way, the boys will follow up this morning. More coffee?"

"Sure." Guthrie handed his cup to Alisdair.

The door opened and the desk sergeant approached them.

"Mr Guthrie, this came in during third shift. They called to make sure it was given to you first thing." He handed a piece of paper to Guthrie. It was a print out of an email.

"Thanks."

Guthrie started to read. Alisdair sat down and put the fresh cup of coffee in front of him.

"Thanks," Guthrie repeated.

"What's that?"

"A lab report from forensics."

"Oh, good. I was hoping they would get back with something quickly."

"You know about this?"

"Eh, yes. Sorry I didn't say."

"You didn't say what, Alisdair?"

Alisdair squirmed a little in his seat.

"Come on. Out with it."

Alisdair swallowed. "You were in a bit of a mood yesterday, if you remember?" Guthrie raised is eyebrows. "You told me that if I wanted to be a detective..."

"I remember."

"Well, I did a little digging. I was filing the report on the fire and I had a hunch. I guess more of a roll of the dice."

"What do you mean? We're done with the fire. Don't sidetrack us with the fire, Alisdair. Hell, we have enough to be getting on with!" Guthrie's voice became louder and louder. "We need to move on."

"Just let me explain. I wanted to know if there was a connection between the fire and the Gant murder."

"Seriously? Why on earth would you think that? The fire was an accident. You know that. Why would you even begin to think that, Alisdair?"

Alisdair looked down at the table. "I... I don't know."

Guthrie tossed the sheet of paper on the table. "Sorry. I shouldn't have gone off like that."

"That's okay, Tom. I was just trying to do *something*, you know?"

"I know. Sorry."

Guthrie stood up and gathered what was left of his breakfast. "You done?" he asked.

"Aye."

He picked up Alisdair's plate and carried them over to the counter. Dumping the carry out container in the bin he turned to Alisdair. "Where do these plates go?"

"Just leave them there. I got them from the canteen. I'll take them back in a little while."

Guthrie nodded and walked back to the desk. Alisdair was reading the email. Guthrie took a mouthful of coffee and almost spit it out in surprise when Alisdair shouted.

"Holy shite!"

"What?" Guthrie spluttered. He had spilled some coffee on the desk. He grabbed one of the paper napkins from breakfast and started to wipe up the mess.

"This!" Alisdair shook the paper in the air between them. "This!" he repeated.

"What?"

Alisdair's face had turned red. "It's a match. It's a bloody match!" he slapped the paper down on the desk and jumped up from his chair.

"A match for what?"

Alisdair picked up the paper again and turned it for Guthrie to read.

"I was going through the inventory of the warehouse fire when I was submitting the report. Something struck me as being familiar. I didn't know at first what it was -- a gut feeling, you know?"

"Oh, I know," said Guthrie sarcastically. "And I know just how much those can get you in trouble."

"You'll know that sometimes you just have to do it anyway -- act on your gut."

"Okay, okay. What does this tell me?" Guthrie said, pointing at the paper in front of him.

"I sent a runner to Dundee yesterday morning with my foul weather jackets and asked forensics to analyse the lining with a sample of the white material our fire victim was bedded down on in the warehouse."

"How did you get that fabric?"

"I just drove over there and took some."

"Oh, you did, did you?" Guthrie's face was a scowl.

"Aye. The door was still unlocked. I just cut a piece and sent it with the jacket. I asked them to tell me if it was close, nothing too detailed. I wanted a quick answer I could either follow up or dismiss, and it's a bloody match."

Guthrie sat back and started to process what Alisdair was telling him. "Let me get this straight. The liner from the jacket is a match for the material in the warehouse?"

Alisdair nodded. "The report says they'd need to look a little closer, but they're confident that the material is essentially the same."

"We have a connection between Ogilvy and the warehouse?"

Alisdair nodded again.

"What the hell does that mean?"

This time Alisdair shrugged.

"Who's the owner of the warehouse?"

"It's in the report. I forget who it is, but we have it."

Guthrie scratched his chin. "Right. You get hold of the owner and ask him what he knows."

"I'm not sure I should be the one, Tom. You have the experience. I'm afraid I might miss something. If this is more than a coincidence, I don't want to screw it up. Heaven knows we've missed one or two things already."

"No. I want you to go talk to him."

Alisdair took a deep breath and exhaled through his mouth. "All right. What are you going to do in the meantime?"

"I'm going to talk to Ogilvy."

"Are you sure you want to do that?"

"What do you mean?"

Alisdair hesitated, then said, "I know you have a feeling about him, but we've got..."

"A gut feeling, Alisdair. A hunch. Look how it paid off for you." Guthrie smiled, but Alisdair could see it was anything but innocent. Guthrie was plotting something.

"I just don't want you doing or saying something that will get you in trouble. That's all."

"I appreciate your concern, but if you're referencing my *unorthodox policing methods*, I would think you know me well enough by now to know I can exercise restraint."

All Alisdair could do was try and hold back a chuckle. "You're sure you want me to interview the warehouse owner?"

"Yes. And don't worry about me. I'll be fine."

"Aye. I bet you will."

FIFTY-TWO

Teri Donaldson was at her position behind the reception desk of Ogilvy Outerwear. When she saw Guthrie walk in, she didn't smile.

"Mr Guthrie. Are you here to slap desks and intimidate people?"

"No," Guthrie replied walking up to her. "I'm sorry about your step-father." Teri looked down at her computer screen but said nothing. "How is he?"

"He's fine, I suppose. He'll be out of the infirmary in the next day or two."

"That's good. Did he tell you anything about who may have done it?"

"He doesn't know. In fact, he told me he said as much to you yesterday."

It was Guthrie's turn to look down, avoiding eye contact.

"Aye, that's right. I just wondered if he had remembered anything new, that's all." He could see she wasn't falling for the line and reckoned he would just be wasting his time if he kept on. He decided to get to the real reason he was back at the clothing factory. "Anyway, I was just wanting to see if I could speak to Mr Ogilvy."

Teri clicked her mouse a few times, bringing up a calendar. "Looks like he's free for half an hour before the morning production meeting. Just let me see if he's in his office."

Teri put on a headset and dialled Ogilvy's extension. "Mr Guthrie is here. He'd like to talk with you." She listened to the answer. "No, just Mr Ogilvy." Pause. "Okay. Uh-huh." She punched a button on the phone, ending the call then looked up to Guthrie.

"You know the way. You can go on through."

Before Teri finished the sentence, Guthrie was heading to the door that opened onto the hallway leading to Ogilvy's office. "Thank you," he said without looking back.

Once in the hallway, he took an opportunity to look to his left and to the factory floor. The machines he had seen that first day, and the times since, coming to interview Ogilvy, were still there, of course, but this time he saw more. He saw a large roll of white liner material being fed onto one end of a process. *That Alisdair*, he thought. *Clever lad*.

At the end of the corridor he knocked on the office door and waited for an answer.

"Come in."

Inside, Ogilvy was sitting behind his desk. He didn't seem to be working on anything, rather just waiting for his guest to arrive. Guthrie sat down without being invited to do so.

"On your own this time? No official police presence?"

Guthrie turned up the corner of his mouth, in a half smile. "Oh, you can consider this an official visit, Mr Ogilvy."

"What can I do for you this time, then? I am quite busy

this morning, and I'd appreciate it if you could keep this fairly brief."

"Yes, I understand you have a production meeting this morning. How are sales, by the way?" The verbal tennis served to overtly heighten the immediate state of tension between them.

"I'm sure our sales figures are not the reason you're here again this morning. How is your investigation going? Have you come to report success?"

Guthrie was already tired of the small talk.

"As a matter of fact, I have."

"You've found Bobby's killer then?"

"I'm afraid not quite." Guthrie held Ogilvy's stare for three seconds. Years ago, he had learned that three seconds was the perfect length of time for a *police stare*. Anything less came across as weak. Anything longer was bordering on provocation. Three seconds was the Goldilocks Zone for stares. Ogilvy looked away. Guthrie smiled.

"I wanted to talk to you about a couple of things."

"Okay. Go ahead."

"First," Guthrie held up one finger, "I want to know why you ran over your brother-in-law yesterday when you left the Commercial Inn."

"What? How dare you!" Ogilvy immediately stood up. His chair was pushed back against the shelving unit, knocking over a book and making a couple of crystal glasses rattle. "You're seriously accusing me of trying to kill Douglas? You're out of your mind!"

Guthrie remained motionless in his chair. "You were meeting with him. You left before he did, with enough time to wait for him to exit the building. What am I supposed to think?"

"You're supposed to think that I may have been long

gone, and someone else ran into him." Ogilvy stood behind his desk. He had turned a deep shade of red and both firsts were clenched.

"Please, Mr Ogilvy, do sit down."

After a second, Ogilvy turned to grab an arm of his chair. He pulled it close and slowly sat down.

"Thank you," said Guthrie.

"I don't appreciate the accusation, Mr Guthrie."

"And I don't appreciate the runaround I've been given for the past few days." Guthrie's voice had risen several levels. As he talked, he leaned forward and rested both forearms on the large, mahogany desk. "You and your family have caused me nothing but headaches. You've deliberately misled this investigation and I am not going to put up with it any longer."

Ogilvy's face remained crimson, but he refused to say anything in response.

"As far as I'm concerned, you are as guilty as anyone."

"And how, exactly, do you come to that conclusion?"

"Your company's on the verge of bankruptcy. You've had to cut costs just to survive. You've fired an important member of staff -- forget about the fact he's family -- because he cut loose what was probably your most important supplier, and the head or your R&D has been heard arguing with that same supplier shortly after they were reinstated. Seems pretty clear to me that you are losing your grip on your company and you lashed out at the one person you rely on to come up with new products. New products that would help you stay afloat."

"Mr Guthrie, I suggest you think about what you just said." Ogilvy's voice was quiet, but wavering. He was trying to keep his anger in check. "You are accusing me of murdering the one person who could *help* turn this company around. Why would I do that? Why would I take the life of someone who has provided this company, provided me, with several years of excellent service, incredible work?"

Flecks of spittle landed on the dark wood of the desk as he spoke. It was obvious he was a moment away from going off like a nuclear explosion. Guthrie didn't want to let up. This was the first real emotion he'd seen from Ogilvy. He knew he was getting somewhere.

His heart started to pound as though it was going to beat right out of his chest. He realised his jaw was clenched and his fists, just like Ogilvy's, were balled so tightly the knuckles were white. His instinct was telling him to push. Push Ogilvy to the breaking point. The point at which he tells Guthrie exactly what happened, just to spite him.

"Okay. Let's pretend you didn't try to murder your brother-in-law as well-"

"Don't even-!"

But Guthrie kept going. "You must have some idea who would want to do something like that."

Ogilvy remained immobile, frozen in rage, almost unable to look away from Guthrie.

"A business rival? A neighbour who didn't get his lawn-mower back? A bookie? A jilted lover?"

"That's enough, Mr Guthrie."

"I'm not sure it is. You haven't given me any help with the list of potential suspects."

"Douglas was well respected in this town and in our industry. I seriously doubt anyone would have it in for him."

"Oh come, come. Everyone has at least one person who doesn't care for them."

"Enough to kill them?"

"You'd be surprised. I stayed at a bed and breakfast

once, and thought the host was trying to free up my room early by serving porridge that tasted like it was laced with fertiliser."

"If you have anything serious to say, or would like to ask relevant questions, I suggest you do so. Otherwise I would prefer you to leave so I can get on with my day." Ogilvy's face was still the colour of an old telephone box.

"Do you have any vans?"

"What?"

"Do you have any vans you use to, say, deliver products?"

Ogilvy looked confused. He stuttered as he replied. "Eh... Yes... Yes, we do. We have two here at the factory."

"Are they here now?"

"No. I don't think so. One is in for its M.O.T. The other is on a delivery up in the northwest."

"Were they here yesterday?"

"The one on the delivery has been out for a couple of days. Not due back until tomorrow. The other was-"

Guthrie interrupted. "What colour are they?"

"What...?"

"What colour are they?" Guthrie gave him no time to stall. He wanted an answer quickly.

"They're both white, but- "

"Oh, they are, are they?"

What exactly...? Then it dawned on him. "Are you seriously asking because you think one of them was used to try and kill Douglas?" Ogilvy laughed. It was a loud, belly laugh.

"Am I amusing you, Mr Ogilvy?"

"You are, Mr Guthrie. You are so funny." He continued to laugh.

Guthrie thought it went on too long. A little too forced for his liking.

"You think it's funny that I ask relevant questions? That's what you wanted me to do, and now you're laughing at me? I'm hurt, Mr Ogilvy."

"I doubt you would know what a relevant question was. Do you know what a relevant question is?"

"Hmmm. Let me see. That one was, for starters."

"You're full of shite, Guthrie!"

Here we go, thought Guthrie, *a little crack*. Dropping the 'mister' and swearing -- two signs he's about to lose it. Guthrie decided to start pushing harder.

"Which van were you driving when you tried to kill your brother-in-law? The one in the garage right now?"

"I wasn't driving a van."

"M.O.T. my arse! It's in the shop getting the dents repaired. The dents caused by hitting Douglas Mitchell."

"I wasn't driving a van!" Ogilvy shouted.

"Oh, you were the passenger?"

Ogilvy could only throw his hands up in the air.

"Who was your accomplice, then? Who were you in the van with?"

"Get out! Get out of my office right now!" Ogilvy stood up and pointed to the door. "I want you out of here in thirty seconds, or I'm calling the police."

"The police, eh? Aren't you forgetting something? I am the police."

"Aren't you forgetting something? You're not either, not really. And, therefore I can still have you arrested for threatening behaviour."

Guthrie resisted the temptation to jump across the desk and belt the stuck-up, self-righteous pillock, deciding that he would try and catch him out by changing tack.

"Why was the liner material you use in your jackets found at the scene of a death this week?"

Ogilvy screwed his eyes shut and shook his head. "I beg your pardon?"

"You heard me. Why was the material you use in, of all things, the police foul weather jackets found at the scene of a fire which caused the death of a man this past Saturday?"

"I have no idea what you're talking about. What fire? What man?"

"You mean to tell me you haven't heard about this second death in a week, here in Arbroath. A town that sees, on average, what, no suspicious deaths a year? That didn't make the local newspaper? You didn't hear about that? I find that hard to believe, Mr Ogilvy."

"I remember something about a fire at some building on the Montrose Road. Wasn't it some homeless person falling asleep while smoking?"

"See! I knew you kept abreast of the deaths and attempted murders here in the town."

"I'm warning you, Guthrie."

"Okay, okay," Guthrie responded, holding his hands up. "I'm still waiting for the answer, though. Why was a pile of your liner material sitting in this warehouse? Essentially the only thing in the warehouse, I might add."

"I don't know. I don't know where the warehouse is."

"Yes, you do. You told me a minute ago exactly where it is."

"That's because I remember seeing something about it, or, or hearing it on the news. I have no idea why our material was there, if indeed it was our liner material. We don't produce it. Our supplier does that."

"Advanced Fabrics?"

"Yes," said Ogilvy. "Perhaps you should ask them?"

"Who owns the warehouse?"

Ogilvy's frustration was growing with the apparent lack of understanding from Guthrie. "I. Don't. Know. Anything. About. The. Warehouse."

"Fair enough," Said Guthrie. He stood up and walked over to the door. "I will be checking on your vans, by the way. And your connection with the warehouse."

"Get out!"

Guthrie opened the door and stepped out of the office. As he closed the door behind him, he called back, "Thank you for your time, Mr Ogilvy."

The door had barely closed when the sound of a crystal tumbler hitting the wall of the office echoed along the corridor.

FIFTY-THREE

Alisdair was sitting in a small, first floor office just off the High Street. He had made the short walk from Gravesend in sunshine, but that was no indication of how the weather was going to play out for the remainder of the day.

"Mr Bell, Thank you for your time this morning."

"No problem." Morris Bell was a short, scruffy man, who reeked of cigarette smoke.

"First," continued Alisdair wanting to get straight to the point, "I want to ask you about your association with Advanced Fabrics."

"Advanced Fabrics?" Bell scratched his unshaven cheek. "Oh, aye! That's Harry's company, right?"

"Mr West, yes," confirmed Alisdair. "How long have you been doing business with him?"

"I'd say about ten years, or so." He scratched the side of his nose, then looked at his fingernails as if he was looking to see if he had caught whatever was causing the itch.

"What exactly is your current business relationship with Mr West?"

"He rents space in the warehouse. You know, the one

that caught fire? Bloody homeless man, eh? Serves him right for breaking in and smoking in my place." At that, he picked up a packet of cigarettes lying on the table and lit up.

Alisdair tried not to show his disgust of the man, but couldn't resist a little prod.

"I assume you refrain from smoking in your facility, considering your feelings?"

Bell looked at Alisdair as if he had just insulted his grandmother.

"My place. I'll do what I want."

"Quite," said Alisdair. He continued. "Mr West rents your warehouse to do what?"

Bell exhaled a cloud of cigarette smoke. "He stores stuff there."

"What kind of stuff?"

"All kinds of things. Depends on what he's got going at the time, you know?"

"Such as?"

"You know, just whatever he needs to at the time. He just needs the space."

"You've no idea what he uses your facility for on a daily basis? You never step foot in the place and see what's going on?"

Bell looked affronted at the suggestion that he didn't know what was going on with his business. He sucked on his cigarette and puffed a large cloud of smoke from the corner of his mouth. He narrowed his eyes as he looked at Alisdair.

"Harry has several businesses and he stores whatever he needs, whenever he needs."

"Which of his businesses use the warehouse?"

"His material place, obviously."

"Advanced Fabrics," Alisdair clarified.

"Aye."

"Others?"

"He has a contracting firm. They do joinery, finish work, that sort of thing. Pretty high-class stuff too from what I've heard." Bell scratched his face again. "Harry even told me they even do boat repairs. Yachts, classic boat restoration. Ties in nicely with the joinery, I suppose. Lots of wood on a boat. Probably a lot of money in it too if I know Harry." Bell's laugh turned into a loud, rasping smoker's cough.

"Mind you, I remember when a boat 'round here was a thing you worked on, not played on. There's but a fraction of the fishing boats now. Not like twenty years ago. You could walk across the harbour, from one side to the other, just by going from fishing boat to fishing boat. Aye, those days are long gone now, though." He looked beyond Alisdair with a far-off gaze. "Not any more. Harbour's a bloody marina now. All yachts and pleasure boats now. Hardly a working vessel among them, and then they're just wee lobster boats."

Being a local, Alisdair could remember the sights and sounds as well as Bell. He had to agree. "Sounds like you miss those days."

Bell scrunched the butt of the cigarette into the ashtray. He leaned forward. As he talked, Alisdair got a nose full of his stale breath.

"I was on the boats since I was a boy. Fourteen I was. Loved it. My family were all fishermen. I used to help at the fish market when the boats came in. Couldn't wait to get on as a crew member. Was never any good at the school 'cos I knew what I wanted to do, knew where I was going to end up." He sat back again and held his arms wide.

"Now look at me, eh? Bloody businessman, wishing I'd paid more attention to those classes. Forced into it when the

EU started with the quotas. Then the cost of keeping the boat seaworthy was hardly worth the effort. Eventually sold up and started buying property. It wasn't as if fishing was ever going to provide for a decent retirement."

Bell laughed and then started to cough. He didn't cover his mouth. Alisdair pushed his chair back a few inches, trying to stay away from whatever Bell was coughing up. He brought the conversation back on target.

"He has a couple of companies, Mr West?"

"Aye, he does."

"Do you know the names of the others?"

Morris Bell stuck an index finger in his ear and wiggled it around. "Hmmm. Sorry, no I don't."

Alisdair decided to move on. "Mr Bell, you say you rent out space to Mr West for whatever he needs it for?"

"Aye, that's right. Whatever he needs."

"And you've no idea what he uses the space for?"

"Sorry, son. What part of this don't you understand? He pays me rent. He pays it regular. He's happy, and I'm happy. What's it got to do with me what he uses it for?"

Alisdair was trying to determine whether Bell was just a bad businessman, or if he just didn't care, as long as the rent cheque arrived on time. "Mr Bell, I'm just trying to understand the circumstances around Mr West's use of your building, that's all."

"Put yourself in his shoes, son. You have a couple of businesses and, every once in a while, you have a load of, I don't know, building material that needs to be stored for a job. Timber, doors, insulation. You're looking for a place in town. Morris "Rocky" Bell's your man."

"Rocky?" Alisdair asked.

"That's what everybody calls me. You know, after the lighthouse?"

Alisdair rolled his eyes. "Of course. The Bell Rock."

Bell folded his arms and grinned widely. The nicotine-stained teeth, what remained, appearing between his lips like a line of over-ripe bananas.

"Getting back to Mr West," Alisdair went on, "what do you know about his business relationship with Ogilvy Outerwear?"

Bell's brow furrowed. "I didn't know he had one."

Alisdair recorded the fact in his notebook.

"Here, isn't that the place that bloke worked for? The one who was murdered? Out at the cliffs?"

"Yes."

"Are you saying Harry's connected to that?"

"Mr Bell, I'm not saying anything. I'm merely asking if you knew of any connection between Mr West and Ogilvy Outerwear."

"Now, son, I may be some thick, old fisherman, but I know exactly what you're saying." He picked up the packet of cigarettes and tapped on the end until one came out. Alisdair remained silent -- a trick he had picked up from Guthrie. "I thought you had come here to talk about the fire at my warehouse, so I can get my insurance claim sorted, and now you're..." He paused. "Wait a minute. Are you telling me you think I had something to do with it? Is that why you're here?"

Bell was now physically agitated. He lit the cigarette and puffed away on it as though the only way he could breathe was through the tobacco and filter.

"Mr Bell, please. I am just asking questions as part of the normal investigation. I'm certainly not accusing anyone of anything."

"Doesn't sound like it to me, son."

"I assure you, I'm only here to straighten out some facts

and gather additional information." Alisdair let the comment settle on Bell. In the meantime, he tried to interpret Bell's mood and state of mind. Was he nervous that he thought he was being associated with a murder, or was he twitchy because he *was* associated with one? Alisdair needed to find out.

"Mr Bell, I need you to answer just a few more questions for me, then I'll be out of your hair."

Bell avoided eye contact with Alisdair and kept staring at the wall. "Aye, okay."

"Very good. First, you said you didn't know about any connection between Mr West's company, Advanced Fabrics, and Ogilvy Outerwear, correct?"

"Aye."

"Second, do you know of any personal connection between Mr West and Mr Ogilvy?"

Bell thought. "No."

"Are you sure?"

"Aye. Aye. Perfectly."

"Right. Now you don't know what Mr West stores at your warehouse?"

"No. Not unless I just happen to go up and see what's there at the time."

"How often do you check on the warehouse? On average?"

Bell drew on the cigarette and then blew out a large, blue-grey cloud which mixed with the other smoke above their heads. The room was slowly filling from the ceiling down with the stuff. Alisdair couldn't wait to get out of there and into the fresh air.

"Och, probably twice a month. More if I have my own stuff to store."

"And have you had to store anything there recently?"

"No. It's been a couple of months since I've had anything there."

"Everything in the warehouse at the time of the fire belonged to Mr West, correct?"

"Aye, that's right."

"No other clients?"

"For that building? No. It's only six or seven months old. Haven't had any real, long-term prospects for it."

Alisdair closed his notebook. He was sure Bell was telling him everything he knew and wasn't hiding anything. A refreshing change, he thought. He pocketed his notebook and stood up, almost disappearing into the cigarette smoke.

"Well, thank you, Mr Bell. We'll be in touch if we have any more questions."

"Aye. Okay."

"I apologise if you were under the impression I thought you had anything to do with the murder of Bobby Gant. That's not why I'm here."

"No. I understand. Like you said, you have to ask a lot of questions to a lot of people."

Alisdair smiled weakly and was about to turn towards the door when Bell asked, "But you never told me why you asked about the connection between Harry and that company -- Ogilvy, right?" Alisdair nodded. "And what that has to do with me."

Alisdair weighed up what to say. Then, "Mr West's company is a supplier to Ogilvy Outerwear. You do business with Mr West. We're just checking out everything we can, that's all."

Bell's demeanour noticeably shifted to more of a relieved posture. Alisdair hoped he hadn't misjudged the man, but he was confident he didn't know about the connection.

"Thanks again for your time. If we have some more questions, we'll contact you."

"Okay. When will I know about the insurance claim, though?"

"I'm not the right person to ask, I'm afraid. That's between you and your insurance company."

Bell sighed.

"Thanks again," repeated Alisdair as he walked out of the office. Outside, he was relieved to take in the fresh air. Unsurprisingly, the sunshine had been tamed by several dark clouds, threatening to let loose their load of rain on the town. Alisdair wasn't opposed to the idea. The time in Bell's office was all he could stand and the heavens washing off the streets would serve to cleanse his mind too.

The walk back to Gravesend took him past Nayte's coffee shop. He decided to stop and get a latte to go. Elaine was working and he managed to snag a pastry on the house, much to his embarrassment.

Walking out of the shop, he felt the first of the rain. He hoped the worst of it would hold off until he made it back to the station. It was only five minutes, but that was more than enough time for the weather to decide it was going to ruin everyone's pleasant morning and dump its store of rain on the pedestrians.

He barely made it. He made his way to the incident room. Guthrie hadn't made it back from his visit to Ogilvy. Sal's report included nothing new, other than the press conference had been set for six so it could be picked up in time for the television news, and details included in the morning papers.

While he was waiting for Guthrie, he entered the details of his conversation with Bell into the system.

FIFTY-FOUR

Guthrie entered the incident room and headed straight for the coffee pots. Alisdair got up from his desk and joined him.

"Well?" Alisdair asked. "How did you get on?"

Guthrie stirred in a spoonful of sugar and almost drowned the mixture with enough vanilla flavoured artificial creamer to turn the dark brown liquid as white as the polystyrene cup.

"Ogilvy has a white van at his company. Two white vans."

Alisdair raised an eyebrow, but said, "And so do half the businesses round here. You've seen the list. I know what you're thinking, but chances are it's a coincidence. Anyway, doesn't he drive a Jag?"

Guthrie ignored the question. "I'm not one for coincidences, Alisdair."

Alisdair shrugged. "I know, I know." He walked back to his desk. Guthrie followed and hovered beside him as Alisdair took his seat.

"Did you see them?"

"Hmmm?"

"The vans at Ogilvy's. Did you see them?"

"No. One's been on a delivery for a couple of days, the other is in for its M.O.T. today."

"You've not seen them?" Alisdair sat back in his chair.

Guthrie shook his head slightly as he took a sip of coffee. When he had swallowed, he said, "No, but before I left I got the address of the garage from Teri Donaldson."

"Do you want to go and take a look?"

"Already did. On my way back here."

"And can I assume by the sheer lack of celebration that there was nothing to make you believe it was involved in a hit and run?"

Guthrie looked at his coffee and shook his head. Alisdair laughed.

"Bloody hell, Alisdair, I know that bugger is up to something."

"But once again, we've nothing to go on."

"I thought I had him."

"What do you mean?"

"I thought I had him there for a minute. I pressed him hard and he didn't like it."

"I'm not surprised. Your chats with suspects are almost legendary."

Once again, Guthrie chose to ignore the remark. "I saw the anger in the man, Alisdair. I saw him boil over. You should have seen his face when he realised why I asked him about the vans."

"I'm sure it wasn't pretty." Alisdair looked around the room, then lowered his voice almost to a whisper. "I can imagine you out-and-out accused him of attempted murder. Well, did you?"

Guthrie took another sip of coffee. This time he

nodded. Alisdair rolled his head back and closed his eyes. "Tom, you can't just go around accusing people of serious crimes, provoking them."

"How else are we going to cut through all the shite these people are hiding behind? Tell me that."

Alisdair was quiet. He started tapping on the computer keyboard. Inside he knew Guthrie was right. Everything about these people was screaming cover-up.

"The only thing I know to do is rattle these buggers until they crack."

"And we all know where that got you."

The look Guthrie shot Alisdair's way would have melted granite. This time, Guthrie didn't have to respond verbally. His point was made and received.

"Sorry, Tom. That was uncalled for."

Guthrie sat on the corner of the desk. He reflected on Alisdair's comment and knew it was right. In no more than a handful of seconds, several memories flashed across his mind's eye. Times he had done the very same thing with suspects and informants.

"No. I deserved that." He looked across the room and at the rain outside. "Ach! It's the only way I know how to deal with people like Ogilvy, Mitchell and the rest."

"Meaning?"

"Oh, you know. People who have power, wealth. They have all this stuff and money and they think the likes of you and me are there just to do their bidding. What's a lowly copper to them, Alisdair? Huh?"

Alisdair kept typing, not wanting to look away from the screen. His mind was filled with times his father had come home from work and complained about the job. Brown-nosers, arrogant colleagues, the injustices of working on a police force that seemed to be more obsessed with its own self-preservation, than solving the problems of crime.

When he had joined the service, he was determined to do what he could to not fall victim to the internal politics, and work hard to do real policing. But the realities had quickly set in. In-fighting, paperwork, and public perception, on top of political correctness, seemed to be stifling the work he wanted to do.

"I know, I know," was all he could say.

"What about you? How did you make out with the warehouse owner?"

"You mean, Morris *Rocky* Bell?"

"Oh, I do, do I?" said Guthrie.

"Aye. He's a former fisherman. The Bell Rock lighthouse... therefore..."

"Oh-kay." Guthrie smiled and shook his head. "Apart from his dubious nickname, what did you find out?"

"Quite frankly not a lot. He got out of the fishing business when the fleet here in town started to decline. His business owns several properties, mostly storage or warehouses."

"What about Ogilvy or West? Connections?"

"Again, not much. He's done business with West over the years. Didn't click at first with him that Advanced Fabrics was the name of West's company. He did say that he knew West had a couple of concerns, one being a joinery place. Also does some refurbs on boats, what with all the wood. Everything in the warehouse right now belongs to West."

"Any connection with Ogilvy?"

"Nope. He'd heard of the company and Gant's murder. Got a little nervy when he made that connection. He thought I might be thinking he was caught up in it."

"And do you?"

Alisdair thought. "No," he said eventually. "No, I'm sure there's nothing there to chase."

Guthrie considered Alisdair's answer. He was a sharp young man and Guthrie felt confident that had there been something, Alisdair would have picked up on it.

"Okay."

Alisdair pointed to the computer monitor. "I've already entered my notes in the file." Guthrie just nodded. Alisdair continued, looking for some direction. "Do we need to do some more digging with Ogilvy on the white vans? We already have a couple of the boys going through the long list of local vehicles."

"No," Guthrie responded. "I think that's a dead end as far as a connection with Ogilvy is concerned. Advanced. Do they have vans, white ones?"

Alisdair laughed, "No. I checked myself before I went over there. If only, eh?"

Guthrie puffed and looked around the incident room then at his coffee. He picked up a paper from the in tray on Alisdair's desk. He began, almost absent-mindedly, scanning the page. It was the inventory list from the warehouse fire.

"I thought we were done with this?"

"We are, I've already entered all of that into the system. I just need to file the paperwork and other documents."

Guthrie put the sheet of paper back on the stack. He drained the last of the coffee and tried to decide if he wanted another. He looked down at the paper in the in tray again. The list of items on the inventory seemed to blur together -- except one: *Rope.*

He put down the coffee cup and picked up the sheet.

"Alisdair?"

Alisdair looked up. "Uh-huh?"

"Pull up the SOCO report on Gant."

Alisdair frowned, but clicked his mouse a couple of times, then typed what he needed to bring up the Gant file on the screen. A few more double clicks and the report filled the monitor. Guthrie slid off the desk and bent down behind Alisdair trying to focus on the small text.

"Can you expand the window and scroll down?"

Alisdair complied.

"Keep going down," Guthrie said. He waved a couple of fingers in a repetitive downward motion. "Stop. There. What does it say?"

"Where?"

"There," Guthrie tapped the screen.

Alisdair read the line. "Wrists tied to metal rings. Rope material, nylon, light blue in colour. Approximate diameter one point five centimetres."

Guthrie put the piece of paper down on the keyboard in front of Alisdair.

"Look." He pointed at a line of the numbered list on the warehouse fire inventory.

Alisdair read aloud, "Nylon rope, light blue. Two lengths, each approximately four feet. Diameter, one point two five centimetres. Bloody hell!" He turned in his seat. Guthrie was looking at him with a questioning on his face.

"Well?" asked Guthrie.

"I remember exactly what it looked like, the one at the warehouse."

"I do too," said Guthrie, "but I can't remember the rope at the Gant scene."

They looked at the screen until Guthrie said, "Evidence storage. Where is it?"

"The room at the end of the corridor is where we've

been keeping the physical evidence in the Gant case. We've nothing on the warehouse fire."

"Alisdair, go and get the rope from the scene."

Alisdair left the room to secure the key from the desk sergeant.

Guthrie turned and shouted at Sal. "Sal, I need the photographs of the warehouse fire."

"Yes, sir. You want them printed out?"

"Please," Guthrie responded. Sal nodded and turned back to her monitor. He sat down in Alisdair's chair, elbows on the desk. He leaned forward and put his head in his hands, the palms rubbing his eyes. He knew what this would mean if there was a match. A solid connection between West's company and Gant's murder.

He stopped rubbing his eyes and stared at the monitor just twelve inches from his face. He could barely focus on the words. Alisdair had only been gone a few minutes, but Guthrie had already grown impatient.

"Bloody hell, Alisdair. Where are you?" he said to himself.

Just then, the door opened. Guthrie looked up expecting to see Alisdair. Instead, Buchanan entered the room and looked around. He spotted Guthrie.

"Tom," he said. "What's the latest? I need a briefing before this afternoon's press conference. You know Brian Campbell is coming up from Dundee."

The Chief Inspector's name caused Guthrie's chest to tighten. He knew Campbell had vouched for him since leaving the force. If he screwed up on this investigation, Campbell would have a difficult time trying to convince anyone Guthrie was fit for purpose for any future jobs.

"Remember what I said yesterday, Tom, about today being your last opportunity to make some progress, or-"

"I remember!" Guthrie cut Buchanan mid-sentence. The annoyance in his voice was obvious.

"So? Do you have an update for me? Anything new from yesterday?"

There was a war going on inside Guthrie. He wanted to tell him they may have found another connection, just to see the look on his face, but he just didn't like the man, and not telling him would satisfy a completely different desire.

"Tom? I need to know what the latest is."

"Ah, we've got nothing for you. Sorry."

"I didn't think you would." Buchanan glowered at Guthrie. His neck quickly turning red above his collar. He then turned on his heel and marched towards the door.

Just before he reached it, Alisdair opened it, saw his boss, and backed up to allow Buchanan to leave the room.

"I want you at the media briefing. Eighteen hundred hours," Buchanan said without slowing.

Alisdair barely got, "Sir," out of his mouth before Buchanan brushed past him and into the corridor. He leaned into the room and waved the key to the evidence room at Guthrie, who nodded, stood, picked up the empty coffee cup and threw it in a bin under the desk.

"He seemed like he was in a fine mood," Alisdair said, as they walked down the corridor to the evidence room.

"He asked if we had anything new for him."

"You told him about the rope?"

"Nope."

Alisdair stopped. "What?"

Guthrie turned. "I told him we had nothing new to add to his press briefing this afternoon. Are you coming?" Guthrie thumbed over his shoulder. "You have the key."

Alisdair stood as if rooted to the spot. "You didn't mention anything about the rope?"

"No. Here, give me the key." Alisdair handed it over.
"Why not, Tom?"

Guthrie made it to the evidence room without answering and unlocked the door. He reached just inside the door and felt up and down the wall for the light switch.

"Ah-ha. That's better." He disappeared inside.

Alisdair caught up. "Tom, I may be completely new to all this detective nonsense, but I'm pretty sure something like this should be shared with Buchanan."

Guthrie looked up and down along a series of shelving units that were positioned against each wall in the small room. "Where are you?" he said to himself. He had checked the first shelving unit when he found what he was looking for. "Here you go."

"Tom?" Alisdair's voice was sounding a little desperate. "Why didn't you tell Buchanan?"

Guthrie grabbed the large, thick plastic bag containing the two lengths of rope that were used to tie Bobby Gant's wrists to the rings at the foot of the cliffs. As he walked past Alisdair he said, "Come on, let's take a closer look." He stopped at the door. "I have half a day left on this case unless I come up with something solid. Something that points pretty convincingly to a suspect. This," he held up the bag, "could be what we've been looking for. But I'll be buggered if I'll let Buchanan steal the glory in front of the press and Brian Campbell."

"It's just about getting the glory is it?" Alisdair almost shouted the words. His anger and frustration with Guthrie had reached a new level. Just when he thought he had the measure of Guthrie, at least figured out what motivated him, he was confronted with the truth, the real Guthrie. The Guthrie that he read about in the reports. The officer who was forced to retire because he was unwilling or incapable of changing and following protocol.

Guthrie smiled. "Of course not. It's about screwing Buchanan too." He walked out and back towards the incident room.

Alisdair's head fell. His heart started to beat as if it wanted to burst out of his chest. What was the emotion? He couldn't decide if it was anger or supreme disappointment.

"Alisdair? C'mon, son!" The shout came from along the corridor. He locked the door from the inside and turned off the lights. Heading back, he wondered if he should confront Guthrie about giving the information to Buchanan, or to just go directly to Buchanan himself. By the time he reached the incident room he had decided nothing. He would wait to see if there was a potential match with the ropes and what Guthrie's reaction was.

Guthrie was already sitting at a desk. He rummaged through a couple of drawers before he found an old wooden ruler, broken at one end.

Alisdair stood behind him. "Same colour," he said.

"Yes, but there are light blues and light blues. It is nylon, though." With one hand Guthrie pinched the plastic of the bag around the rope. Holding the ruler in the other he tried to get a read on the diameter. "I make it one and a quarter centimetres."

"Coincidence?"

Guthrie looked up at Alisdair. "There you go again! You and your coincidences."

Alisdair took the bag from Guthrie. He turned it over in his hands. It was heavy. Both lengths had been placed in the bag and sealed. "What now?" he asked. "Forensics?"

Guthrie took the bag back from Alisdair and put it on

the desk. He took out his phone and opened the camera application. "Probably, if it's a match with the warehouse." He snapped a couple of pictures, then put the phone back in his pocket. "But first, we've got to get a sample of that rope."

Alisdair sat on the edge of the desk. "Who does it point to? Bell? West?"

"We can't be sure, Alisdair. I trust what you thought about Bell, but we need to get them both in here for a formal interview. Get uniforms to bring in Bell. You get down to West's place and bring him in."

"Which one?"

"Huh?"

"Which one? I interviewed the son, Devon. The owner is Harry West."

"Hell, bring them both in. We can't afford to choose one over the other at this point. I'm going to go over to the warehouse and find that rope and see what we have. If it's close, and I have a feeling it is, we'll get it over to forensics."

"Okay." Alisdair rose from the desk and walked over to Sal in order to arrange for the uniforms.

Even though the thought of a possible match would mean a definitive link between Gant's murder and either the West's or Bell, Guthrie couldn't help thinking about having to talk to Jacquie again. He sat, staring at the evidence bag. His eyes slowly went out of focus. He then realised he was looking through the bag, through the desk and into a space beyond the incident room. His mind was filled with short-lived images of Jacquie that played like a slideshow -- their first encounter at the lab, drinks at the hotel, the pub in Brought Ferry, the brake lights of her car. He suddenly came back to the present. He breathed in, noisily, and stood up.

"Right. I'm off to the warehouse. I'll meet you back here."

FIFTY-FIVE

The warehouse was quiet. The door had been forced by the fire service to gain access to the building and the lock had yet to be replaced. Guthrie had to go back to his car to find a small torch and returned to find the interior still almost empty and looking like nothing had changed since his first visit. Probably why Bell was in no hurry to repair the broken lock.

He swept the dark interior with the weak light from the pen-sized torch. He couldn't remember where he had seen the rope. It had to be at this end of the building, as he had walked from the door to the scene of the fire along one wall.

He retraced his steps from a few days before. A single SOCO overshoe was lying against the wall just inside the door. He could see the grey light from outside through the hole in the roof above the far corner. Guthrie slowly walked towards the spot.

Shining his torch along the wall, his eyes were becoming used to the overall gloominess of the building. The light from the torch seemed to be getting dimmer.

"Shite," he said, and hit it against the palm of his hand. The light momentarily brightened, but then faded again.

He picked up the pace, hoping there was nothing in his way that would see him trip and nose-dive onto the concrete floor. As he approached the area the fire had consumed, he saw the remnants of the cardboard boxes and liner material. Beyond the scorched heap, in the corner, were off-cuts of wood and other building materials, and there, lying behind a scaffold was the rope.

Then his torch died.

"Bugger!"

His eyes had not fully adjusted to the low light. He had read somewhere that it takes around fifteen minutes for your night vision to become effective. He didn't have the time to stand there, so he gingerly made his way over to the corner. At least the light coming in through the hole in the roof was a little brighter, making it slightly easier to navigate the odd bits of wood and cans of paint.

When he reached the rope, he remembered about the torch feature on his phone. He reached into his pocket. The phone wasn't there. He patted his pockets in turn. Nothing. Then it struck him. He had been charging it on the way over. He must have left it in the car. Guthrie took a deep breath and exhaled slowly, trying to keep his anger and frustration in check.

He couldn't tell how long the rope was. It wasn't coiled up tidily, rather it looked as if it had been thrown into the corner, along with all the other bits and pieces, the scaffold propped up against the wall in front of it. Guthrie reached through the scaffold and grabbed it. He stood up and carefully began gathering it into several loops. He thought about the possibility of forensics, but quickly decided, *bugger it*. He needed to know if it was a match. That would be good enough to connect Bell and West to Gant, and with that connection they could start to push for an answer. *The* answer.

Thankfully, the rope was only a few feet long. He walked back along the wall and out into the evening.

Once inside his car, he placed the rope on the passenger seat and picked up his phone. He unplugged the charging cord and opened the photo file. The last picture was the one he took of the rope at the station. He reverse-pinched the screen with his thumb and forefinger, zooming into the rope. He held the phone next to the rope lying on his passenger seat. He didn't want to raise his own hopes, but it looked close, really close.

He opened the camera application and snapped a picture of the rope, for no other reason than just in case. Next was a quick text to Alisdair.

Have rope. Looks good! See you back at station.

Starting the car, he turned on the heater. The temperature was beginning to fall as the evening took a hold on the day. Reluctantly, Guthrie knew he had to call Jacquie to set up forensics. He looked at the phone in his hand. The screen was still showing the text he had sent to Alisdair. He could just text her, which would save him having to talk to her. After all, he was just giving her advanced notice of the request to analyse the rope. He didn't actually need to talk to her. He congratulated himself on his reasoning.

Need to send a rope for analysis. May be connected to Gant case. Same rope used to tie wrists?? Will have a runner bring it to the lab this evening. Appreciate results ASAP.

Guthrie read the text before pressing the send button. Too formal, businesslike? He looked up, through the windscreen. The lights of the traffic cast moving shadows of the small trees lining the main road across the field beyond

Guthrie's position. He didn't want to come across as a prat, but he needed Jacquie to know this was all business.

He added *Thanks* at the end of the message and pressed send.

He plugged in his phone and backed out of the parking space. He needed to get back to the station and get stuck into the interviews with the West's and Bell.

The media briefing.

He had forgotten about that. He stopped the car and looked at his watch. It had just gone four, the briefing was at six. He could make it back to the station and have time to start the interviews, but he would need to go in with all guns blazing and not waste any time if he was going to get anywhere prior to the briefing. He picked up his phone again and called Alisdair. It rang out to voicemail.

"Alisdair. I just wanted to make sure you are on your way back to the station. I want to be able to interview these guys before the briefing at six. Let me know. Cheers."

He hung up, but before he could put the phone down it vibrated in his hand.

"Alisdair."

"Tom, it's me, Jacquie."

Guthrie was caught off-guard. A shiver coursed through his body, but it wasn't the chill in the air.

"Uh, hello, Jacquie. Did you get my text?" he said, not knowing how to play the conversation. *Keep it professional, Tom*, he thought to himself.

"Yes." Jacquie paused. "How are you?"

Guthrie closed his eyes. He could have at least asked her the same thing, instead of launching into business. *Idiot.* "Oh, I'm okay, thanks. Busy with all this stuff, obviously. You?"

"I'm fine."

Guthrie was at a complete loss for what to say. He wasn't sure if she wanted an apology, for him to act as if nothing had happened the other night, or to start sobbing into the phone. He was hopeless at this kind of thing. Whatever she was expecting him to say, he knew she was expecting him to say something.

"Sorry about..."

"Look, Tom," Jacquie interrupted, "I know how things are, what with the pressure of this murder. You don't have to say anything."

Guthrie swallowed. "I was going to say I'm sorry about needing the forensics done on this rope this late in the day. I'm sure it'll cause you and your staff some overtime, but I need the results as soon as I can."

"Oh. Oh, yes, of course. Yes, your request for our lab services."

Guthrie pinched the bridge of his nose as he listened to Jacquie back-pedal.

"Yes, sorry," he continued. "I really need a result, and this may be just what we've been looking for."

"I'll have someone here waiting, then."

"Thanks."

"Right then. I'll have the lab phone you when we have something."

"Thanks. Any time, even if it's late."

"Of course."

The conversation was forced and awkward. Guthrie just wanted to hang up and get back to the station. He knew he had blown any chance of Jacquie actually wanting to talk to him any more than she had to, and he couldn't wait to finish the call and put her out of her misery.

"Look, I need to get back to the station..."

"Yes. Sorry. I'll have someone call you."

Jacquie hung up.

"Bugger!"

He tossed the phone on the passenger seat and drove out to the main road, turned right and headed back towards the station.

The sky was quickly turning dark. It was still another couple of hours before the sun set, but it was as if God had decided to call it a day a little early. The greyness of the late afternoon rain was a reflection of Guthrie's mood, which had turned immediately after talking to Jacquie. And where the hell was Alisdair? He had better be waiting for him when he got back to the station.

His stomach growled. A combination of hunger and irritation. When was the last time he ate anything? He wanted to stop at the bakery Alisdair had taken him to almost a week before, but he didn't have the time. It was probably closed anyway. He'd have to settle for something from a machine.

As he negotiated the roundabout in front of Morrisons supermarket, his phone lit up and started buzzing. He looked at the screen. Buchanan.

Guthrie figured he could wait. He'd be back at the incident room in a couple of minutes. Buchanan was probably working himself into a lather wondering where he was with the media briefing less than two hours away. The thought of letting him stew, even for a few short minutes longer, made one corner of Guthrie's mouth curl up in a half smile.

FIFTY-SIX

More than an hour had gone by and still Alisdair had not returned to the station. The briefing was scheduled to start in a little over thirty minutes. Two television crews had arrived and were setting up in the conference room on the ground floor.

Guthrie had called Alisdair's mobile several times and it had rung to voicemail. He tried again.

"Alisdair. Where the hell are you? Call me back. The briefing's in half an hour and I wanted to get some time with the Wests." Guthrie hung up.

Bell was sitting in one of the interview rooms protesting about his time being wasted. Guthrie had left him there while he tried to get in touch with Alisdair, the only compromise was allowing him to smoke, which was strictly against the rules, but Guthrie didn't want to take the time to argue. Bell was left to wait.

Guthrie, however, was beyond the point of waiting any longer.

"Sal!" he yelled across the room.

Sal turned and took her headset off. "Yes?" she said sweetly, as if to point out Guthrie's harsh tone.

"Sorry," he said. He walked over to her. "I'm worried about Alisdair. He's been gone an awfully long time. Have you heard from him?"

"No, I haven't."

Guthrie sighed loudly. "I sent him to pick up the owner of Advanced Fabrics, and his son, Harry and Devon West. Could you call Advanced and check to see if they're on the way back?"

"I can. Hold on."

Sal turned to her screen and put the headset back on. She clicked her mouse and typed into a search bringing up the main number for Advanced Fabrics. Another click of the mouse, and she dialled the number.

"Hello, this is Police Scotland. I'm calling from the station here in Arbroath. I was wondering if one of our officers is still with you." She paused, listening to the answer. "Yes, I can hold." Sal looked up at Guthrie who nodded.

"Yes, I'm still here. I see. Okay, and what's that address?" She scribbled on a notepad. "No, that's grand, thank you. Uh-huh. Bye."

Sal tore the page from her notepad and handed it to Guthrie. "The receptionist said Alisdair was round there, but he was sent to Mr West's home. That's the address." She pointed at the paper in Guthrie's hand.

"Can we get someone down there to check on him?"

"I'll have a couple of the lads round them up."

"Thanks, Sal."

Just then Buchanan burst into the room.

"Where's Alisdair?" His voice boomed across the room.

Guthrie handed the piece of paper back to Sal, then faced Buchanan. "Just rounding him up now."

"You do realise, don't you, that the media briefing starts in twenty minutes?"

"I do."

"Then get him downstairs now." Buchanan punctuated the demand with a pointed finger.

"Do you still want me to sit in?" Guthrie asked.

"I've had second thoughts about that, Tom. I'm not sure I want a civilian there. The optics of it wouldn't be good. Besides, unless you come up with a confession in the next," he looked at his watch, "eighteen minutes, I would say you'll be off the case anyway."

Guthrie didn't respond. He wished he could just tell him what he thought of the man, but instead looked at Sal, who could do nothing but stare at her monitor. He was grateful that he didn't have to sit in front of the press.

"I do need to talk to you after the briefing and before you leave for the day."

"Whatever. You can find me here, I'm sure."

"Very well." Buchanan left the room.

Guthrie looked around the room to find something on which to take out his anger. The wire waste basket by his right foot was the unlucky object and it found itself skidding across the polished floor, stopping only when it reached a filing cabinet.

"Bugger!"

Sal had been patched through to a couple of uniforms in a car on the airwave radio. She gave them West's address and told them to get there in a hurry.

"You all right, sir?" she asked Guthrie.

"Aye. Sorry about the bin." Guthrie walked over and picked it up. The thin mesh was dented where he had made contact with it. He picked up the balls of paper and biscuit wrappers that were strewn across the floor and placed them in the wounded receptacle.

"Is that true, what the Inspector said, about you being replaced?"

"I'm afraid it is, Sal."

Sal was a quiet, but efficient member of the incident room team. The rest of the crew were your typical police officers. Young and full of banter and themselves. Guthrie was sure he had been the same, many moons ago, but the bravado and toilet humour of those who had been seconded to the investigation, had gnawed away at Guthrie for the last week.

Sal, however, was good at what she did and didn't brag about it. She went about her duties without complaint, and it was only ever apparent when you took time to think about it. It was like a clock. You rely on it; you don't think about it. You look, you see what it says, and you go on. It only hits you, you only ever pay attention to it, when it stops working.

"I was given a deadline and it looks as though I'm almost there with nothing to show for it."

"Well," said Sal, "if it's any consolation, I think it's a bunch of balls."

Guthrie laughed. "I appreciate your support."

"No, really. What do they expect? I just don't get it." She shook her head.

"Well, in the world of serious crime, the quicker the better, I'm afraid. The longer a case drags out, the harder it is to get a result."

"And there is another thing."

"Oh, yes?"

"You've made a big difference in Alisdair."

Guthrie was caught out by the comment. "What... what do you mean by that?"

Sal spun her chair round to face Guthrie. Off came the headset and she folded her arms. "He's matured."

"In a week? I'm not sure I buy that, Sal."

"No, I'm serious. He's changed."

Guthrie cast his mind back. The black lab retriever. "He did seem a little over-enthusiastic when we first met," he said.

"Exactly. He was all over the place, probably because he wanted to do something more, be something more than walk the High Street. I could see the potential in the lad. He just didn't know how to use his smarts."

"It wasn't my idea to assign him to the case. You know that, don't you? It was Buchanan."

Sal's brow furrowed. "Hmmm. Buchanan is smarter than I give him credit for."

Guthrie laughed again. "Sal, you're a dark horse yourself."

"Just here to help." She winked at Guthrie before switching her focus to her screen.

Guthrie walked back to his desk, or at least the desk on which he had stacked used paper cups and some paperwork over the past several days. It was across from Alisdair's. As he was about to sit down and put together a plan of action to interview Bell, he changed his mind. He walked around and sat at Alisdair's desk.

The space was the opposite of Guthrie's and more like his home than his own work space -- clean and organised. Documents were stacked neatly in the wire in tray. A couple of pens and a yellow pencil lay, arranged in order of size, on the right side, a notebook beside them.

Guthrie picked up and flicked through the notebook. It was arranged by date and Alisdair's handwriting was in two colours, black and blue. Reading a page, Guthrie assumed that initial notes were taken using a black pen, then it appeared Alisdair made notes later in blue, indicating thoughts, questions, and action items.

He placed the small, black book back in its place beside the pens, noting the ends of their respective tops were black and blue. Guthrie smiled to himself, but the emotion quickly faded as he thought how unlike Alisdair it was to ignore calls and texts. He looked at his phone. Still nothing. What in the world was Alisdair doing?

"Sir."

"Yes?"

Sal's face reflected a concern. Guthrie walked back across the room towards her.

"We had a car on the north side of town, closest to Harry West's home. They made their way over there and just checked in. They said there was nobody home."

Guthrie threw his head back. "Well where the bloody hell is everyone?" He was tempted to attack the wire basket again, but managed to stop himself, instead tensing every muscle in his body.

Sal coughed, clearing her throat then said, "They said the only thing there was one of our pool cars."

At first Guthrie didn't comprehend what Sal had just said, but then the implication finally settled on him.

"What did you just say, Sal?"

She finished typing something into a form on the computer screen in front of her.

"Sal?" Guthrie repeated.

"Sorry, I was just double-checking something." She turned and said, "I said there was nobody at Harry West's place -- just one of our pool cars. I was checking to see who had signed it out."

Although Guthrie knew the answer, he still asked, "And?"

"Alisdair."

"Bugger," was all he could say. He just stood there. Sweat started to form on his brow and under his shirt collar.

"Are they sure there's no-one about?"

"Pretty sure. I'm listening into the Airwave comms between the uniforms on the scene and the control room. They're taking another look round, but there are no other vehicles and there doesn't appear to be anyone in the house."

Guthrie's body temperature was rising further, making him sweat even more. He wiped his forehead with the palm of his hand then ran it across the top of his head. His mind was racing. Harry West. Devon West. What is going on?

"Sal, whoever you talked to at Advanced Fabrics, what exactly did they say?"

Sal closed her eyes as she spoke. "The lady said that Alisdair had asked to see Mr West and he was told he wasn't there, but at home. Alisdair asked about Devon West and she said he was with his father. Alisdair asked for the address and said he would catch them there."

Guthrie started to pace back and forth behind Sal. "I trust you, Sal, but get back to Advanced Fabrics and make sure that's exactly what she said. I want to make sure we're not missing something there."

"Like what?"

Guthrie was surprised she questioned him. "I... I don't know," he barked. "He was just supposed to bring them in. It's not like he was going to pay them a social visit and they were going to head out for an early dinner."

Sal's face reddened. "Okay."

Guthrie realised his mistake and put a reassuring hand

on Sal's shoulder. He walked back to Alisdair's desk and took a seat. He stared at the black monitor, his faint reflection looking back. His eyes slowly went out of focus as he replayed things in his mind. Where would they go? Why would they take Alisdair? What would they want with him? It was obvious to Guthrie that Alisdair's enforced silence was down to him being abducted by one or both of the Wests.

He couldn't believe he was even thinking that. A police officer had probably been abducted. *Shite*.

The sweat was flowing like a burn down his spine. Sal was talking to someone. He looked down at the desk. Alisdair's notebook. He opened it and flipped to the last page to contain Alisdair's handwriting. The entry was from Sunday. Probably why it was here and not with Alisdair.

Bugger.

Sal called over to him. "Apparently, Alisdair had called Advanced on his way over there. At that time, both Harry and Devon West were at the factory, but left just before Alisdair arrived."

"Everything else, just as you described?"

"Yes, sir."

"Thanks."

The door to the incident room opened and the imposing figure of Chief Inspector Brian Campbell entered, followed closely by Buchanan. Guthrie's heart tried to claw its way out of his body through his throat.

"Ah, Tom. How are you?"

"I've been better," was all he could think to say.

The two men shook hands. "I understand that you've not had much luck on the Gant murder."

Guthrie's heart was still making its way upward. "I suppose you could say it's been a rather frustrating week or so." He looked over Campbell's shoulder at Buchanan, who stood with his hands clasped behind his back and with a look of disapproving disdain, like some irritable headmaster.

"Yes, well you know how I feel about your ability, Tom, but we really need to get a result, and Ian has filled me in on his recommendation to request additional resources from Serious Crimes."

"Brian, you know I don't think that's necessary, don't you?"

"I understand your enthusiasm, but frankly, no matter what I think of your personal abilities..." Buchanan sniffed behind the Chief Inspector. "...I have to consider the input from the officer ultimately tasked with, and responsible for, the successful outcome of this investigation."

"Oh, come on, Brian. You know there's more to that request than just objective results. Ian has been after my blood since before I left the force."

"Since before you were forced to retire because of your unsatisfactory performance, you mean?" said Buchanan.

"Oh, shut your face...!"

Sal slowly turned in her seat. She had never heard anyone talk to Buchanan like that.

"Now, gents," said Campbell. "let's not make this a personal matter."

Guthrie snorted. "It's already personal, Brian."

"Sir," Buchanan stepped forward, "whatever history Mr Guthrie and I have," *There was that Mister again*, thought Guthrie, "I assure you that my recommendation is based purely on a lack of forward progress on the case. This is exactly the reason you are here this evening."

Guthrie sat down at Alisdair's desk.

"Tom," Campbell continued, "I want to talk to you

immediately after the media briefing. We'll have time to discuss this at length, okay?"

"Aye, fine." Guthrie was slumped in the chair. His arms were folded tight across his chest. What did he care about any of it at this point? The notebook and pens in front of him changed his focus back to Alisdair.

As if Buchanan was reading his mind, he asked, "Where's McEwan?"

Guthrie realised Buchanan didn't know. For whatever reason he had assumed he would know what was going on. The media briefing and Brian Campbell were obviously his priority for the moment.

Guthrie looked over to Sal, who just raised her eyebrows in a you're-on-your-own-with-that-one look. Guthrie swallowed.

"We don't know where he is."

"Has he gone down to the briefing already?"

"No," another swallow, "we think he's been taken by someone he was bringing in to interview."

The silence was broken by Campbell.

"I'm sorry, who has been taken where by whom?"

Guthrie provided an answer before Buchanan could speak. "Constable Alisdair McEwan is my liaison. He's been working closely with me this week and I asked him to bring someone in for questioning. He wasn't returning my calls and we found out he went to the individual's home. We sent a car over there and just found out that no one is home and Alisdair's pool car is in the driveway."

As Guthrie recounted what had happened, Buchanan's face was turning scarlet.

"Why the hell was I not informed about this?"

"We only just found out before you came in."

"This is great. This is just great!" Buchanan's voice

filled the room.

The door behind them opened and the head of a uniformed sergeant appeared.

"Sorry to interrupt, sir. Five minutes until the media briefing."

Without turning around, Buchanan responded, "I'm very well aware of the time sergeant, thank you."

The officer looked around the room then quickly retreated back into the corridor.

"What have you done?"

"Nothing as of yet. We asked the uniform at the house to double-check. Nothing."

"Who's house?" Campbell asked.

"Harry West, owner of a company called Advanced Fabrics."

Buchanan had already walked over to Sal and was barking out instructions.

"Get everyone we have available over to this West's house."

"Yes, sir."

"And put a call in to trace any vehicle West owns."

"Sir."

"How long has Constable McEwan been ignoring your phone calls?"

Guthrie looked at his phone. "Almost two hours."

Buchanan looked like he was going to explode. "For heaven's sake!" He looked at Guthrie and asked, "When did it dawn on you that something was amiss, Tom?"

The last thing he wanted to tell Buchanan was the truth: that he'd had a gut feeling when Alisdair didn't quickly respond to his first text. "Uh, I don't know. I suppose when I returned to the station and he wasn't back yet."

"Why was he on his own anyway?"

"Because we don't have the resources to send everyone out two-by-two, hand-in-hand like they're going out for play-time at nursery school." Guthrie wasn't about to justify why to anyone, least of all Buchanan.

"I'm just asking a simple question, Tom. I don't need the attitude."

"And I don't need to be questioned like it's my fault."

"All right," interrupted Campbell. The big man stepped in front of Buchanan and held up an index finger in the direction of Guthrie. "None of this is solving the issue."

He focused on Guthrie. "Any idea where this West would have taken him?"

Guthrie thought and what he came up with he didn't like. He had to say it, however. "Frankly, no. And who's to say who has Alisdair? It just happens his car is at Harry West's house."

"What do you mean by that, Tom?" Buchanan asked.

"I mean it could be any number of people."

"Really?" Buchanan laughed. "Like who? He went to pick up West, he went to West's home, and now he's missing. I think that's a pretty good place to start."

Guthrie shook his head. "I have been accused of jumping to conclusions and not being open to alternative possibilities, and now the opposite argument is being used against me. What do you want me to say? What do you want me to do? Harry and Devon West..."

"Devon?" asked Campbell.

"The son," Guthrie answered, then continued. "Harry and Devon West haven't been on our radar at all during this investigation."

"Then why bring them in?" Buchanan asked.

Guthrie conceded the point. "There's a connection between Ogilvy Outerwear and Advanced Fabrics beyond the obvious. We needed to get West, and or his son, in for a formal interview."

"What's the connection?" Buchanan asked slowly.

Guthrie switched to looking at Campbell as he explained. "Advanced is a major supplier to Ogilvy. West has a couple of businesses and he uses a warehouse for storage. That warehouse is owned by a man called Bell. Bell is in the interview room."

Buchanan threw his hands up. "Why is no-one telling me any of this?"

Guthrie ignored him and went on. "The warehouse just happens to be the one that went up in flames and in which an unknown male died. The fire investigation concluded that he had been smoking and fell asleep. We were going through the inventory of the warehouse and found a connection with the Gant murder."

"Again," Buchanan exclaimed, "why am I just now hearing this?"

Campbell turned to Buchanan. "Let him finish, Ian."

"We believe the rope that was used to tie up Gant is the same as the rope we found at the warehouse."

"Believe?" Campbell asked as he raised an eyebrow.

"At this point, yes, but I've already sent it to Dundee for analysis."

Campbell turned his attention to Buchanan. "Ian, we have a media briefing. I suggest we keep the same plan we had prior to these revelations. No mention of Constable McEwan, though. We mustn't do anything that could compromise his safety, if he is in trouble -- and we've yet to confirm that."

Buchanan was about to protest but was silenced by a look from his superior officer.

Campbell continued. "Tom, you need to make damn

sure we find McEwan. If what you say is correct, and what I think you're saying is that there's a high probability West or his son is mixed up in Gant's murder, then we can't waste time arguing about protocol. We need to get everyone on task."

Guthrie smiled inwardly. He had always respected Brian Campbell and knew that he was a no-nonsense leader, who despite having to play the political game required to reach and maintain his senior position, he had done it in a way that reflected his genuine care for those under him, and the pre-modern copper he was when you stripped away all the fancy braid on his formal uniform.

Buchanan wanted to complain, but again Campbell waved him off.

"Ian, you and I need to keep to the script for the next half an hour. When we're through, we'll come back here and find out what our next steps are. Tom, I'm counting on you to get everyone organised."

"Yes, sir."

"Sir?"

The same sergeant as before appeared at the door.

"We're coming, sergeant," said Campbell. He almost pushed Buchanan to the door, with a hand on his shoulder.

As soon as the door had closed behind them Sal called across the room.

"Sir?"

Guthrie sat up in the chair. "Yes, Sal?"

"Sergeant McDonald is at West's house. He reported that they're convinced no-one's there."

"Tell me something I don't know, Sal,"

She took a deep breath before saying, "Okay. He says they've found what appears to be blood on the floor of the garage."

FIFTY-SEVEN

Guthrie had almost sprinted out of the incident room when Sal had told him about the discovery of blood at West's house. He had shouted only one instruction -- have Buchanan interview Bell as soon as the media briefing was over.

He raced to the car park. Fumbling with the key he cursed not having a modern car with remote locks. Once behind the wheel, however, he sat and caught his breath. What's the point of going to the house, he thought. If no-one's there, what good does that do?

He stretched his neck and let his head fall back against the headrest. *Think, Tom. Where could they possibly be? Where would they go?*

The warehouse? No. Guthrie immediately dismissed the idea. Too much had happened there recently. Back to Advanced? No. People would still be there.

He hit the steering wheel. "Think!"

What did Alisdair say about West? Were there any clues? Ach, who are you kidding? This is going to be like finding a rowing boat in the Pacific. He grabbed the top of the wheel and slumped forward, forehead on his hands.

Suddenly, there was a feeling in his chest. Before his brain had communicated mentally, it had caused a physical reaction.

Boat. Boat. What had Alisdair said about boats?

Then the connection was made. Guthrie turned the key in the ignition and the old car fired up. Where he was going was close enough he could probably walk almost as quickly as driving.

The sun was setting, not that it mattered. It was almost dark. Black clouds had sucked the sunlight from the day hours ago. Guthrie turned the headlights on and backed out of the parking space.

Turning left onto the main road leading to Dundee, his journey was only going to last a few short minutes. He headed to the harbour.

He wasn't sure where the boat yard was. He parked in a small, public car park overlooking the inner harbour. The few boats were a mix of small working vessels and pleasure craft. Yachts were moored along several floating jetties, a row of street lights illuminated the foreground with their orange glow.

Guthrie looked to his right. There was a modern structure housing a restaurant, and beyond, the old lifeboat shed. To his left an access road connected to the outer harbour. He decided that was the better bet.

He took out his phone and called Gravesend. When the call was answered he asked to be put through to Sal.

"Sal, it's Guthrie."

"Yes, sir."

"Anything else come through from the West's house?"

"No. I've asked them to let me know first if anything changes."

"Very good. Make sure you tell Buchanan to talk to Bell."

"Sure."

"And have Campbell do whatever he needs for us to gain access to the house. We need to go by the book on this."

"I assume you think Alisdair's not in the house then?"

"I don't think so. God, I hope I'm right about that."

"That also tells me, and from how you phrased your instruction to have Campbell okay entry to the house, you're not on your way there."

"Sal, you're wasted making calls. You're right. I have a hunch I'm following up."

"You going to tell me where? I don't want to have to tell Inspector Buchanan we've lost another one."

"Anyone ever told you, you have a dark sense of humour?"

"Comes with the job, I guess."

"I'm at the harbour."

"Okay." Sal paused. "Be careful."

"I will. I'll check in later."

Putting the phone away he half walked, half jogged along the cobbled road. Dozens of lobster pots, stacked like small pyramids along the edge of the harbour wall, were the only things preventing someone from just walking off the road and into the water a dozen feet below.

Passing the old fish market building on his right, the outer harbour opened up in front of him. It was darker here. A solitary boat was tied up, the top of its cabin barely rising above the level of Guthrie's feet.

To his left a temporary construction wall masked a new up-scale residential development. He walked quickly, following the curved barrier and came to a small bridge. It allowed access to the far side of the harbour. The stone wall beyond was at least twelve feet high, six feet across its flat top, and kept the North Sea at bay. It reached back to the right, ending, after a hundred yards, in what appeared to be a miniature lighthouse, marking the entrance to the harbour.

More importantly to Guthrie, the bridge crossed the slipway from a boat yard.

He approached the high, metal gates of the yard, the navy-blue paint peeling and flaking. Patches of rust and red and yellow from previous coats were barely visible in the darkness. Guthrie realised just how quickly the darkness had descended. The wind had picked up and the cold air on the back of his neck was telling him that the rain was on its way.

The gates were unlocked and slightly ajar. He pushed on one and it complained with a low, metal screech. Inside, the yard was practically empty. There was one notable exception, however. A small, white commercial van was parked beside a portacabin office. Guthrie's pulse raced. Things were starting to fall into place. Perhaps his hunch was right.

He walked up from behind the van and peered through the driver's side window. The small cab was empty and separated from the back by a solid partition. He moved around the nose of the vehicle and put a hand, palm down, on the bonnet. It was warm. It was also dented above the headlight.

Looking around, the yard was small. An old fishing trawler, so prevalent in any harbour along the coast only twenty years ago, was perched on wooden blocks at the top of the single slipway. The portacabin office was dark. It appeared to be empty, but although the blinds in the window to the left of the door were open, from where Guthrie stood there was no clear view inside.

He slowly climbed the three wooden steps to the door. Leaning over the shaky handrail he eased closer to the window. He pressed his nose against the glass and blocked out the light with one hand. All he could see was darkness. He tried the door handle. Locked.

If not the office, then if someone was still around, where would they be? The only logical answer was the boat. He turned. From his position on the top step he could now see a faint light coming from inside the wheelhouse. Guthrie really didn't want to go on the boat.

Shite!

FIFTY-EIGHT

An ancient wooden ladder, looking like it had been used by Noah in one of his projects, and propped against the side of the old boat's hull, gave Guthrie access to the deck. Stepping over the gunwale he stumbled on a coiled rope. Catching himself he cursed under his breath, then cursed the darkness.

It would have been easy to use the torch on his phone, but the last thing he needed to do was advertise his arrival should there be anyone around. His eyes were not quite used to the darkness, but he could pick out shapes on the deck. Various piles of lumber were stacked where the deck was being repaired. Remnants of the original fishing gear and equipment were still in place, promising to catch Guthrie's shins if he wasn't careful.

He stood still and quiet. Apart from the distant sounds of the traffic from the other side of the harbour, the only thing he could hear was the wind whistling through the ropes and wires of the boat's jibs.

The door to the wheelhouse was open. Carefully making his way towards it, now he was on the deck, he could see the light he had seen from the ground was actually coming from a hatch leading below.

He was still not convinced there was anyone around. The van could have been dropped off; the driver long gone. Still, the feeling in his stomach said he was just trying to convince himself.

Might as well get on with it.

Stepping across the threshold, the smell of wood filled the wheelhouse. The radio and navigation equipment took up places on slanted tabletops on three sides of the cabin. The hatch leading below deck and source of the light was in one corner. Slowly, Guthrie inched forward and looked over the edge. An almost vertical, ladder-like set of stairs led down into the belly of the vessel. Again, no sounds could be heard bar the wind.

Guthrie puffed his cheeks and slowly breathed out. He backed down the steps, holding on to the brass hand rails on either side. At the bottom he turned. A single bulb seemed to cast more shadows than light. The space had been gutted as part of the renovation work being carried out on the boat, but it was still clear that where he was standing had been a galley. The room was only twelve feet by twelve feet, enough to meet the needs of a handful of fishermen. A table to the right, surrounded by a couple of fixed bench seats, a cook top, and a small sink were still in place. Looking around, there was nothing, no one. Another deep breath. He had obviously misjudged this one.

He started back up the steps, resigned to heading to West's house when, just as he was level with the floor of the wheelhouse, his head was snapped around by a blow to the temple. His grip on the hand rails loosened and he fell back into the galley, landing in a heap on the wooden floor.

Almost as soon as the pain registered, he blacked out.

He didn't know how long he was unconscious, but when he came to his head was throbbing like the worst hangover he ever had. He reached up and explored his skull. No blood, but the entire right side of his face and head was tender to the touch. As bad as his head felt, he had bitten his tongue and that particular delight was sending sharp pains shooting through his mouth.

He sat upright, slowly, cautiously. Everything seemed to be working. He wiggled his toes. All fine. He looked around, but his neck complained.

"Ah, bugger!" he said aloud, wincing, and rubbed his neck.

Once he had taken stock of his physical condition, his brain started to function on a higher level. Guthrie realised, for the first time, he wasn't alone on the boat, but he was sure he didn't want to stick his head into the firing line again. He had no choice, however. The only way to get above deck again was through the wheelhouse. He sat, pressing his tongue to the roof of his mouth in an attempt to dull the pain. It wasn't working.

Sitting on the cold, wooden floor wasn't going to help either. He had to get out and after whoever levelled him. There was nothing else to do, no other option. He had to take the chance that whoever it was didn't want to hang around and was long gone.

He wondered how long he'd been out. Did it really matter?

Guthrie stood up, slowly at first, but once he was sure no other part of his body was going to complain about being vertical, he quickly took the two paces to reach the foot of the steps. Looking up he could see the dark contours of the wheelhouse ceiling. He hesitated before placing a foot on the lowest step. He strained to hear any indication that someone may be waiting for him, but all he could hear was the wind.

Pulling himself up the steps, he emerged into the wheelhouse. He half expected another blow, but none came. Relief flowed through his body on a wave of adrenaline. His heart was pounding harder than after a four-coffee breakfast.

Then he started to shake. Thinking he might pass out, he grabbed his knees, closed his eyes and consciously kept his breathing under control. Straightening up, he found the edge of a counter and steadied himself. The feeling quickly passed, but the light-headedness remained.

He looked out of the door and down to the yard. The rain had started. In the darkness he saw something move behind the van parked beside the portacabin. Guthrie instinctively moved as far back into the wheelhouse as he could, into the shadow of a corner, without giving up his line of sight to the van. He stood still, heart racing. He thought he must have been spotted. Whoever tried to take his head off knew where he was, and they were sure to be watching.

The fact that someone was there, assuming this was the person who tried to take a chunk out of the side of his head, seemed to indicate he hadn't been unconscious for any great length of time.

He watched the figure in the darkness. Guthrie couldn't make out any details other than it was a man. He could tell by the way he was moving. He was wearing a heavy coat, the hood pulled up over his head.

The van was facing Guthrie. The rear doors were open, and the figure had disappeared directly behind the vehicle, obviously doing something inside. Guthrie knew that if he was going to make his move off the boat, now was probably the best time. He crept towards the wheelhouse door, crouching low, keeping the van in sight, but trying to stay hidden in the darkness.

The rain was making it slick under Guthrie's feet. He made his way back towards the ladder, his right hand steadying himself against the outside of the wheelhouse. When he reached the ladder, he saw that it would be impossible to climb down without being spotted. His attacker could easily see him, and he would be vulnerable for the time he was making his way down to the concrete of the slipway.

There had to be another way off the boat. He looked around. One more quick glance at the van. Nothing. He walked across the deck to the opposite side of the boat and looked over. Left. Right. No ladders or gangplanks. Turning back, he saw the rope he had stumbled on when he first climbed aboard. He picked up the coil. It was heavy, soaked by the rain.

Still bent over, he carefully backed up across the deck to the far side. There was a little movement from the van. An arm appeared from behind the door. Guthrie stopped, but the arm disappeared just as quickly. The rain was now pounding off the deck. He hadn't noticed, but he was drenched.

He screwed his eyes shut, tightly, refocusing himself on getting off the boat unseen.

Guthrie put the rope down at his feet. He took one end and threaded it through a gap and back over the top of the gunwale. He pulled it through another four or five feet then knotted it back on itself. Picking up the coil he threw the rope over the side. It landed with a wet splat on the slipway. Guthrie looked over his shoulder. He was far enough away that the sound hadn't carried, or it had been drowned out by the wind and rain.

Now came the part he wasn't looking forward to. Twenty feet of wet rope stood between him and the ground, but he knew this was the only way he could get off the boat without being seen. He tugged on the rope, checking the security of the knot. He wished he had stayed in the scouts longer than he had all those years ago, but the knot held. With the rope in both hands he sat on the rail and swung both feet over the side. It wasn't going to be easy and he just hoped he could keep his grip and not fall. He took a long, deep breath through his nose and pushed off, swinging around so he straddled the rope, facing the hull.

He inched himself down, hand over hand. The hull of the boat curved away from him to the point where he could no longer steady himself against it. Wrapping one leg around the rope, he flashed back to gym class and having to climb up what seemed, at the time, to be an impossible height. He wondered if that had anything to do with his fear of heights. At least that one skill from his childhood had come in handy.

He reached the sloping ground and hopped twice as he released the rope from his leg. Another deep breath. This time, however, out of relief versus nervousness.

He ran up the slipway to the bow of the boat. He knew he had to make it across the yard as quickly as possible. As he was deciding how to do that, the man appeared from behind the van. His back was towards Guthrie. He was saying something, talking to someone. Guthrie couldn't make out the words. The man reached back into the van. His body language indicated he was agitated. Then Guthrie saw something that made the hair on the back of his neck stand on end.

Alisdair. His hands were tied behind his back. He was hunched over and walked with a limp.

"Shite." Guthrie said out loud, but not loud enough to be heard. The man grabbed Alisdair and spun him round, facing Guthrie. He couldn't be sure, but it looked like Alisdair had suffered his own beating. Alisdair was pulled backwards before being told to stop at the foot of the steps of the portacabin. The man opened the passenger door and, reaching in, pulled out a shotgun.

FIFTY-NINE

Guthrie's mind started to race. He needed to get Alisdair away from the man, but how?

Alisdair stood while the man took the steps to the door. He reached into a pocket and found some keys. The shotgun was pointed at Alisdair's back.

Guthrie knew the best time to move closer was now. He quickly made his way towards the van. He took a chance that Alisdair's kidnapper kept his focus on unlocking the door long enough to allow him to reach the cover of the vehicle. He didn't take his eyes off the man as he ran across the yard, but Alisdair saw him.

When Alisdair realised who the figure running towards him was, he raised his head and his eyes opened wide. Guthrie reached the safety of the van and positioned himself behind the right side of the bonnet. He still had no idea what he was going to do. He didn't want to give himself away too quickly. That much he did know.

"Tom?"

Guthrie couldn't believe it. Alisdair shouted his name out.

"Tom!"

The hooded man spun round, dropping the keys. "Who's there?"

The man's face was still hidden by the hood of his coat.

"Who's there?" he repeated.

There was nothing for it, Guthrie had to show himself. He stood; hands held up. The man descended the steps and stood behind Alisdair. He prodded the barrel into Alisdair's back, causing him to take a half step forward. Guthrie's heart missed a beat.

"Look," Guthrie said, "Why don't you just let Alisdair go and you and I can work this out."

"I think we're past working things out, don't you?"

Guthrie shrugged. "It's over if you insist on kidnapping a police officer. If you let him go, then who knows."

The man took Alisdair's arm. They walked sideways, passing behind the van. Guthrie still had his hands up. He too walked to his right until he could see them again.

"Don't try anything, okay?"

"Aye, okay. I'm just worried that you might do something silly, that's all."

Guthrie couldn't place the voice. He had heard it before.

The rain was really coming down now. It was as if the drops were not content with just hitting the ground, but bounced back up and tried again. Guthrie could feel the cold water running down his neck. Everything was drenched. The cold water was running down his face, making him blink, getting into his ears.

Alisdair was man-handled backwards as they headed towards the wall of the boat yard. Stone steps led up to the far end of the bridge and the access road. Still backing up, they made their way to the top. Alisdair stumbled several times. At one point it looked like he was going to fall over the rail. With his hands behind his back, climbing the steps backwards was not easy.

Guthrie moved with them. He wondered why the man would want to leave the relative safety of the yard. Yes, the weather had turned lousy, it was dark, but it was still early. The probability of people being around the harbour would be high. Perhaps taking this stand-off into a public place would make sure Guthrie didn't try anything.

On reaching the top, they quickly disappeared from sight. Guthrie ran to the steps and climbed them two at a time. He stopped just below the level of the road, fearing yet another blow to the head, or worse, was waiting for him. Satisfied that he was safe, he completed the climb and emerged at the side of the road. To his left, five hundred feet away, he could see the Old Brewhouse pub. To his right, a similar distance away, was the end of the harbour wall. Thirty yards in that direction he spotted Alisdair, still being forced along.

The outer harbour was hemmed in to Guthrie's left by the sea wall. Steps similar to the ones he had just climbed, allowed access to the top of the wall. The steps were spaced every fifty yards. Alisdair and his kidnapper had reached one and were climbing them.

Guthrie checked behind him. The closest steps were just a short distance away. Without thinking, he ran over and climbed them. The top of the sea wall was uneven and slick. Patches of lichen made the walkway even more treacherous -- one mis-step and you he would fall down to the cobbled road, or into the sea. Neither one would be a pleasant experience.

Carefully, he ran as quickly as he could, trying not to think about the consequences of a fall. The wind had picked up and on top of the harbour wall, the rain mixed with the salt, sea spray from the waves crashing against the stonework. He reached Alisdair, the other man still behind him.

"Look, let Alisdair go. Put down the weapon and let him go."

The man shoved Alisdair closer to the seaward edge of the wall. Guthrie instinctively reached out, even though the pair were still twenty feet from him.

The man kept the shotgun pointed at Alisdair. With his free hand, he reached up and pushed the hood back off his head. Guthrie swallowed. He knew he should have recognised the voice.

John Ogilvy stood smiling at him. The smile was like his voice -- not quite right. A little off.

"Mr Guthrie. I'm sure you're happy to see me. I've been on your hit list ever since our first meeting."

"I suspected you knew more than you were telling us. That's for sure."

"Oh, I've told you everything I thought you needed to know," Ogilvy replied.

"What we needed to know is for us to determine though."

"Perhaps."

Guthrie took a step forward.

"Now, now, Mr Guthrie. Let's not put Alisdair in any more danger here, eh? So close to the edge and all."

Guthrie backed up a step. "So. Did you kill Bobby?"

Ogilvy laughed. "You still have no idea, do you?"

"No," he said, "I guess not. You have to admit you gave us a bit of a run around." He took a step forward. "It would be nice to get a straight story out of someone for a change."

"Perhaps you were asking the wrong people the wrong questions?"

"I'm sorry, Mr Ogilvy, but it seems to me I was asking the right people the right questions but getting no answers." Another step.

"Did you ever work out why?"

Guthrie frowned. "Why?"

"Yes, why. Why was Bobby killed? Did you figure it out?"

"Why don't you tell me?"

Guthrie saw that a small group of people had gathered and were watching what was going on. Two teenage boys in tracksuit bottoms, rain coats and baseball caps were standing beside a man with a dog on a leash.

"Ha!" Ogilvy exclaimed. "You don't know, do you? You don't *know*."

Guthrie had to keep Ogilvy engaged, keep him talking. "All right, let me tell you what I think."

"Okay. Let's see how good you are."

Guthrie took another step forward, narrowing the gap to just a few feet. Ogilvy caught the movement and warned him.

"That's close enough."

"I think Bobby Gant almost ruined your business. Bobby and your brother-in-law, Mitchell. The business had been in decline for some time and the one product keeping you afloat was almost screwed up by the decisions of those two individuals."

"Interesting. Go on."

Guthrie swallowed. The wind whipped around him, making him take a step sideways and catch his balance. The six-foot-wide surface seemed to shrink with every gust. He continued, shouting above the noise of the wind and sea.

"There wasn't much you could do to your brother-in-law at the time, other than ask him to leave -- he is family after all -- but Bobby Gant was a different story. Bobby, a trusted employee, had screwed your company, screwed you."

Ogilvy was smiling through the rain at Guthrie.

Guthrie continued. "He screwed you and put your company in a position that could mean Ogilvy Outerwear would go bust. And you couldn't let him get away with that. Someone had to pay. Right?"

"That's almost believable," Ogilvy said, "but not exactly how it went down."

"Oh, come off it, Ogilvy," Guthrie shouted. "You killed Bobby Gant. You know it, I know it." Guthrie was sore, wet, and fed up with the crap Ogilvy had given him for the last week. His emotions were getting the better of him. He took another step towards the two men.

In an instant, Ogilvy swung the shotgun up and over Alisdair's head, and pointed it at Guthrie. Guthrie hit the cold, wet stone just before Ogilvy discharged a barrel. Guthrie looked up in time to see Ogilvy take the shotgun in both hands and use it to push Alisdair to the edge of the wall.

"Ogilvy!" Guthrie yelled.

Alisdair resisted the push, but with his hands tied behind his back, he couldn't fight back and keep his balance. A second later he disappeared into the black North Sea.

SIXTY

Guthrie had to make a split-second decision.

As soon as Ogilvy pushed Alisdair over the edge, he turned and ran down the steps. The small crowd of onlookers scattered when Ogilvy waved the shotgun towards them as he ran back across the bridge.

Guthrie's first reaction was to take off after Ogilvy, but he knew immediately he had to get to Alisdair. He looked over the edge. The water was as black as the sky. The rain was now coming down in sheets. Salt-laden spray from the waves mixed with the rain and stung Guthrie's eyes as he scanned the water. The drop to the surface was about twenty feet. He had no idea how deep the water was, or if there were rocks hidden by the waves as they crashed against the wall.

"Alisdair! Alisdair!"

Guthrie could barely see the waves, never mind spot Alisdair among them.

"Alisdair!" he shouted again.

Then he saw him. Alisdair's head appeared above the water. He gulped for air before being overcome by another wave. He was fifteen feet from the wall, but with every wave he felt as if he was going to be smashed against the red sandstone. Guthrie looked around for a life ring. Nothing. Alisdair appeared again in the darkness. All Guthrie could make out was the contrast of his face and white shirt against the black water.

Alisdair was struggling. The only way he could keep his head above the waves was by kicking his legs, trying to tread water, but with his hands tied behind his back, the effort was enormous.

Guthrie knew he wouldn't last much longer. Adrenaline kicked in. The only course of action was to jump in. He took off his jacket and let it fall down onto the cobbled road. One of the teenagers was still there, looking up. Guthrie yelled at him.

"Phone nine-nine-nine!"

Guthrie focused again on Alisdair. The waves had pushed him closer. Now only a few feet from the wall, the next wave scooped him up and bashed him against it. Guthrie knew he couldn't take much more. He had to jump now.

"Bugger!"

He took a couple of steps back then, after a short run, launched himself into the void above the waves.

He hit the water, went under, but quickly surfaced. The water was freezing. The bitter cold shocked him as he gulped for air, as if the sea knew what he was doing and was working against him. A wave crashed over his head. Salt water filled his mouth and he spat it out before grabbing another lungful of air.

"Alisdair!"

He spun himself around trying to find the young officer.

"Alisdair!"

Another wave. This one moved him back, closer to the wall. The darkness closed around him. The wall blocked any light from the harbour. Then he saw him.

"Alisdair!"

He was only a few feet away. Guthrie kicked his legs to propel him towards his colleague. The sea was doing its utmost to push him back. Every wave seemed to make the distance double, but Guthrie made it to Alisdair just as he was sinking back below the surface. He grabbed him under the arm and pulled him into his shoulder.

"I've got you. It's all right."

Alisdair didn't respond. His eyes were barely open and, even in the darkness Guthrie could see that his skin was deathly white.

"Hang on, Alisdair. Hang on!"

Guthrie wrapped one arm around Alisdair's chest and tightened his grip. Laying back he kept Alisdair's face above the water using the life-saving technique he had first learned all those years ago in high school. He oriented himself so he was looking towards the wall, the expanse of the North Sea behind him.

Guthrie could see nothing that would help them escape the cold water. The wall was a dark mass stretching, as far as he was concerned, forever in both directions. He knew he had to get them out of the water. His fingers were tingling, beginning to go numb. He was starting to shiver. A sure sign of hypothermia taking hold. The more he had to work to keep them both afloat, the quicker he would feel the effects of the cold. His body was going to protect its core and restrict the blood flow to his hands and feet. Then his arms and legs. Soon he would find it difficult to keep hold of Alisdair.

The relentless sea picked them up in a wave and moved

them closer still to the wall. Close enough that Guthrie had to push off the stone with both feet. The net result was imperceptible as the next wave did the same.

How was he going to get out of the water? The only thing he could think of was to try and make his way around the end of the wall and into the calm waters of the harbour, but that was crazy. The harbour entrance was easily a hundred yards away. There was no way he could make it, but what options did he have?

He hooked Alisdair under one arm and across his chest, keeping his head above the water, and began to kick. They were at a forty-five-degree angle to the wall. The movement of the sea forcing him back towards the wall as he countered by swimming against it.

After twenty strokes his heart was racing, lungs burning. He was swallowing almost as much water as he was gulping in air. He was getting too much of the one and not enough of the other.

Because of the lack of any references, he had no idea what kind of progress he was making. Everything was dark. Everything except Alisdair's face. Even in the low light, it was still parchment-like. He was also not helping to kick. In fact, he was not doing anything.

Guthrie was shivering constantly now. "We're getting there, Alisdair," he said, more to reassure himself than Alisdair. But he knew, even without looking behind him, that they were getting nowhere.

Guthrie was losing the feeling in his legs. He knew he was kicking, but there was no sensation. He persisted, but he was finding it difficult to keep his head above the surface. He started to panic. He wanted to cry. The thought seemed to lodge itself in his mind. Why cry? He should be mad. He should surely want to scream out in anger. Anger! That's what he needed to channel. He began kicking hard again, but a wave, the largest one so far, picked them up and smacked them into the wall.

"Argh!" Guthrie screamed. His right arm, the one supporting Alisdair, took the full force of the collision. Even through the pins and needles, the pain was sharp. What little strength he had was now gone and Alisdair slipped from his grasp.

"No!"

Alisdair slid down Guthrie's body and disappeared beneath the surface. Then he felt him catch against his foot. Guthrie hooked Alisdair using both legs, but that meant he was unable to stay afloat. Instinctively, he filled his lungs with as much damp air as he could before going under.

Once below the surface, it seemed calm. The noise of the wind and waves faded to a muted rumble, and all motion slowed. But it was black. It was as if Guthrie had descended into a water-filled cave. What little light there was at the surface was gone only a few inches below.

Guthrie still had Alisdair between his legs -- barely. He was starting to slip away again. No longer having to expend his energy on staying afloat, however, Guthrie raised his knees to his chest. In fact, because of the mass of Alisdair's limp body, it was actually the other way around. The net result was that he could reach down and quickly found Alisdair's shirt collar.

Sure, that he had an adequate handhold, Guthrie released the grip of his legs and kicked. Kicked harder than he had ever done. He had only been submerged for a few seconds, but already his chest was burning and the desire to take a breath was overpowering.

Kick.

Kick.

Guthrie looked up towards the surface. A flickering light danced above him. He had to be close.

Kick.

Kick.

When his head broke the surface the air in his lungs was let loose with a cry and he gulped in deeply to fill the void. He tilted his head back until it touched the water and his legs came up to support Alisdair's body. He wrapped his free hand under Alisdair's armpit and cupped his chin, keeping his head above the water.

He looked around and panicked. He could see nothing. Nothing but the surface of the sea within a few feet of him before it merged into the blackness of the night. He realised he had been turned around and the harbour wall was now behind him.

"There!"

The shout came from above and to Guthrie's left. A beam of light landed on him.

"There! There they are!"

Guthrie manoeuvred until he was facing the wall. The light shone in his face and blinded him. He jerked his head away as if he had been punched. Whatever night vision he had was now gone.

"Help!" he shouted.

Another blinding light landed on Guthrie as he struggled to stay afloat. His legs were burning, and he felt as though he couldn't breathe fast enough to satisfy his body's desire for oxygen.

He blinked away the water from his eyes and through the white spots in his vision, caused by the lights, he could make out several shapes on top of the harbour wall. One jumped and landed in the water only a few feet from him. The swimmer reached the pair and grabbed Alisdair.

"No!" shouted Guthrie.

"It's all right. I've got him."

"No, no!" Guthrie barely got the second word out before his head went under. He quickly surfaced and spat out a mouthful of cold, salty water.

"Let go, sir, I've got him," repeated the swimmer.

Guthrie didn't want to let go. He didn't want to leave Alisdair's fate to someone else. He wanted to say no again. Tears started to fill his eyes. The stark, white light of the torches shining down on them became brilliant starbursts through the tears. He knew, however, that he had to release his grip. He couldn't do this on his own.

He let go and Alisdair and the swimmer disappeared behind the crest of a wave.

Suddenly, a life belt splashed into the water a few feet ahead of him. At first, he didn't know what is was, then a shout from above said, "Reach for the life belt!"

Guthrie's right arm was numb. His legs felt heavy. He was so tired. If he could only stop for a moment. Guthrie slowed the frequency and power of his kicks. Between each one, as he leaned his head back, he couldn't stop his face from going under the water. Another kick and push with his arms, and he would surface and breathe in. A pause, and down again.

Kick. Breathe.

Pause.

Kick. Breathe.

Pause. Longer this time.

Kick.

Pause.

Blackness.

SIXTY-ONE

The siren echoed off the buildings and the lights were reflected in the rain-soaked surfaces as the ambulance made its way to the end of the access road, before turning and heading to the infirmary.

Alisdair had been hauled out of the water and immediately checked for vital signs before being placed in the back of the ambulance and driven away.

Guthrie had come to in the back of a police car. He didn't recall how he made it out of the water. He was wrapped in a thin metal blanket, like a runner at the end of a marathon. He was still soaking wet, the foil blanket wasn't doing much, but the car's heater was pushing out hot air like a furnace. The door was open, and a paramedic was kneeling down, looking in at him.

"How are you?" he said.

Guthrie blinked twice, trying to focus on the voice. He shivered violently, and immediately his left leg cramped up.

"Argh!"

"What?" the paramedic asked.

"Cramp I think," said Guthrie. He reached under his thigh and rubbed the muscle. The tension and pain quickly faded. His thoughts turned to Alisdair. "Where's Alisdair?"

"Sorry, sir, who?"

"Alisdair. The other police officer. The other one who was in the water. Where is he?"

"Sorry, sir. I think he must have been the one taken to the infirmary."

"Is he okay?"

The paramedic shook his head. "I don't know. I just heard what was happening on the radio as we arrived."

Guthrie felt sick and light-headed. He closed his eyes and rested his forehead against the back of the headrest in front of him.

"You all right, sir?" the paramedic asked.

"Aye. Fine."

But he wasn't fine. He was far from fine. He could hear Buchanan's words in his head, and he suspected he had been right. Why did he send Alisdair off on his own to pick up the Wests? If he had sent him with a uniformed officer, this would never had happened.

Buchanan's voice said, "I hope you're not too worse for wear after your swim?"

Guthrie frowned then realised Buchanan had replaced the paramedic and was leaning in, bent over, at the car door. He was still wearing his dress uniform from the media briefing.

"I think I ruined another perfectly good pair of shoes on this case."

Buchanan's face showed no reaction.

"They think Alisdair's going to be fine."

Guthrie's eyes welled up again. "Good." He sniffed and rubbed his nose with the back of his hand.

Buchanan stood up, dug into his pocket, and produced a handkerchief. "Here," he said offering it to Guthrie. "And no, I've not used it."

Guthrie took it and blew his nose. "Thanks."

Buchanan nodded and then went on. "We have some witnesses that told us there was a gun involved. Do you know who it was?"

"Ogilvy," was all Guthrie could say. His voice was quiet. He had forgotten about Ogilvy. "Bloody Ogilvy."

Buchanan turned and shouted at a uniform. A young PC trotted over.

"Yes, sir?"

"Organise some men and get over to the house of a Mr John Ogilvy. The incident room will have the address."

"Yes, sir."

"Do it now, but I just want you to take up positions around the house. Ogilvy threatened Mr Guthrie here, along with Constable McEwan with a firearm, so I'm going to call in a firearms unit before we confront him. I just want to make sure if he's home, he doesn't leave without us knowing."

"Yes, sir," the constable said for the third time, then turned and jogged over to a police car.

"We'll pick him up, Tom."

Guthrie couldn't help himself. "Do you really think he's going to go home after he's just tried to drown a police officer and shoot me, witnessed by a handful of onlookers?"

"Don't start, Tom. It's the most likely place-"

"How did he get here?" Guthrie cut Buchanan's response before he could finish his thought.

"What?"

"How did he get here?"

"What do you mean, how?"

Guthrie swung a leg out, forcing Buchanan to take two steps back, and then got out of the car. He stood, unsteadily, then leaned back against the vehicle. His legs felt weak and the blood drained from his head making him feel light-headed.

"Have you checked the boat yard?"

"The boat yard?" echoed Buchanan.

"Yes, the boat yard. How did you know to come here?"

"One of the witnesses dialled nine-nine-nine."

"No, I mean how did *you* know to come here? Why did *you* come here? You were in a media briefing. Even if there was a gun involved, you wouldn't normally attend the scene."

"The caller told us that you were talking about the Gant murder. I checked with the incident room and was told you'd gone to the harbour. I didn't have to put two and two together."

"Only the harbour, yes? You don't know about the boat yard?"

"No."

"Shite!"

Guthrie threw off the foil blanket and headed off towards the swing bridge over the slipway and to the boat yard. The water in his shoes squelched between his toes. Every step caused pin pricks of pain to shoot up his legs.

"Guthrie!" Buchanan shouted after him, but he didn't stop.

Buchanan took off after him and motioned for a handful of uniforms to fall in behind, as he ran after the sodden Guthrie.

"Tom!" But he was already across the bridge and rounding the wall, heading for the yard gates.

When Guthrie got there, they were open. The small,

white van was still just inside the yard, its double rear doors open wide. His lungs burned as he gasped for air, still weak from his swim. He grabbed his knees and breathed deeply and quickly. Buchanan and three uniforms ran up beside him.

"Tom, if you think he's still here, don't you think it's a little foolish to run off on your own? Especially after your last solo effort required a team of men to pull you out of the North Sea?"

"He's not here, Ian."

"Exactly what makes you think that?"

Guthrie pushed his body upright. "I'm not one hundred percent sure." The remark got a grunt from Buchanan. "I'm pretty sure he drove here in that, though." He pointed at the van. "When I got here, the engine was still warm."

Buchanan indicated that the uniforms take a look around, warning them to be careful. They spread out and slowly walked around with their torches making sweeping arcs around the sloping yard.

"What was in the van?" Buchanan asked.

"Alisdair was back there. I saw Ogilvy take him out. They were about to go into the office when they spotted me."

Buchanan cautiously walked over to the van. On reaching the open doors he turned on his torch and lit up the interior.

"Tom?"

"Huh?"

Buchanan turned back to Guthrie and, indicating with a nod back over his shoulder, said, "You might want to see this."

Guthrie was puzzled. He forced his legs to take the

steps towards the van. Buchanan aimed his torch and lit up the interior of the small cargo compartment.

"Bugger."

Buchanan's light shone on a body. A dark, red stain covered the front of what was a crisp, white shirt. One arm was stretched out above his head, showing a grey patch of dirt at the elbow.

"Do you know him?" Buchanan asked.

Guthrie couldn't quite see the man's face. He stepped forward, making sure he didn't touch the van, and peered in. He was older, probably in his seventies. From the style of his clothes he certainly appeared to have some money -- not a working man, thought Guthrie. However, he didn't recognise him.

"I don't," Guthrie answered, "but if I were to guess, I'd say it could be Harry West."

Buchanan sighed. "Makes sense. McEwan goes to pick him up at his home, there's blood found there, McEwan and West can't be found, you turn up here where Ogilvy has McEwan..."

"That's what I'm thinking," Guthrie said. He turned his back on the van and looked around the yard. "He's not here."

"Ogilvy?"

"Aye. He's long gone." He followed the light from one of the officer's torches as it picked out a pile of wood at the far end of the yard.

"Where, though?"

Guthrie thought. "He can't be far. I'd put money on him being on foot."

Buchanan whistled and called over the uniforms searching the yard. When they had gathered around the inspector, he began issuing orders. After the officers had dispersed, a plan was in place to keep searching the yard, but also to round up every available resource to begin a search of the entire harbour area and beyond. Buchanan had an officer with an airwave set call in a request for a firearms team and additional officers from surrounding areas to supplement the search efforts.

"We will find him, Tom."

Guthrie shivered, the chilly evening air reminding him that he was still in wet clothes. "I hope so, Ian. I hope so."

The inspector took in the dripping Guthrie. "I say we get you back to the station for now and into some dry clothes. Then you can head home."

"No, I'd rather-," Guthrie protested, but was cut off.

"Yes. Tom. You've done quite enough. You need to call it a day."

Guthrie looked up. Low clouds picked out by the street lights were speeding across the town. The smell of the rain lingered in the air.

"That's me is it? I'm done with the case?"

Buchanan scowled. "We both know what the parameters were, Tom."

Guthrie kicked at a pebble at his feet.

"Get over to the station and they'll find you something dry to get you home. Call me in the morning." With that, Buchanan turned and headed for the closest uniform, barking orders.

Guthrie slowly walked through the gates of the yard and found the closest police car, looking for a lift. No one paid him any attention, as those who were not busy with some task or other, were gathering around Buchanan, who was pointing in various directions, obviously taking charge of the search for Ogilvy.

He walked over to the lone ambulance. They were

packing up their gear and about to leave. He had to catch them before they left as his jacket, with his keys and phone, was in it. The paramedic checked on him again, much to Guthrie's annoyance, but they offered him a lift back to the station. He refused. His car was parked around the corner.

SIXTY-TWO

Sal had managed to find, from one of the civilian staff, a tracksuit that almost fit Guthrie. The pair of trainers, secured from a plastic tub of lost and found, however, could have been Guthrie's own they fit so well. At least he was warm and dry.

"What a bloody state this whole thing is," said Sal as she handed Guthrie a cup of coffee. "Have you heard anything about Alisdair?"

Guthrie took a sip before answering. "No, I haven't. Not yet."

Sal sat at her desk. "I'll call the infirmary and see what I can find out."

"Thanks." Guthrie looked around the empty incident room. Everyone who could be spared was down at the harbour. A sickly feeling rose in his stomach. There was nothing else he could do.

"Look, Sal, if you find out anything on Alisdair, give me a shout on my mobile. I'm going to head home. Not much I can do here."

"Of course. You'll be the first to know."

Guthrie smiled and raised his coffee cup in thanks. Picking up a bin bag containing his wet clothes, he walked out and down to the car park.

Four minutes later he was passing the harbour. He slowed as he craned his neck to look back to the left. He could see several yellow jacket-clad officers slowly making their way along the side of the harbour, checking the stacks of lobster creels. Two officers were walking along the jetty between the rows of small craft in the inner harbour's marina facility.

Approaching a roundabout, Guthrie saw a car slowing to give way as he approached. As he passed, he couldn't believe what he saw.

In the instant it took Guthrie to recognise the Jaguar and saw Ogilvy behind the wheel, Ogilvy had pulled in behind him on the roundabout.

Guthrie slammed on the brakes taking Ogilvy by surprise. Ogilvy had no time to react and the Jag smashed into the back of the little MG. Guthrie flicked the gear lever into neutral and jumped out. On seeing Guthrie, Ogilvy reached over to the passenger seat and grabbed the shotgun. Cracking it open he expertly loaded two cartridges and hit the window button on the door's armrest.

Guthrie was already two steps away from the car when the shotgun appeared. He threw himself down just as a blast from the weapon shattered the relative quietness of the evening.

Ogilvy threw the Jaguar into reverse. The chrome rear bumper from the MG was pulled away from the car and the lens from one of the Jaguar's headlights scattered in pieces on the roadway. Ogilvy punched the accelerator and the car's wide rear tyres struggled for grip on the damp surface then squealed as they purchased and moved the car around the MG. Guthrie rolled away to avoid being run over, half expecting another shot to come his way, but Ogilvy didn't want to hang around. The car slid around the roundabout and headed back towards town.

Guthrie stood up. He was facing the harbour and saw several officers running towards him, but he didn't want to wait either. He jumped back into the car and prayed that the collision hadn't done so much damage that he couldn't drive it. Selecting first gear he let out the clutch and the car moved forward.

"Yes!"

He knew the old car was no match for Ogilvy's powerful ride, but he had to follow. He had to try. Once around the corner the road was a straight shot past the station at Gravesend. He hoped he could spot Ogilvy's distinctive rear lights which would give him a decent chance to stay within reach. Passing the station, he saw Ogilvy's brake lights as he slowed for a pedestrian crossing. Was he heading back to his house? The next turn should tell him. Left would take him that way; straight on, towards the warehouse on the north of the town.

Guthrie's foot was planted on the accelerator pedal, pushing it through the floor. He willed the little car to go faster, but it struggled to accelerate, and a grinding noise had developed in the rear. Strangely, he thought about all the work he had put into it.

The lights of the pedestrian crossing changing from green to yellow brought Guthrie back to the matter at hand. "Bloody hell!" he shouted, angrily. He slowed, but only slightly. He couldn't afford to be stopped by the light as he'd lose Ogilvy. He pressed the horn in the middle of the steering wheel. An old lady had already stepped into the road when Guthrie sounded the horn. Startled, she stopped quickly and as Guthrie sped through the now red light, she raised her fist as he passed.

Ahead, Ogilvy's brake lights came on as he approached another roundabout. Guthrie saw a car, with the right of way, heading towards Ogilvy, who should have stopped. The Jaguar, however, hit the car square in the passenger side door, locking the two cars together. Guthrie was still two hundred yards back but could see that Ogilvy was trying desperately to gun the engine to free the car. It was hopeless. He jumped out and started to run. Guthrie spotted him in the yellow of the street lamps.

Guthrie reached the crash scene. He stopped, got out, and ran over to check on the occupants of the second car. A young woman sat in the driver's seat. A baby in a car seat behind her was crying.

"Are you okay?" he asked the woman.

"Aye."

"Do you have a mobile phone?"

"Eh... Aye... Aye, I do." She rubbed her forehead and adjusted the mirror to see the child.

"She looks fine," said Guthrie, in what he hoped was a reassuring tone. "Call nine-nine-nine, all right?"

"Aye, okay. Is my baby okay?"

"She's fine. She's all cocooned in that car seat. But call nine-nine-nine and get the ambulance coming."

Guthrie couldn't wait any longer. Every second he stood there Ogilvy was getting away. But he was on foot and not getting anywhere quickly. He wondered if he should get in the car and follow, but he decided to just start running.

He had seen Ogilvy head up the hill to his right. He took off in the same direction. He thought he saw Ogilvy half way up the hill on the other side of the street, but he wasn't sure. With no other option, he stuck to his plan.

In the distance behind him he could hear sirens, but his mind quickly refocused on his legs. They had immediately started to burn as soon as he took off running. His ordeal in the sea, barely an hour earlier, had taken more out of him than he realised. The paramedics had given him some glucose tablets to quickly raise his energy levels, but asking his legs to work hard again felt like an impossible task. With every step it seemed like his heel was smashing into the pavement and shattering his bones. His lungs were burning, and he struggled to breathe. The same sensations from his swim.

He had to stop. Bending over, he put his hands on his hips. "Bloody hell."

He looked up. Ogilvy was crossing the street at the top of the hill. Guthrie willed himself to start running again. His pace was slow -- he could probably walk faster -- but he didn't want to let Ogilvy escape again. The hill seemed steeper than it actually was. Every muscle protested each step -- his neck, his arms. It was as if he could pick out each muscle as it contracted and stretched.

A couple of older men walked out of a pub and looked at the figure of Guthrie in the tracksuit, struggling to make it to the top of the incline. They offered some encouragement as he approached, thinking he was on some sort of keep fit regime.

"On yersel', son!"

"Bugger off," was all Guthrie could manage as he passed them.

At the crest of the hill he stopped and leaned against a signpost. Every breath hurt, but he was gulping for air.

His quarry had crossed a grassy area and was heading for the Abbey's visitor centre. The building was locked up. He made for a side car park and a set of metal steps leading to a back door. Guthrie had to wait for a car and two vans to pass before he could cross the street. Each time he stopped made it more difficult to resume the chase, but the thought of catching Ogilvy was enough to fight through the pain. Catching Ogilvy meant getting the man that had thrown Alisdair into the sea. He wasn't thinking about what he had done to anyone else, even taking a shot, two shots, at Guthrie was set aside for the act of trying to drown his colleague right in front of him.

The sound of sirens grew louder. The strobe of blue lights reflected off the brown stone of the buildings. At least someone else knew what was going on.

A low hedge was in Guthrie's path. His first thought was to jump over it, but he was too exhausted, he knew that if he tried, he wouldn't make it, even though the plant was only two feet tall. As he reached it, he stopped and stepped through it. The stiff branches dug into his legs. Guthrie swore under his breath.

To his right a police car pulled up. The passenger door opened and he recognised the officer as one from Montrose drafted in to the investigation.

"Sir?" he shouted.

Guthrie pointed to the steps. "Over the wall. Get over the wall. Ogilvy."

The officer stood looking across the visitor centre car park. "We heard a gunshot. Is he armed?"

It dawned on Guthrie that he forgot to check Ogilvy's car before he left the collision scene at the roundabout. "Eh, I'm not sure." He tried to picture Ogilvy running up the street. Did he look like he was carrying a shotgun? "I don't think so." He rubbed his eyes. "I'm not sure."

The other officer from the car was now with them. He looked at his partner and nodded before they ran towards the Abbey wall. Guthrie blew out his cheeks and knew he had to follow. He jogged over to the car park. The uniforms had already climbed the steps and were looking over the wall. Guthrie could only concentrate on not falling over. His legs felt like lead and yet made of wet noodles.

He tackled the steps one at a time using the handrail to pull himself up in an effort to ease the strain in his leg muscles. The officers had already disappeared over the wall.

The steps could have been Mount Everest and Guthrie was scaling it without oxygen. Everything in him wanted to take the steps two at a time, but his body was leaving him in no doubt that mind over matter was not on the menu this evening.

He finally reached the top and looked over the red sandstone wall, the top of which was chest high. On the other side was a drop of some nine or ten feet. He could see the two officers walking slowly around the open ground of the ruined Abbey, the light from their torches bouncing off the walls and stubs of columns long demolished.

Guthrie stretched his arms out along the top of the wall. The rough stone seemed to taunt him. *You're not getting past me*, it said. *You've nothing left. You're done, finished. Leave the chasing to those who can still handle it.*

Bloody walls. He was sick of them. He turned and slowly slumped down. He wrapped his arms around his legs and rested his forehead on his knees.

The events of the night, the week, crowded in on Guthrie. He had let Buchanan get to him, force him into a corner. He had reverted to his old self and thought he knew better. Worst of all, he had allowed Alisdair to be taken by Ogilvy.

And now he had let Ogilvy get away -- again.

He looked up. It had started to rain. The last thing he

needed was to get wet. He stared at the passing traffic. From where he was sitting, he could see back down the hill and could make out the roundabout and an ambulance.

Then, out from the space below the steps, a figure emerged.

Guthrie's heart skipped then started to pound in his chest. Ogilvy. He had been hiding behind some bins. He stood just beyond the shelter of the metal stairs and looked left and right, like a deer venturing out into the open, making sure no one was around.

Guthrie watched him through the railings. He had to act and act now. He knew he didn't have the energy for another foot race. Slowly, he pushed himself up using his hands against the wall behind him. Ogilvy was breathing hard. The run up the hill took its toll on him too.

Guthrie stepped forward. He was immediately above and behind Ogilvy. He could hear the blood rushing through his body, was breathing hard, and was afraid that Ogilvy could hear the same.

It was now or never.

A police car, siren blaring and lights flashing, came screeching around the corner and slid to a stop in front of the visitor centre. Two uniformed officers jumped out of the car.

Bugger, Guthrie thought.

Ogilvy crouched down and waited to see where the two men went. They headed for the locked main door and pushed and pulled on the handle. Guthrie watched and rolled his eyes.

He focused on Ogilvy again. *He's going to make a run for it*, he thought. This time it really was now or never.

In one move, Guthrie stepped forward, grabbed the railing and swung his legs sideways and over. He landed on

Ogilvy's back and they fell to the ground. Guthrie's knee had contacted the small of Ogilvy's back, causing him to groan loudly. Guthrie tried to grab his arms and pull them behind his back. He held his grip on one, but Ogilvy managed to wrench his left arm away. He tried to push himself up, but Guthrie swiped him across the head with a backhanded fist.

Ogilvy continued to struggle, but Guthrie managed to straddle him and while keeping Ogilvy's right arm behind his back, forced his head to the damp brickwork pavement.

"If you think I'm going to let you go, you're an idiot, Ogilvy," Guthrie said.

"Screw you!" Ogilvy yelled.

Guthrie pushed Ogilvy's cheek into the ground. "Just lie there and shut up, huh? You'll have plenty of time to talk when you explain why you murdered innocent people and tried to kill a police officer."

Ogilvy squirmed, but Guthrie's weight held him fast. "Nobody's innocent, Guthrie. You should know that."

"You're not. I know that much for sure."

He tried again to free himself from under Guthrie. "Get off me!"

"I've been on you from the start, and if you think I'm going to change now, well you are as dumb as I suspected."

Ogilvy said nothing, just snorted. Guthrie looked back to find the two uniforms. "Oi! Over here!"

A torch beam swept around a couple of times then picked them out of the dimness. The officers ran over. One grabbed Ogilvy's free arm and whipped it around his back, causing him to complain with one or two choice words.

"I have him, sir," the officer said, and Guthrie could do nothing more than roll off Ogilvy's back and onto his own.

"Bloody hell, lads. What kept you?"

SIXTY-THREE

Guthrie exited the toilets having just spent fifteen minutes under the hand dryer trying to dry himself for the second time that evening. Sal had tutted and tried to stifle a laugh when he walked into the incident room.

He headed to the interview room where Buchanan had already started the formalities with Ogilvy. He had managed to convince Buchanan to allow him to be part of the process. Buchanan was holding fast to the argument that Guthrie was no longer on the case as of the time of the media briefing, but Brian Campbell came to his rescue and overruled the inspector -- much to his obvious displeasure. Guthrie knocked on the door and went in.

Ogilvy was sitting behind a desk. His hands were clasped together and in his lap. He was looking down at them as if they held the answers to the situation in which he now found himself. Buchanan sat across from him, a pad of notepaper on the desk between them. Guthrie closed the door and took up a position against the wall behind Buchanan. The inspector looked behind him and said nothing to Guthrie.

"For the purposes of the recording," Buchanan said, "Mr Tom Guthrie has entered the room."

Guthrie smiled at the back of Buchanan's head and stood beside a uniformed officer positioned next to the door.

"Mr Ogilvy, you do understand that you are in a very serious situation here, don't you?" Ogilvy remained motionless. "You are being charged with several counts of serious crimes, including the murders of Mr Bobby Gant and Mr Harry West, and the attempted murder of two others, one of whom is a police officer." Still no reaction from Ogilvy. Buchanan sighed. "Mr Ogilvy, I need you to tell me exactly why you decided to kill these people."

Nothing.

"Mr Ogilvy," Buchanan continued, "why did you kill Bobby Gant?"

Ogilvy stared at his hands. Buchanan was quickly becoming frustrated with the lack of answers. He decided to change direction.

"Okay, why did you kill Harry West?"

Guthrie spotted a twitch from Ogilvy. It was almost imperceptible, but West's name caused Ogilvy to clench his fists just a little. Guthrie decided to jump in with a question of his own.

"Mr Ogilvy. By my reckoning you can be charged with two counts of murder, four counts of attempted murder, several deadly threatening charges, reckless driving, trespassing, and a few other bits and pieces I'm sure we'll throw in for good measure. Now, I bet you know that out of all of those, the murder charges are, shall we say, the pick of the bunch."

Buchanan rolled his eyes and asked, "Where, exactly, are you going with this, Mr Guthrie?"

Guthrie ignored him.

"Mr Ogilvy, you are on the hook for a long time behind bars for those two murders. Bobby has sunk your company and you wanted nothing more than to see him punished for that. Punished in a way that made you feel good that he knew what he had done to you. You came up with a plan to make sure that happened. You were going to make sure that he would never again do what he did to your company."

Ogilvy's jaw tightened. Guthrie knew Ogilvy didn't like him. He knew that he wanted to tell him everything. He flashed back to the scuffle in the Abbey car park -- Ogilvy arguing with him about how everyone was guilty of something. He knew Gant was guilty of causing the company to have financial issues. Or was it all Gant's fault?

Guthrie frowned. What could Gant do, or know, that would be so catastrophic that Ogilvy would want him dead? He pushed himself off the wall and began to slowly walk around the desk.

"Your company was on the rocks. The only thing keeping your company afloat were a couple of products. You needed to cut costs, and you tasked your brother-in-law with that."

Guthrie had completed a circuit of the room and was once again behind Buchanan.

"Tom, where is this going?"

"Just hold your horses, Ian," he answered before continuing. "But that deal, the deal with the new liner supplier, was not what you wanted, right? That's why you changed back to Advanced Fabrics. The whole mess ended in you and your brother-in-law having a bit of a family feud and you firing him, or him resigning, depending upon whether I believe you or your brother-in-law, before you tried to hit him with a van."

"I did not." Ogilvy's voice was barely audible.

"Sorry, what?" asked Buchanan, who sat up and leaned on the table. "What did you say?"

"I said I didn't try to run over Douglas."

"That's what you say," said Guthrie.

"Look, how many times do I have to tell you? That wasn't me, right?"

Guthrie pressed, "But you did kill Bobby."

"No."

"No?" Guthrie said in what he hoped was an incredulous voice. "Then who did? Who had any reason to kill him other than you?"

"West."

Buchanan looked at Guthrie. "Harry West?" he said.

"Yes."

"Why?"

Ogilvy didn't answer.

"Why, Mr Ogilvy?"

Guthrie walked behind Ogilvy and leaned on the back of his chair. His stomach started to turn over.

"West is mixed up in this more than just through a hit and run."

Buchanan cocked his head to one side. "Explain."

Guthrie was still right behind Ogilvy. "You know, John, I think I believe you. You didn't kill Bobby Gant."

The knuckles on Ogilvy's hands turned white as he forced them together even more tightly.

"John!" Guthrie shouted, startling Ogilvy and causing him to jump. "Harry West killed Bobby Gant. Bobby, someone everyone got along with, who did his job well, conscientiously. The one person who found out about the liner material not meeting spec."

"What?" said Buchanan.

Guthrie just shook his head dismissively. "He told you,

and you had West's company removed. Advanced Fabrics was in just as much trouble as your company. Who orders fabric from somewhere other than China nowadays, right? Guthrie pushed on. His gut was telling him he was heading down the right path. The details they had found out were beginning to gel together in his head.

"West's company was pushed out of something that meant big money. You told me so yourself. West found out who told you and decided to beat up Bobby and leave him to drown, didn't he? Didn't he?"

Again, the shout made Ogilvy flinch. He raised his head and looked at Buchanan.

"Yes."

"West killed Gant." Buchanan said. "You're saying that it wasn't you, but Harry West?"

"Yes."

Guthrie could see it now. "West killed Bobby and he did it why? Because it wasn't a lesson for Bobby, was it? No. How could it be a lesson for him? After being beaten and tied up below the high tide line, the lesson would be pretty short, wouldn't it? No. The lesson was meant for you. It was a message to *you*. Harry West wanted to tell you that you could never back out of your deal with him again."

"He told me he would make sure my entire family paid for it," Ogilvy said. He talked quietly. His voice was smooth, and his tone was measured like he was having a conversation over brandy in some swanky club.

"When we cut them, Harry was furious. He didn't like being cut out of the patent deal. He left me in no doubt about his intentions were we not to reinstate their contract. When we did, Bobby found out that they had switched the liner material. Bobby demanded they provide the original design. He was trying to protect the company. I knew Harry killed Bobby."

"Then why the bloody hell didn't you come to the police?" Buchanan spat.

Guthrie raised a hand. Normally that reaction would be his and the calm, collected one in this situation would be Buchanan, but he'd had enough shouting for the day.

"Am I right in saying that when he tried to kill your brother-in-law you snapped? You had had enough?"

Ogilvy took in a deep breath of the musty air of the interview room.

"I should have taken the information I found out about the liner material and self-disclosed on the contract. I just couldn't. Too many people were relying on me to pay their bills every week. I had to keep the business going." Ogilvy seemed to be calm now that he had decided to talk.

"Douglas found out about the real reason why we had to switch the contract back to Advanced. Douglas and I argued about it and we decided that he could survive without being a part of the company. It was a cost-savings. Without his salary we could continue to pay a couple of our production employees."

"You didn't fire him?"

"No. I told you that for no other reason than I didn't know what else to tell you to keep the real liner issue under cover. Whatever was going on, I had to keep the truth hidden until we sorted it out."

Buchanan pushed himself and his chair back from the table, causing the legs to screech on the polished floor. "You thought that saving your company was more important than telling us the truth in a murder investigation?"

"I know what that sounds like..." Ogilvy dropped his head again. Guthrie was afraid he would clam up and they would lose momentum. He jumped in before Buchanan could do any more damage.

"When West tried to kill Douglas, you decided enough was enough, huh?"

Ogilvy was quiet.

Shite, thought Guthrie. "I can see that," he went on. "You'd had your fill. Your business was in poor shape, you were trying to do right by your employees and West was the last straw. You snapped and decided to teach West a lesson. I probably would have done the same."

Ogilvy sniffed. "I've worked my whole life to make that company what it is. What it was. Bloody economy goes into the toilet and cheap competition was killing us. West was the last straw, right enough. He wasn't going to get away with it. I had to kill him."

Gotcha.

Buchanan smiled.

The interview went on for another two hours. Ogilvy slowly told them about conversations with West and how he threatened not only Ogilvy's family but his business. Ogilvy had no choice left but to end the threat. Guthrie almost felt sorry for him. He was trying to do the right thing by doing the wrong thing, but that was the point at which sympathy goes out of the window.

"And Constable McEwan was just in the wrong place at the wrong time. Is that right?" Buchanan asked.

Ogilvy seemed to be tired now. "You could say that. I had just loaded West into the van and was heading back to the boat yard when he arrived. I was hiding behind the van. He didn't see me, but he did see West in the back. I panicked and jumped him. We struggled, but I managed to hit him with, with, something. I can't even remember. Something from the van."

"What about Devon West, Harry's son?" Guthrie asked.

"Huh?"

"Devon West left Advanced Fabrics with his father after Constable McEwan paid a visit to the factory earlier today. Where was he?"

Ogilvy looked genuinely puzzled. "Douglas dealt with him." After a pause, he said, "I only dealt with him once."

"He wasn't at the house when you went over there?"

"No."

"Where is he?" Guthrie asked Buchanan.

Buchanan raised an eyebrow.

Guthrie turned back to Ogilvy. There was something niggling him about Ogilvy's behaviour. It had been too easy once he had cracked and decided to answer all of their questions. Ogilvy's demeanour had changed too. This calm personality was not exactly what Guthrie had come to expect from him. This was just weird. This was too easy.

Guthrie knew that Ogilvy had flipped. The pressure had built up over the past several months in the business. He had done everything he could to save it, to help his employees, only to see it be thrown into turmoil by West. The very act that Ogilvy despised in West was played out by him when he eventually cracked.

Then something else clicked with Guthrie. He sat on the edge of the desk beside Ogilvy.

"John?" he said in a quiet voice. "You said you went back to the boat yard from West's house, correct?"

"Yes." Ogilvy was once again staring at his hands in his lap.

"Why did you go there?"

"I needed to pick up my car."

"Aye, the Jag. Nice cars those. Always fancied one myself."

Buchanan shook his head.

"You went *back* to the yard to get the Jag?"

"Yes."

"Why did you go there the first time?"

"I knew West owned the yard and I was looking for him."

"Looking for him with a shotgun?"

Ogilvy didn't respond.

"John? You went to the boat yard to find Harry West, yes?"

"Yes. But he wasn't there."

"But the yard was open, isn't that correct, Mr Ogilvy?" asked Buchanan.

"Yes."

"Who was there? If the yard was open there must have been someone there? Someone in the office, someone working in the yard?"

"The office was locked, but there was someone there."

"Who?" Guthrie prompted.

"Devon West."

Guthrie closed his eyes. "Devon West?"

"Yes."

"I'm sorry, John, you just talked to Devon West, asked him where his father was and left?"

Ogilvy paused before answering. "No."

"Then what happened, Mr Ogilvy? Buchanan's voice was stern, like a headmaster.

Ogilvy wiped his nose with the back of his hand. "I shot him."

When he heard the words, Guthrie slouched. "Is he still at the yard?"

"No."

"Where is he, Mr Ogilvy? What did you do with him?"

Ogilvy shifted in his chair. "I wrapped him in a sheet of some kind. You know, just stuff I found right there. Then I dumped him into the Brothock Water that runs behind the yard. I thought he would be washed out to sea and no one would know." He sniffed again.

Guthrie looked at him. This was not the man he interviewed just a few short days ago. The man who seemed to have and be in control of everything was now sitting beside him, looking all the world like he had lost a foot in height and a hundred pounds in weight. His hair was tousled, and his face was still covered in grime from their struggle. But Guthrie also realised that what appears at the surface is almost never what lies beneath.

Buchanan told the uniform to get a team to look for the body, then turned to Ogilvy and coldly, in a matter-of-fact way, formally charged John Ogilvy with the murders of Harry and Devon West.

SIXTY-FOUR

Alisdair had been taken to Ninewells Hospital in Dundee as a precaution. The facilities there were better than the infirmary in Arbroath; if there were any complications, they would be better suited to deal with them.

Guthrie was shown into Alisdair's room. He was told not to stay long -- it was the middle of the night, after all.

Alisdair lay beneath the white sheets, propped up slightly by two oversized pillows. He was asleep and breathing deeply. A couple of machines stood to the side of the bed, monitoring Alisdair's vital signs. Guthrie didn't know what they indicated, but hoped it was normal.

Alisdair was going to be fine. The nurse said that he had suffered from mild hypothermia and was lucky not to have drowned.

"I heard someone jumped right into the water and kept him afloat until the police arrived. Probably saved his life."

Guthrie did what he was told and didn't stay long.

SIXTY-FIVE

Guthrie unlocked his front door and entered the dark flat. Without switching on a light, he walked into the kitchen where he dumped two plastic bags; one containing his wet clothes and one his dry. He then found the bottle of Auchentoshan. He really should shower, but the thought of getting wet again sent a shiver down his spine. He poured himself a healthy measure and added a little water.

He opened one of the bags and found his phone. It indicated four missed calls and one voicemail. All four calls were from Jacquie, as was the voicemail.

He walked over to his chair facing the window and sat down. The whisky left its mark on his throat on its way down, but he felt better for it. Staring out the large window it seemed as though the darkness of the flat merged with the outside. From his bedroom he could hear the soft ticking of a clock. Outside was still. No wind. No waves. No sirens. No shouts.

He looked at his phone again and clicked on the voice-mail alert. His eyes went out of focus as he looked at Jacquie's name, but then he made a decision.

He swiped the screen with his thumb.

Delete.

SIXTY-SIX

Wednesday, 16th April, 2014

"One regular white coffee, one single espresso, and two coffee towers."

"Thanks, Elaine," Alisdair said to the waitress. She smiled, turned and walked behind the counter.

"Here's to being back in uniform, then," Guthrie said, holding up his fork.

"Cheers," Alisdair responded, "but I'm not sure Inspector Buchanan would approve."

"Ach, what's he going to do? It's almost two. You're technically off duty in less than fifteen minutes. Besides, he'll never know. So how are things?"

"Okay. Still feel a twinge every now and again, but generally fine."

"No serious side effects? No webbed feet?"

Alisdair laughed. "No. Nothing to stop me from walking the beat."

Guthrie sensed a note of disappointment in Alisdair's reply. "You hoping to get out of uniform any time soon?"

"I don't know, Tom. I've put in the paperwork and Buchanan said he would certainly give me the highest recommendation."

"Well, that's a plus."

"But I'm not going to hold my breath."

"You don't know how to hold your breath. I can attest to that!"

"Shut up!" Alisdair said, through a mouthful of cream and pastry.

Guthrie took a mouthful of coffee. "You'll get it. Just have a wee bit of patience."

"Aye."

"I'll tell you what, I'll call Brian Campbell, put in a good word."

"You don't have to- "

Guthrie cut him off. "I know I don't *have* to, but I *want* to. You're wasted in uniform." Guthrie pointed his fork at Alisdair, and a piece of cream flew off and landed on Alisdair's uniform sleeve. "Shite. Sorry."

Alisdair acted as if an entire bucket of cream had been dumped on him. "Now Buchanan will wonder why I have a stain on my uniform. You know what he's like."

Guthrie turned red and grabbed a napkin. "Sorry, Alisdair. Really."

Alisdair chuckled.

"You bugger," said Guthrie. "Just for that, you can phone Campbell yourself."

"Sorry, Tom. Couldn't resist. Should've seen your face."

The two men sat in silence as they enjoyed the desserts and coffee. They watched the comings and goings of the customers -- the same crowd of older women on which Guthrie had remarked during their first visit.

Alisdair spoke up first. "Hey! I heard your MG took a beating. Was it bad?"

"Bad enough it's off the road."

"Oh, no. I'm sorry, Tom. You put so much work into that didn't you?"

"I did, yes."

"So, what are you driving? Did you have to buy another car?"

"I did." Guthrie spooned the last of his coffee tower into his mouth.

Alisdair sat, waiting for more details.

"What?" said Guthrie.

"Never mind 'what?' What did you get?"

"A Jag."

Alisdair put down his spoon and sat back with a look of disbelief. "A Jaguar?"

"Well, you know, I did like Buchanan's loaner."

"And you were almost killed by someone who not only drove one, but drove it into the back of your MG."

Guthrie looked at Alisdair as if butter wouldn't melt in his mouth. "What?"

"Oh, nothing. That's great. Just the last thing I thought you'd buy."

"It has heated seats!"

SIXTY-SEVEN

Back at his flat, a red light on Guthrie's answer machine was blinking steadily. He pressed play.

Tom, Jacquie. I just wanted to say sorry for whatever I have done or said. Please call me back. I'd like to talk. Perhaps a coffee. Nothing much. You know what I mean. Anyway, please call me. Right, well, I hope you're okay. Bye.

He deleted it.

His mobile rang. The caller I.D. told him it was the main Bell Street number.

"Hello. Tom Guthrie."

"Tom, this is Detective Inspector Bill Riddle, Police Scotland. I was wondering if you could come down to the office right away. We'd like to use you on a murder case."

Guthrie's pulse quickened.

"Ah, okay."

"Sorry, Tom, but I understand you know what it's like round here at the moment. Brian Campbell told me to give you a ring."

Good old Brian Campbell, he thought. "Aye, no problem. I can be there in half an hour. Is that okay?"

"That's fine, Tom. I assume you know the drill when you get here?"

"Yes."

"Okay. Just have them call for me and I'll come down and get you."

"No problem. See you in a little bit."

"Thanks."

Guthrie's phone beeped twice as the line went dead.

"This retirement gig is turning out to be busier than working."

ACKNOWLEDGMENTS

ALLAN WOULD LIKE TO THANK...

Robert L Mann:

Former Tayside Police officer—and my Dad—for the little snippets of insight from the good old days of policing.

Mike Baxter:

Independent Forensic Science Services Development & Management Consultant, and former Head of Operations—Forensic Services—East, Scottish Police Services Authority, and Head of Police Forensic Science Laboratory Dundee (PFSLD), for the insight to the forensic labs and its politics.

ABOUT THE AUTHOR

Allan lives in Georgetown, Kentucky.
He and his wife, Christy, have three
daughters, Katie, Emily, and Maureen.
Allan grew up on the East coast of
Scotland, and has been a professional
pilot his entire career. He thought
writing books would be much simpler.
He was wrong.

    TOOLS OF THE TRADE, the first in a trilogy of full-
length novels featuring retired detective Tom Guthrie, is
part of the *Angus Murders Mystery* series set in the area
Allan knows best—Angus.

 facebook.com/AllanLMann

twitter.com/AllanLMann

 instagram.com/AllanLMann

Wrung Out

Murder in the Sma' Glen

Printed in Great Britain
by Amazon

44794120R00205